*"Stop play[ing] ... this ... [can't fall]*
*understand, ... [g]*
*of you. It ...*
*y ...*

She still couldn't breathe or think properly. She was furious that she needed to leave one hand against him to steady herself. She was furious at him for being right. And for being so bloody self-righteous.

And for being steady on his feet as he regarded her.

And then she realized he was trembling. She could feel it beneath her palm.

He was a seasoned rogue, and that kiss had shaken him. Suddenly this unnerved her more than the kiss itself.

"Is that why you do it?" she asked softly. Ironically. "To lose yourself?"

Swift anger kindled in his eyes. "Have a care."

She took her hand away from him finally, slowly, as if he were a rabid dog and would lunge at her if she made any sudden moves. She was steady on her feet now. Her breathing had nearly resumed its usual cadence. She couldn't yet back away; he maintained a peculiar gravitational pull. She could still feel the warmth of his body on her skin. She wondered distantly if she always would. As if she'd been branded.

"What if I want to be lost?" she whispered.

## By Julie Anne Long

# Julie Anne Long

# Between the Devil and Ian Eversea

AVON
*An Imprint of HarperCollinsPublishers*

This is a work of fiction. Names, characters, places, and incidents are products of the author's imagination or are used fictitiously and are not to be construed as real. Any resemblance to actual events, locales, organizations, or persons, living or dead, is entirely coincidental.

AVON BOOKS
*An Imprint of* HarperCollins*Publishers*
10 East 53rd Street
New York, New York 10022-5299

Copyright © 2014 by Julie Anne Long
ISBN 978-0-06-211811-0   5415 4579   06/14
www.avonromance.com

First Avon Books mass market printing: April 2014

Avon Trademark Reg. U.S. Pat. Off. and in Other Countries, Marca Registrada, Hecho en U.S.A.
HarperCollins® is a registered trademark of HarperCollins Publishers.

Printed in the U.S.A.

10 9 8 7 6 5 4 3 2 1

# Acknowledgments

MY DEEPEST GRATITUDE TO my darling editor, May Chen; my stalwart agent, Steve Axelrod; the talented, hard-working staff at Harper Collins; and all the wonderful readers who let me and everyone else know how much my books mean to you.

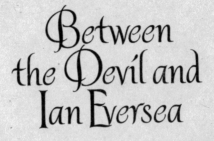

Between
the Devil and
Ian Eversea

# Chapter 1

✣

IF INNOCENCE HAD A color, it was the rain-washed silver-blue of Miss Titania Danforth's eyes.

Her spine was elegantly erect against the back of her Chippendale chair, her hands lay quietly in her lap; her white muslin day dress was as spotless as an angel's robe. She would have in fact been the picture of serenity, if not for her lashes. They were black, enviably fluffy, and very busy. They fluttered up. They fluttered down. They fluttered up again. Then down again. As if she could only withstand the potent gaze of the Duke of Falconbridge in increments.

A bit the way a virgin might sip at rotgut gin, the duke thought dryly.

Then again, even grown men found him disconcerting. Disconcerting was what the duke did best, without even trying.

Two hours earlier Miss Danforth's companion hired for the ocean voyage to England—a redoubtable barrel-shaped woman of middle years whose name the duke had promptly forgotten—had delivered her along with nearly a dozen trunks, and with an irony-tinged "Good *luck*, Yer Grace," departed with startling haste. No teary, lingering good-byes between her and Miss Danforth. But then, long ocean voyages could play havoc with even a saint's nerves, and familiarity was a well-known breeding ground for contempt.

And now that Falconbridge had seen his cousin's daughter, he was certain no luck was necessary. Her faultless breeding was in every word she spoke. Her voice was pleasant, low and precise, with a very becoming husk to it.

But her beauty astonished.

As if to affirm his conclusions, a great sheet of afternoon light poured in the window and made a corona of her fair hair. She might as well have been wearing a bloody halo.

On the whole, however, sheltered women irritated him. He never knew what to say to them. They taxed his patience. But the future of this particular sheltered woman was now his responsibility, thanks to an almost-forgotten promise he'd made many years ago.

A promise his cousin had seen fit to immortalize in his will.

The surreptitious press of his wife's knee against his stopped him from sighing aloud or muttering under his breath or any of the things she knew he was tempted to do. He reflected for a moment on the multitude of glorious things that could be communicated with a knee press. That he was known, loved, fortunate beyond all reason, and could afford to be charitable when the beautiful, gloriously kind young woman at his side on the settee was his. Genevieve was never dull. She'd never had a prayer of being dull, having been raised an Eversea.

Fortunately, he'd done most of his underbreath cursing when the succinct, ever-so-faintly harried letter from Miss Danforth's solicitor had arrived two months ago.

Genevieve said brightly, "I understand the crossing from America can be . . ."

She paused as two footmen appeared in the doorway, their knees wobbling under the weight of a profusion of brilliant hothouse blooms stuffed into an urn.

"For Olivia?" Genevieve said this almost with resignation.

"Yes, my lady."

"I think there might be a little room on the mantel."

The footmen shuffled into the room and hoisted the urn up with little grunts. Miss Danforth followed their progress to and fro with wide, wondering eyes.

The long stems continued quivering for a time after they departed.

"I was saying," Genevieve continued smoothly, "I understand the crossing can be grueling indeed, but the sea air seems to have agreed with you. You look radiant, Miss Danforth. What a delight it is to meet such a pretty cousin!"

Miss Danforth glowed. "You're too kind! Truly,

the crossing from America was mercifully un-
eventful. I understand I come from hearty stock."

The lashes went up again and her eyes were
limpid. She looked about as hearty as a blown
dandelion. He humored this transparent attempt
at flattery with a faint smile. "Certainly, Miss
Danforth, our stock, as you say, has withstood
any number of buffetings over the centur—"

"... *aaaaannnnnnnn* ... !"

He swiveled his head. High-pitched, very faint,
very sneaky, a sound floated into the room. It
was impossible to know from which direction it
came. It waxed and waned, a bit like the whine of
a diving mosquito.

He glanced at his wife, who was sporting a
faint, puzzled dent between her eyes.

Miss Danforth, on the other hand, remained
unruffled. She gave no appearance of having
heard a thing, unless one counted a slight further
straightening of her spine. Her eyes were bright
with curiosity now. Perhaps she thought men of
his advanced age—he had just turned forty—
naturally acquired twitches and tics, and she was
prepared to be sympathetic and tolerant.

"Your home is remarkably beautiful," she said.
"And so very grand."

"We're so pleased you think so," Genevieve
said warmly. "I loved growing up here. Falconbridge is indulging me in a hunt for another home
nearby, so we can live near my family for at least
part of the year. But I cannot wait to show you the

grounds! Though I'm certain it will all seem rather tame compared to America, Miss Danforth."

Miss Danforth's laugh was like bells. "I daresay it isn't as exciting as you might think, though it certainly is different from England. Oh, and I do hope you'll come to call me Tansy! All my friends do."

Both Genevieve and the duke paused. There *was* a bit of American expansiveness to her manners, as if all those wide-open spaces across the ocean caused them to stretch indolently, the way one slouches in a chair when no one is about to impress. The duke smiled faintly.

"We'll have such fun introducing you to society, Tansy," his wife indulged. "How exciting New York must be, but oh, we do manage to have a lovely time here! Do you enjoy dancing? We've a splendid array of activities planned for you."

"Oh . . . well, I fear I'm a bit of a wallflower. Life has been a bit . . ." She cleared her throat. ". . . a bit quiet, you see, for the past year or so."

The lashes stayed down and there passed a little moment of silence. For they did see. Her parents had been killed in a carriage accident a little over a year ago, her older brother had died in the War of 1812 before that, and that left Miss Danforth alone in the world. Save, of course, for the duke, who was now charged with marrying her off to a title spectacular enough to match the girl's fortune, which would only be released to her in its entirety when the match was made. Her future, essentially, was in the duke's hands.

So dictated her father's will.

His cousin had decamped from Sussex to America when the girl sitting before him was only eight years old. The duke had always hoped to see him again, for they'd been close, and the duke's close friendships were few.

"*. . . aaaaaaannnnforth . . . !*"

Bloody hell—there the sound was again. So eerie, nearly ghostly, it almost stood the hairs on the back of his neck on end. He whipped his head about again. But not before he saw Miss Danforth's eyes fly open wide, then give an infinitesimal guilty dart toward the window and back again.

He narrowed his eyes at her.

Her smile never dimmed. Her hands remained neatly folded in her lap. She met his gaze bravely.

"Perhaps a sheep fell into a drainage ditch?" Genevieve suggested into the ensuing silence. "Poor thing."

"*. . . oooooooove you . . . !*"

The sound was quite discernible as a voice now. A *man's* voice.

"Per . . . perhaps it's the wind?" Miss Danforth had tried for casual, and almost but not quite succeeded. "Wind" was more a squeak than a word.

Miss Danforth jumped when the duke stood abruptly.

"I'll just have a look, shall I?" He crossed the room in three strides. He pushed the window open and a stiff breeze hoisted the curtains high, like a villain brandishing his cape.

He peered out. On the green, far below the window, a man was down on his knees, his hands clasped in the universally understood gesture of beseeching, his head thrown back so far his mouth looked like a little dark O. And from this O issued howls of what sounded like tormented passion.

"Miss Daaaaaanfooooorth! I loooooooove you! Please just one word, I beeeeeggg of you! Do not forsake me!"

The duke eyed this pathetic scene for a moment.

And then he turned around very, very slowly, and stared at the now silent and very wide-eyed Miss Danforth.

He was silent for so long that when he launched his brows upward in a silent question she jumped. "Does that voice sound familiar, Miss Danforth?"

She cleared her throat.

"Oh . . . dear. That does sound like Mr. Lucchesi. He was a passenger on my ship, and I fear he may have nurtured a . . ." Pretty color flooded her face. ". . . a *tendre* which I assure you I do not return, though I took great pains to ensure I was all that was polite and my behavior was all that was appropriate. He must have . . . he must have somehow followed me from the ship."

Probably her open American manners were at fault. Although, admittedly, Lucchesi wasn't bellowing "Tansy!"

". . . *pleeeeeeaaaaase* . . ." The forlorn word drifted into the window.

"He's Italian," Miss Danforth added into the ensuing dumbstruck silence.

"Ah," said Genevieve sympathetically, as if that explained everything.

Miss Danforth shot her a look of gratitude.

"These things happen," Genevieve embellished.

At this, her husband's eyebrows shot upward again.

"Not to *me*, of course," she hastened to add. "But my sister Olivia . . . well, you've seen the flowers." She waved in the general direction of the mantel. "Men have always thrown themselves at her feet. They're forever sending flowers. They make embarrassing wagers about when she'll be married in the Betting Book at White's and . . ."

She trailed off when she saw what was no doubt incredulity writ large on her husband's features.

"Careful, my dear," he said. "It's beginning to sound like an endorsement."

She grinned at that and he grinned back, and there passed an infinitesimal moment during which they were the only two in the world.

Miss Danforth's voice intruded.

"I am so terribly sorry to inconvenience you, when you've been so kind and welcoming!" Miss Danforth's hands wrung. "I never dreamed . . . that is, I could not anticipate . . . to follow me onto your grounds! I am *appalled* that—"

The duke held up a hand. "Do you wish to speak to Mr. Lucchesi, Miss Danforth?"

She shook her head so vigorously the two blond curls flagellated her cheeks like a cat-o'-nine tails.

"Do you wish *me* to have a word with Mr. Lucchesi?"

"No! That is, I'd rather you didn't. That is . . . Oh, I wish he would just go away." She ducked her head again. And said nothing more.

He did sigh then. Mother of God, but she was the veriest babe. The girl was a danger to herself. The sooner he could hand this one off to an appropriate husband, the better. It ought to be a simple enough matter to accomplish, but he would need to keep her out of trouble until that happened. That sort of thing shouldn't present too much of a challenge. Intelligent rogues were afraid of the Duke of Falconbridge and the stupid ones could be dispensed with easily.

One particular rogue, however, warranted a personal warning.

He turned to his wife. "My dear," he said idly, "do you suppose your brother is in Pennyroyal Green at the moment?"

She didn't need to ask *which* brother.

IAN EVERSEA ROLLED over and opened one eye. Mercifully, he'd awakened before the usual dream could really get its talons in, which was one reason he awoke in a cheerful mood.

As he always did after that dream, he stretched his legs and flexed his arms, grateful he still pulled air, grateful he still possessed all his limbs.

Not to mention *another* appendage.

He sighed a long, satisfied sigh and opened his other eye.

The window next to him framed a perfect half of a moon and a few stars. It was evening.

Which meant he'd better leave soon, or he'd ruin his unbroken record of never staying an entire night through.

He rubbed at his ear. "Funny," he muttered.

"What is funny, *mon cher*?" came a sleepy, French-inflected purr next to him. She was the other reason he'd awoken in a cheerful mood.

"My ear is hot."

Monique propped herself up on one elbow and peered at him through her great cloud of auburn hair. A position that mashed her large and delectable breasts together and reminded him of the pleasures of pillowing his head there. An embarrassment of riches, those, just inches from his nose.

"What is it they say when your ear is hot? Someone must be talking about you." She reached out a finger and trailed his ear with it.

"Someone," he murmured with satisfaction as he rolled over to Monique to pull her into his arms and continue the marathon of lovemaking, "is *always* talking about me."

# Chapter 2

❧

POOR GIANCARLO.

It was now nearly midnight and Tansy couldn't sleep. She shoved aside an explosively colorful flower arrangement—they seemed to be *everywhere* in this house, apparently thanks to Olivia Eversea— dominating a little table near the window.

She stepped out onto the little balcony into the star-strewn Sussex night. She tried to imagine him down on his knees on the green. He'd likely have been scarce more than a speck of white linen seen from the distance of the third floor window. Mother of God, what a terrible moment—sitting very still, beaming like a loon at the duke and duchess, while the words *bloody hell bloody hell bloody hell* clanged over and over in her head as realization set in. She'd never dreamed he'd *follow* her from the docks, let alone appear beneath the Duke of Falconbridge's window to bellow things like "forsake," of all words. Wherever had he *learned* it? His chief attraction, apart from his liquid brown eyes, had been his mellifluous murmured Italian (which he never suspected she mostly understood) interspersed with charmingly fractured English. He must have been reading English poets or some nonsense when he wasn't romancing her on deck. She didn't know how reading poetry could ever lead to anything good.

The Duke of Falconbridge had done little more than flick an eyebrow and—poof!—Giancarlo had somehow been spirited away. She'd been assured she would never have to worry about him again, and the duke and duchess (the duchess primarily) had gone on to talk about other things and other people, so very many people, all family members, in a voice of such warmth, and she'd been spared any queries about her association with Mr. Lucchesi. Because the duke was likely confident he'd ended it.

A speck, indeed. That was what Giancarlo was to someone like the duke.

The duke. She suspected the duke accomplished more with a flicked eyebrow than most men did in a lifetime of toil. He'd been polite, of course, welcoming, of course, but a bit . . . unyielding. A bit impervious to her attempts to charm. She'd felt a little winded after the conversation, as though she'd been attempting to scale a slippery wall for an hour only to do nothing but slide down again and again. It was probably best to nod and agree a good deal around him. Her father had known what he was about when he consigned her fate to the Duke of Falconbridge.

Tansy supposed he could be considered hand-some, but he must be forty years old at *least*. So astonishing, given that his wife was so very pretty and was hardly older than she was, and she was twenty.

She recalled the glance they exchanged.

It had reminded her of looks exchanged between her parents. Those looks had always felt like a door ajar on a world she'd never be invited to visit.

She'd loved her parents very much and had been loved, too, she knew, but she also known precisely where she fell in the hierarchy of affection in her family.

She suspected the duke considered her a speck, too. A temporary problem to be handed off to another man, whose problem she would then become. A baton of sorts, in the eternal marriage relay.

So be it. She wrapped her arms around herself and gave a little shiver of anticipation. She *wanted* to be married. Imagine what all of her erstwhile friends in New York would say if she became the Duchess of this or the Countess of that. And if someone could find her a duke for a husband, surely it was another duke?

Likely she'd never see Giancarlo again.

She did feel a minute pang of regret. She'd never anticipated it would all reach such an . . . untidy . . . crescendo. It had begun with a variety of glances— fleeting and lingering, sidelong and direct—sent and intercepted. And then, experimentally, she'd timed a pretend slip on the foredeck just as he was passing; her hand had curled over his arm as he helped her to right herself, and as she stammered thanks, standing a bit too close, his pupils had gone huge.

This closeness had evolved into an invitation to stroll on the deck.

She understood enough Italian to know that Giancarlo (his bicep tightened beneath her grip when she accidentally-on-purpose breathed his name for the first time—"*Giancarlo*"—as he helped her to her feet again) was saying things no gentleman should say to any proper lady—reckless, stirring, often baffling things. He would like to kiss her. Her lips were like plums. Her lips were like roses. Her ass was like a peach. Her skin was like a lily. All manner of flora and fauna were represented in his compliments. He would like to do other things besides kiss her. She wasn't familiar with Italian slang, more's the pity, because she expected she'd have gotten quite an education.

She'd even mulled allowing him to do one or two of the things he professed to wanting to do. And with each passing day on the ship the lips of her hired companion, Mrs. Gorham, had gone thinner and thinner and thinner and her underbreath muttered warnings grew darker and darker. But Tansy couldn't stop. She was a virtuoso of flirtation who'd been denied an opportunity to practice her art for far too long, and the whole episode had acquired the momentum of a driverless carriage rolling downhill.

It was probably a very good thing the ship had docked when it did.

She ventured out onto the little balcony outside her window and searched the English sky, but she couldn't find the particular constellation she wanted to see. And though she knew it was ridiculous, it was this more than anything that made her feel bereft all over again, as if she were spiraling aimlessly through the heavens, like so much dandelion fluff, inconsequential, destined never to land.

Somewhere out there in the Sussex dark was the home she'd once known and loved fiercely as a little girl. Lilymont. Sold when her father had taken his family off to America. She wondered who owned it now. Her home in New York had been sold, too, as dictated by her father's will, and though she missed it, in a peculiar way it was also a relief. After her parents died, nearly everything once familiar and beloved—from furniture to flowers in the garden—had seemed foreign, even a little sinister, like props in an abandoned theater.

She needed a home of her own. And she wouldn't have a home, a *real* home, of her own again until she was married.

And now the silence seemed total and fraught, like the aftermath of a gunshot, and the dark outside wasn't the dark of thick woods frilling the edges of the New York estate. Even the stars seemed strange and new viewed from this side of the Atlantic. They called the constellations by different names here in England, she recalled. The Big Dipper was called instead the Starry Plough. She was uncertain about the rest of them, but it wasn't as though she'd learned the Queen's English the way she'd learned Italian.

All she knew for certain was that she didn't like the dark, and she didn't like quiet, and she didn't like to be alone.

She reached for a night robe, thrust her arms into it and tied up the bow at the neck, shoved her feet into a pair of satin slippers, seized her lit lamp and tiptoed down the long marble stairs.

Her surroundings were so unfamiliar it was like moving through a dream, and she liked it. It seemed to carry as little consequence; it seemed as though anything could happen, as though anyone or anything could appear, monsters, dragons, princes, ghosts. She almost wished something would appear, simply for novelty's sake. She'd stopped being afraid some time ago.

She found herself in the kitchen by instinct, as if it was the heart of the house and she'd followed the sound of its beat. A slice of bread, perhaps a cup of something hot. She knew her way around a kitchen well enough to heat a kettle.

Unsurprisingly, a vase of flowers going limp from the heat of the kitchen was in the middle of the kitchen table. For heaven's *sake*. She gave her

head an imperious little toss. Not too long ago
*she'd* collected bouquets as effortlessly as she collected beaux.

A boy on the hearth snored softly, and stirred
and muttered in his sleep. She supposed his job
was to turn the grand haunch suspended on a spit
over the fire. The haunch was near to being licked
at by low flames. It would burn.

"Pssst," she said.

He shot upward, all limbs flailing like an up-
turned spider for a moment until he righted himself, thrust his fists into his eyes and ground them
a bit.

"Cor! I nearly pissed meself, ye scared me so."

"I'm sorry."

He stared at her for a moment. "Are ye an
angel?" was his conclusion. He sounded almost
accusatory.

"Far from it."

"Was I asleep?"

"You were."

"You be an angel then, m'lady, if you saved me
from burning the haunch."

She laughed softly at that. Something about
him—the sense of barely repressed mischief, no
doubt—reminded her of her brother, who had
been everyone's darling. "I imagine you need
your rest, and if you give it a crank now it should
be fine. I'm Miss Danforth, a guest in the house. I
was feeling a bit peckish and—"

"Jordy! I *thought* I heard voices!"

Both the boy *and* Tansy jumped this time. The voice belonged to a small woman who looked as soft and plump and homey as a loaf of rising bread. Rust-colored curls sprang from the confines of her nightcap and were still shimmying on her forehead. Clearly she'd hurried to the kitchen.

"Oh, miss, ye must be Miss Danforth." She curtsied, clutching her voluminous white night robe in her hands. "Mrs. Margaret deWitt at yer service, miss. I be the cook."

"I *am* Miss Danforth, and a pleasure to meet you, Mrs. deWitt. I'm so sorry to disturb you! It's just that I felt a bit peckish, and I—"

Miss deWitt lit up at those words. She *lived* to vanquish hunger and to fuss over young people. "Here now, Miss Danforth, you just sit down and I'll make ye a cuppa and summat to eat. You're a slip of a thing, ain't ye? You ought to have rung and we'd have brought it up."

She was kind. Tansy knew this instinctively; her face, her voice, belonged to a woman who knew her place and liked it well. She felt a temptation to lean toward it, like a flower into the sun. It somehow seemed a safer sort of kindness than the exquisite welcome of the duke and duchess.

"Oh, I couldn't have rung. I didn't want to disturb anyone and the house was so quiet and peaceful and—"

" 'Tis no trouble at all to be awakened. Some of us are a bit restless nights, aye, like mice? Shame on ye, Jordy, for botherin' Miss Danforth."

Tansy smiled at that, imagining herself as a mouse, a nightcap perched on her head, a cup of tea in her hand, pacing in front of a tiny hearth in a tiny hole, sleepless. There were times, especially recently, she wouldn't have minded living her life at the level of the baseboards and having a hole to return to.

When she wasn't thoroughly relishing being the focal point of a given room, that was.

"Jordy didn't bother me at all! He was just about to tell me where to find the bread." She winked at the boy.

The boy beamed at her, enslaved for life.

Mrs. deWitt immediately performed what amounted to a ballet of competence, unwrapping a loaf of bread and a half wheel of cheese, hewing generous slices of each, sliding them onto a plate which she slid over to Tansy, along with the jam pot. She pumped water and heaved a kettle up onto the stove, and Tansy almost closed her eyes at the soothing, familiar, homely sound of water coming to a boil.

"Ye're here to be wed now, ain't ye?" Mrs. deWitt said brightly.

She wasn't surprised the servants would know all about her. It was the nature of servants everywhere to know such things.

"I suppose I am."

Mrs. deWitt nodded. "The duke, yer cousin, I believe, he be a fine man, the finest."

*And the scariest*, Tansy was tempted to add.

"I would go to the ends of the earth for that man. The ends of the earth . . ."

She suspected the cook was trying to reassure her.

". . . despite what some may say about him," she added stoutly. "And don't you believe a word of it."

She *knew* it.

"What do they say?" she coaxed casually.

"And the duchess, our Miss Genevieve, well, she be an angel come to earth," she said as if she hadn't heard Tansy at all, which Tansy very much doubted. "A beautiful lady, and so kind and fair."

Genevieve—the duchess—was, indeed, beautiful. Petite, black-haired, blue-eyed, radiating a calm intelligence and the serene confidence of one who is certain she is loved, certain she belonged, and who was a part of everything she saw here in Sussex.

Tansy fought back an irritable little twitch, as if someone had dragged a hand along her pelt in the wrong direction.

"The duchess is lovely and she's been all that is amiable and welcoming," she said. "I am blessed indeed in my relations."

Mrs. deWitt beamed at her approvingly. "Tea . . . or . . ." She peered shrewdly at Tansy. ". . . would it be a bit o' sippin' chocolate, miss?"

"Oh, chocolate, please!" Despite herself, she gave a girlish clap.

A few moments of bustling later a cup of steaming chocolate was thunked in front of her, and Mrs. deWitt prodded Jordy with a toe because his head was lolling, before thunking her own solid behind in a chair across from Tansy.

"Thank you so much, Mrs. deWitt. It was just what I wanted."

Miss deWitt's smile was triumphant. "I knew it! I know a girl who likes chocolate, m'dear. The prettiest ones do."

Tansy felt her pride settle into place again. "Have you worked for the Eversea family long?"

"I've known Miss Genevieve—Her Grace—since she was a wee thing. She was Miss Genevieve Eversea then. Mind *ye*, now, Genevieve is a beauty, but she's always been quietlike; ye be pretty as an angel yerself," the cook hastened to reassure.

"So I've been tol'—er, that is, you're much too kind."

Tansy rotated her cup of chocolate on the table abstractedly, then stopped. She prided herself on her ability to remain in control of any circumstance, whether it was a ballroom flirtation or an Italian shouting "forsake" up at the window, or reading a message about a carriage accident while the messenger, a curious stranger, looked on and waited for her to regain her ability to speak and breathe and to find a shilling to pay him for delivering the news of the end of her world.

"But 'tis the duchess's sister, Miss Olivia . . . talk about a beauty! She does have a way of turning men into fools for her. And she'll make a grand, grand match, too."

Tansy's pride yanked at its tether. She was used

to stopping conversation when she entered a ballroom. She was used to dropping jaws. *Can you do
that, Olivia Eversea?*

It seemed an awfully long time since she'd been
in a ballroom.

"Miss Genevieve spoke so affectionately of her
brothers and sisters."

"Oh, aye. There's Master Marcus, married to
Louisa, and Colin, settled and raising cattle but
no babies yet. Miss Olivia, she may be married
to a very grand viscount before the year is out,
at long last, bless her poor sore heart. And then
there's Master Ian . . . Ah, goodness, that is quite a
bright moon out the window!" she said abruptly.

Tansy swiveled her head. It was bright, all right,
but such was the nature of the moon.

She half suspected the distraction was deliberate. Who had Mrs. deWitt just mentioned? Someone who hadn't been mentioned by either the
duke or the duchess earlier today, she was certain
of that.

The cook appeared to have abandoned that
thread of thought. "'Twill be a simple thing for
a young lady such as yerself to make a splendid
match. Perhaps even as fine as Miss Genevieve."

She wished people would cease talking about
her as if she were simply a shoe missing a mate.
If it were *that* easy, surely she would even now be
exchanging meaningful world-excluding looks of
her own with one of those smitten swains from
New York? Many of them had vowed eternal love,

and many of them were at *least* as handsome as poor Giancarlo, and one of them had kissed her, because he was bold and she'd dared him. She had liked it, and stopped it immediately because she possessed more sense than her father had no doubt credited her.

Apart from an accelerated pulse, there really had been no consequence. He hadn't captured the whole of her imagination, let alone her heart, for more than a day. And she was certain the man she married should be able to capture both.

Fortunately, she'd made a list of requirements for a husband. She thought the duke would find it helpful.

"You flatter me, surely, Mrs. deWitt," she said.

Mrs. deWitt turned to look at Tansy, speculation written over her soft features. She studied her a moment.

Then she surprised Tansy by reaching over and patting her hand, a familiarity perhaps brought on by the fact that they were all wearing night robes.

"Dinna ye worry about a thing, Miss Danforth."

It was probably a platitude, but it felt, in the dark kitchen, with Jordy somnolently turning the haunch at a soothing rhythm, that Mrs. deWitt had seen into her soul. Suddenly Tansy's throat tightened and her eyes began to burn.

Probably just the steam from the chocolate.

# Chapter 3

⤿

THE NIGHT WAS JUST beginning to give way to dawn when Tansy's eyes popped open.

The cloudlike mattress beneath her wasn't swaying with the motion of the sea. The elegantly furnished room was all slim lines and dark woods and gilt and shades of blue. Not America. Not a ship. *Sussex*. Pennyroyal Green, to be precise.

A stripe of inviting rosy light was pushing its way through a crack between the curtains.

She drowsily slid out of bed, rubbed her fists in her eyes, heaved her heavy braid over one shoulder and followed the road like the road to certainty across the deep Savonnerie carpet.

She gently grabbed a fistful of the curtains, which were gold velvet and soft as kittens, and peered out the window.

The horizon lay before her in strata of colors: first the soft manicured green of the Eversea parklands, above that a dark line of trees both fluffy and pointy, which must be a forest, beyond that a broad expanse of darker green, mounded like a tossed blanket, of what had to be the Sussex downs, and finally a narrow strip of silver. Probably the sea.

The sky was just taking on a maidenly blush. She watched as the rising sun gilded mundane things one by one, as if allotting each of them a turn at glory. First a tall, neat shrubbery, then a white stone bench, then a fountain, then a man—

She sucked in her breath so quickly she nearly choked.

A *bare* man.

Bare from the waist up, anyway.

He was standing on the little balcony next to hers, just feet away.

She ducked back into her room and dragged the curtain over her face, leaving just her eyes exposed, like a harem girl, and leaned forward for a better look. She could only see his back: a glorious burnished expanse of shoulders, a lovely trench of sorts along his spine, dividing two ridges of hard muscle, all of that narrowing into a taut waist.

Suddenly he thrust his arms up into the air, arched backward as though he'd been struck by lightning, and made a sort of roaring sound, like a pagan god calling down the morning. Though she doubted whether a god would sport fluffy black hair in his armpits.

He promptly disappeared back into his room, just as though he'd been a cuckoo popping out of a clock to announce the time.

His roar still echoed faintly.

All in all, not an inauspicious start to a day.

She climbed back into bed. If it was a dream, she wanted it to continue.

CAPTAIN CHARLES "CHASE" Eversea swept into the Pig & Thistle, seized a chair, turned it around backward, straddled it, reached for Colin's ale and took a gulp before lifting a hand to call over Polly Hawthorne, the Pig & Thistle's barmaid.

"Thank you," he said belatedly, gravely, to Colin, dragging the back of his hand over his mouth.

Colin scowled but it was more a formality than indignation. Of them, Chase was older, Colin the youngest, and the Eversea brother hierarchy was an unshakable thing. He wouldn't even dream of protesting.

"Is . . . *regular* sitting passé now, Chase?" Colin asked mildly. "Afraid you can't hold your increasingly aged torso up without the assistance of a chair back?"

"His baubles have grown three sizes now that the East India company has promoted him," Ian said. "He needs the additional support."

"If you accept that position with the company offered to you in London, you, too, can have enormous baubles, Ian. When did you get home?"

"Late last night. Too late for my own room to be ready, apparently, as I'm ensconced on the third floor. Rode in from London. And you know my plans, and not even the lure of a bauble-swelling promotion will change them. I'll be gone soon enough. You'll just have to savor my presence while you can." He'd mapped out five ports of call, and he finally had precisely enough money saved—through scrimping and clever investments—to do it. China, India, Africa, Brazil. He'd pored over his map of the world so often, sometimes he thought it was singed on his retinas. He could see it when he closed his eyes.

"Ian probably needs to put his baubles on ice after the week he spent with Mademoiselle—"

Ian kicked Colin silent. Polly Hawthorne had suddenly appeared at the table.

Pretty thing, dark and slim and young, graceful as a selkie, Polly had nurtured an unrequited youthful yearning for Colin, and never forgiven him for having the unmitigated gall to get married. She still refused to acknowledge his existence, but Ian suspected that at this point it was partially out of habit. You had to admire the way the girl could hold a grudge, he thought. He admired consistency. The women he'd known tended toward the fickle, and though he'd definitely benefited from that more than once, he still didn't like it. It was probably hypocritical, but there you had it.

Ian had watched Polly grow up here at the pub her father owned—the Hawthorne family had owned the Pig & Thistle for centuries. He was protective of her, and of Culpepper and Cooke, and everyone else who made Pennyroyal Green the home he'd known and loved his entire life. Perhaps unfairly, he wanted to be able to come and go as he pleased—to war, to exotic countries—and arrive home again to find all them still here, exactly where they belonged, if a little older.

He smiled at Polly, and she flushed and began fidgeting. Such was the power of an Eversea smile. He wasn't stingy with them. Watching women smiling and flushing never got tiresome.

"Three more of the dark, if you would, Polly."

"Of course, Captain Eversea."

"Mademoiselle *who*?" Chase prompted immediately, when Polly had slipped away again.

"LaRoque." Ah, Monique. He remembered rolling out of bed, her fingernails lightly trailing his spine, as she tried to persuade him to stay. He *never* stayed. With any of them. It was one of his rules. He had another rule about giving gifts—he simply didn't. He wanted a woman to feel persuaded by him as a man. Not to feel bought.

"You haven't a romantic bone in your body," Monique had pouted as he dressed. "Merely a bone of passion." Her command of English was often tenuous, but she'd still managed to more or less sum him up accurately. He wasn't insulted. She still wanted him. Because he did know how to give a woman exactly what she needed.

"Monique LaRoque. The actress?" Chase wondered.

"Impressive, or should I say, unseemly, knowledge of London gossip you have there, Chase. Yes. The actress."

"I've heard of her. My wife once saw her perform."

It was a casual enough sentence. But the words "my wife" were faintly possessive and Chase delivered them as if they were a benediction.

They fell on Ian's ears like an accusation. Colin did the same damn thing with the same damn words. When he wasn't talking about cows. He shifted irritably in his chair, as if dodging a lowering net.

"She's uniquely talented, Mademoiselle La-Roque," Ian said. Perversely. To induce a reverie in the two recently married men.

There fell a gratifying hush.

Colin had always been more innately a rogue, and Ian enjoyed prodding at him to see if the rogue in him was dead, killed by matrimony, or simply dormant. Then again, surviving the gallows could inspire any man to seek refuge in an institution like marriage. Or perhaps he'd gotten a little too used to Newgate after his notorious stay there to ever adapt fully to freedom again.

Finally, Colin asked hopefully, on a lowered voice: "*How* unique?"

Ian simply, cruelly, smiled enigmatically.

Monique *was* talented, but not particularly uniquely. Maneuvering her into bed had been a game involving copious charm, his very best innuendos, and outflirting other men. But not gifts. Never gifts. The conclusion had been nearly foregone, but they had both enjoyed it up to and beyond the moment she capitulated. She was skillful and nimble and soft-skinned and gorgeous and . . . showing distressing signs of devotion.

Which was why Ian was relieved to have an excuse to return to Pennyroyal Green—he'd promised his cousin Adam, the vicar, that he'd lead a crew of men—many of them admittedly a bit motley in character if willing in spirit—in much-needed repairs to the ancient vicarage. If he stayed in London too long, the mamas would remember how eligible Ian Eversea was. But if he stayed in Pennyroyal Green too long, *his* mama might remember how eligible he was, instead of devoting all of her attention to the matter of his sister Olivia. Who was, at last, submitting to a semblance of courtship from Lord Landsdowne, and in fact appearing to enjoy it.

*Appearing.* One never knew with Olivia.

All of the Everseas had been holding their breath ever since. And the flowers from the hopeful—or masochistic—continued to arrive for her.

The bloods who had voted against her in the Betting Book at White's were beginning to perspire a little. No one thought Olivia Eversea would wed ever since Lyon Redmond had vanished, taking, it was said, her heart with him.

Funny, but he hadn't given Monique a thought since he'd returned last night from London. Which was likely ungracious, at the very least. Given that she'd been all he thought about for weeks before that.

If he stayed in Pennyroyal Green long enough, Monique would probably forget about him. He wondered whether this was a relief.

Until he returned to London, that was. And the game began again.

If he wanted it to.

The notion of *that* made him restless, too.

Polly returned with ales and thunked them down.

"Chase is paying," Ian told her. With a brook-no-argument eyebrow lift in Chase's direction.

Chase gamely produced the proper coinage.

"To large baubles and willing actresses!" Ian toasted his brothers cheerfully.

They hoisted their tankards "To large bau—"

Their smiles froze. Their gazes locked on a point over his shoulder.

"What?" Ian swiveled his head to look.

"To large baubles!" the Duke of Falconbridge said easily.

Bloody. Hell.

How did *he* get in here? It was a wonder the entire pub hadn't fallen silent, the way singing birds do when a stalking cat is spotted in the garden. But no: everyone was drinking, talking loudly and making broad, ale-fueled gesticulations, as usual, and Culpepper and Cooke were at the chessboard, and Jonathan Redmond was throwing darts at the board with his usual alarming precision. No one had noticed that an infamous duke wended his way into the Pig & Thistle.

Ian knew firsthand that the man could be stealthy.

His sister Genevieve loved Falconbridge, that much was clear. She had married him, throwing over Lord Harry in the process. And Ian loved Genevieve.

But it was damnably awkward to be tangentially related to someone who had once ordered him at gunpoint to climb out of his erstwhile fiancée's window.

At midnight.

Naked.

It was a testament to Ian's fortitude and general pleasure in risk that he was able to walk all the way home wearing only one boot (the duke had thrown the other one out the window, along with his clothes) and the shreds of his dignity and one half of his shirt, the only other clothing he was able to retrieve in the dark. His turn on the battlefield had prepared him to stoically confront an infinite number of eventualities.

Then again, Falconbridge ought to *thank* him for climbing into this fiancée's window if it stopped him from marrying the wrong woman and brought him to Genevieve.

He was fairly certain the duke didn't see it that way.

He wasn't known as a forgiving man—nobody liked him, apart, it seemed, from Genevieve—and he was known to have a long memory for any perceived wrongs perpetrated against him and for righting the balance no matter how long it took. Genevieve had fervently assured Ian the duke hadn't murdered his first wife, as popular rumor had it, and though in all likelihood he would refrain from murdering Ian for Genevieve's sake, one just never knew.

Ian was hardly proud of the episode. If he'd known he'd wind up related to the man, he would in all likelihood have never climbed that tree to Lady Abigail's window.

The three Eversea men clambered to their feet and bowed to their brother-in-law, with cheerful and polite greetings, and then when they sat again, Colin extended a leg and used it to push out the empty chair next to Chase in an invitation.

Ian shot him a filthy look.

Colin fought back a grin.

Colin, who was the only other person (besides perhaps Genevieve) who knew about his midnight exodus from the window at gunpoint.

The duke settled into the chair, his shoulder within inches of brushing Ian's.

Ian contracted all of his muscles.

Polly appeared as if by magic.

"Try the dark, Falconbridge," Chase recommended.

Chase claimed to actually like the man. But

then Chase enjoyed a number of things Ian found questionable, including goose liver, and puppets made him nervous. He might be a fellow war hero, but his judgment wasn't sacrosanct.

Polly slipped away to do His Grace's bidding.

"What brings you to our humble pub?" This came from Colin.

"I was out for a stroll and when I saw the Pig & Thistle, I seized upon it as an opportunity to see my brothers-in-law in their native habitat."

They all laughed politely, giving him the benefit of the doubt that it was meant to be a joke.

"Chase has been promoted," Ian told him.

"Congratulations, Captain Eversea," the duke said. "Rising in the ranks there, are we? Aiming for a governorship?"

"I don't think my wife would like to live in India, but it's not out of the question."

"I don't think they have any puppets in India, so it's safe," Ian reassured him, and Chase kicked him under the table.

The duke either didn't notice or chose to ignore this non sequitur.

"And Ian has been offered a promotion as well," Chase said. "You did know his rank is Captain, Falconbridge?"

"Ian," Ian said, "is taking a trip around the world, and will be booking passage very soon. And will be gone for quite some time."

"Ah. Around the world you say," the duke mused. "Coincidentally, we have a guest lately arrived from across the ocean. I'm not certain whether Genevieve has told you about my young ward, Miss Titania Danforth, and her imminent arrival from America."

She had. But they'd all forgotten until now. A relative of the duke's, who was to be married off apace to a title approved of by the duke. Something of that sort.

"Miss Danforth arrived yesterday."

"Safely and well, I hope?" Colin said politely.

"Quite safe and well. And a more unspoiled, well-bred, impressionable young woman you'll never meet. It's my sincere hope that, while she's here, you will consider her welfare in the same light with which you consider Genevieve's, and treat her accordingly."

No matter how obliquely stated, Ian knew at once it was a warning.

The man had a lot of bloody nerve. As if he couldn't resist mounting any female in his vicinity. He had *criteria.*

There was a silence at the table, roughly akin to the sort that follows an invitation to duel.

*Don't say it, Ian. Don't say it. Don't say it.*

"Or you'll . . . what?"

Colin and Chase were motionless. He knew they were each holding a breath. In the silence that followed, Ian imagined he could hear the condensation trailing the glass of ale.

The duke said nothing.

"I would die for Genevieve," Ian added into the silence. Grimly.

It was only what was true. He'd put his life on

the line for others more than once. And it was one of the reasons his sleep, for years, had hardly been a peaceful one.

He didn't do it lightly.

The duke finally moved, lifting and sipping at his ale leisurely.

"Well," he said, "let's hope you won't need to die for Miss Danforth."

He drained his ale in a final gulp, then raised his eyebrows in approbation. "Excellent brew. Perhaps I'll have to visit the Pig & Thistle more often."

And with that horrible threat he bowed and took his leave.

"She must be magnificent if the duke thought he needed to *warn* you." Colin was thrilled.

"Nonsense. She sounds dull," Ian said idly. "The innocent ones generally are."

# Chapter 4

❧

THE DUKE SENT FOR Tansy that afternoon, and she smoothed absurdly clammy palms down her skirts before hurrying to a room with a large polished desk in it. He sat at it as though it were a throne, but then, nearly everywhere he sat would seem that way, she thought.

"In all likelihood I don't need to remind you of the terms of your father's will, I'm certain, Miss Danforth, but I'll state them thusly: the entirety of your fortune will be released to you upon your marriage to a man of whom I approve."

Why did he sound like a lawyer? Perhaps that was why her father had entrusted her fate to this man. Perhaps he was capable of communicating only in orders, or by flicking that formidable eyebrow. It was difficult to argue with that eyebrow.

"Thank you. I'm aware of them."

There was an awkward little silence.

"The last time I saw you, you weren't any taller than . . ." He held his hand a few feet above the floor. "You hid behind your mother's skirts. It was at Lilymont."

She smiled politely. If she'd hidden behind her mother's skirts, it was, in all likelihood, the last time she'd ever been shy. He'd probably been intimidating even then. His wife—he'd had a different wife then—had been so pretty, she'd thought. She'd laughed so easily. She'd loved the sound of her mother and the duke's wife laughing together in the garden.

The very word "Lilymont" had started up an ache again. She could see it clearly: the walled garden half wild, colorful and surprising and tangled, like something from a fairy tale, at least from her perspective at three feet tall.

And then she remembered the duke had lost that pretty, merry wife quite some time ago. Which was how he had come to be married to Genevieve.

She stared at him curiously, as if she peered hard enough, she might see some sort of give, something that might indicate that life had battered him a bit. She saw nothing but a sleek, older, inscrutable duke.

"I'm given to understand that you *would* like to marry." He said this somewhat stiffly.

"Yes, thank you." *Of course*, she almost added. She felt herself begin to flush.

When he paused, she saw an opportunity to intervene.

"I thought it might be helpful to make a list of qualities I should like in a husband."

There was a pause, which she thought might be of the mildly nonplussed variety.

"You've made a list," he repeated carefully.

She nodded. "Of qualities I might like to find in a husband."

Another little hesitation.

"And . . . you'd like to share this list with me?"

She couldn't tell whether he was being ironic. "If you think it might be helpful."

"One never knows," he said neutrally.

"Very well." She carefully unfolded the sheet of foolscap and smoothed it flat in her lap, then cleared her throat.

She looked up at him, and he nodded encouragingly.

"Number one: I should like him to be intelligent . . ."

She looked up again, gauging the result of her initial requirement.

He gave an approving nod. "Half-wits can be so tedious," he sympathized.

". . . but not too intelligent."

She was a little worried about this one.

"Ah." He drummed his fingers once or twice and seemed to mull this. "Do you mean the sort who goes about quoting poetry and philosophers? Waxes rhapsodic about works of art? Uses terms like 'waxes rhapsodic'?"

It was precisely what she meant. She hoped the duke wasn't the sort who went about quoting poets and philosophers. She rather liked the term "wax rhapsodic," however. She silently tried it in a sentence. *Titania Danforth waxed rhapsodic about the balcony man's torso.*

"I think I prefer him to be . . . active. To enjoy the outdoors, and horses and shooting and such. I enjoy reading. But I'd rather not pick apart what I read. I'd rather just enjoy the pictures stories make in my head."

And now she was babbling.

She hoped he didn't think she'd sounded ridiculous. It had, rather, in her own ears.

"Do you?" She couldn't tell whether he was amused or thoughtful. "I'm not one for reading a good deal myself. My wife, on the other hand, enjoys it very much. I tolerate the habit in her."

Genevieve did have the look of the sort who would enjoy reading very much, Tansy thought glumly. He did, however, sound a little ironic.

"What's the next item on your list, Miss Danforth?"

"Ah. Number two: I should like him to be of fine moral character."

In truth, she'd added that one because she hoped it would impress the duke. She wasn't entirely certain how he would interpret fine moral character. She wasn't even certain how *she* would interpret it or whether she in truth possessed it. It sounded dull, but necessary.

"Of fine moral character," he repeated slowly, as if memorizing it. "This is helpful in terms of narrowing the field," he said gravely. "Thank you."

When he said nothing more, she looked down at her foolscap again.

"Number three: I should like him to be handsome."

She said this somewhat tentatively. She glanced up. *He* was handsome. Even with the frost of gray at his temples. But perhaps he'd think looks were unimportant when moral fiber was critical.

"Rest assured, I wouldn't dream of binding you to a gargoyle, Miss Danforth."

Excellent! She smiled, relieved. "I wasn't terribly worried, since all of the men I've seen so far in Sussex have been so . . ."

*Gorgeous*, she'd nearly said, in her rush of enthusiasm. Thinking in particular of the balcony man.

". . . pleasant," she completed, piously.

He was silent a moment. She thought the creases at the corners of his eyes deepened. Was he combating a smile?

"Many of them are," he said somewhat cryptically. "The next item would be . . . ?"

"Ah, yes." She returned her eyes to her list. "Number four: Enjoys . . ."

Damnation. This was another delicate one. She looked up at him again. The duke had fine lines around his eyes, which made her think that he might *occasionally* laugh. She'd seen no evidence of it yet. She wondered if he actually enjoyed it when he did, or if he felt it was a social requirement, like bowing and the like.

"A good brandy? Brisk walks at the seaside? Embroidery?" he prompted. She could hear the barely contained patience. A speck, she thought. I am an irritant, a speck, and he is scarcely tolerating me.

"...laughing."

She said it faintly. Almost apologetically.

"Ah," he said thoughtfully. "Well, I fear we may have a conflict between requirement number two and this particular requirement. I'm afraid I'm going to need to ask you to choose only one of them."

Her lungs seized so swiftly she nearly coughed.

Bloody hell. Well, she had only herself to blame for this.

A fraught silence ensued, her breathing suspended as she mulled the consequences in her mind.

And then he brought his palm down with a smack on his desk so hard it made her jump and burst into laughter. He threw his head back and laughed with it.

"Oh, Titania. You look so *stricken*! I am *teasing*. You see, I, too, occasionally enjoy 'laughing.' But I do believe I now know what you would choose if you had to."

His laugh was marvelous, so infectious that she rapidly recovered from being incensed and found herself laughing, too. Though she hadn't quite forgiven him for shaving a year or two from her life with his little joke. She'd imagined her doom a little too vividly.

"Your father was a good laugher," he said when they were both quiet again.

"The best." She dug her fingernails into her palm when she thought tears might prick at the corners of her eyes. They came at the oddest times. Even on the heels of laughter.

"He had a remarkably nimble mind, too. He could debate me into a corner on occasion. We enjoyed it, rather. And I'm very difficult to defeat, mind you."

"I don't doubt it," she said sincerely. But she was half teasing, too.

He smiled.

The laughter seemed to have loosened him, and Tansy recognized something: he was simply a bit stiff, as uncertain of her as she was of him. And he'd experienced a loss, too, when her father died. Someone to whom he'd been close, and she doubted the duke had many bosom comrades. Knowing this aroused her sympathy. She suddenly felt—and this seemed ridiculous, and yet there it was—protective of him.

"He called you 'Titania' in his letters to me."

"The name was his idea, and Mother never could refuse him anything. Then again, it was Mother who persuaded him to return to America. I always thought my name was a bit cumbersome. A bit much to live up to."

"I think you've quite grown into your name."

"Thank you. I think. It was Mother who called me Tansy. Father eventually capitulated."

He smiled again. And it looked so natural, she was relieved to believe he did it often, and not just because an occasional smile was expected of everyone. "But you certainly look like your mother."

"That's what everyone says."

A silence, an easier, softer one, ensued.

"I always hoped to see all of you again," he said gently. As if he knew too much discussion all at once would be unwelcome.

"I do remember you," Tansy told him, a bit shyly. "Just a very little. You were married to someone else then. I remember thinking she was so very pretty, like someone from a fairy tale. And she had such a lovely voice."

"Oh, she was. She *was* pretty. She passed away some years ago."

"I know. I am so sorry."

He nodded shortly.

There had been a baby, too, she recalled, and now she was sorry she'd mentioned it. She remembered her father receiving the letter from the duke. He'd told her mother about it in a few short, devastating sentences, and then repaired to his study, closing the door. As if by being alone he could share his friend's grief.

"But you should know, Titania, that I cannot recall ever being happier than I am now."

She knew it was true. There was really no mistaking it. She would never be able to describe happiness in words, she thought. It was something one witnessed.

And he'd said it because he wanted her to know she could be happy, too.

"I'm glad," she said softly. "Thank you for telling me."

He cleared his throat. "Do you have any more requirements on your list?"

She did.

"Number five: I should like him to be kind."

She looked up, a little worried about that one, too, but less worried than she had been when he first entered his office. She knew now, no matter what was said about him, that the duke was kind. Impatient, perhaps, more than a bit arrogant, perhaps, but one rather expected that of a duke. She felt he was fundamentally kind.

"And that's all I have for now."

He smiled faintly. "Is the list a work in progress?"

"I haven't yet decided."

"Do keep me apprised of critical changes in its content," he said somberly.

She suspected he was teasing her again.

"I shall." She smiled.

"I think we have an excellent chance of finding a match meeting your requirements. Your father was one of the most sensible people I've ever known, and he trusted my judgment. I imagine you'll be spoiled for choice. But I will know which young men are worthy of you, Titania . . . and which ones most definitely are not. But if you have any questions, you may feel free to confide in me."

"Thank you," she said, while thinking, *Good try*. He might be kind, but she also suspected he knew how to curtail fun, and she wasn't *that* naive.

"I'd like to chat a bit again, if you're amenable to it," he added, as he stood, signaling for her to stand, too.

"I would like that."

This, she found to her surprise, *was* true.

THE INTRODUCTION OF Miss Titania Danforth into Sussex society was to begin with a dinner, a little aperitif of a party before the ball—a *modest* ball, is how the duchess described it—to follow that evening. The most amusing people in Sussex had been invited, Genevieve had assured her, and a portion of London, too, and then she'd recited a list of titles both major and minor, both married and unmarried. When Tansy pictured them, they were all attractive. Funny the sort of magic the word "lord" could confer upon a person when it preceded a name. Privately she was now convinced the only way her own name would ever sound anything other than cumbersome would be if the word "duchess" came before it. Duchess Titania. Countess Titania? Lady Titania?

It was only a matter of time, she told herself stoutly.

The modest ball would be followed in a month or so by what Tansy was tempted to call an immodest ball, but which Genevieve referred to as a Grand Ball.

Tansy had been told she needn't do a thing but emerge from her chambers looking beautiful, "which you could accomplish wearing only sackcloth, if you preferred," Genevieve said with her usual generosity and graciousness. "Not that wearing sackcloth is a custom in Sussex."

"Ha ha!" Tansy laughed.

She'd decided to take looking beautiful tonight with the seriousness of blood sport.

And because her own American maid had been terrified at the very idea of making the crossing into a new country with her, Genevieve graciously sent over her own, a girl named Annie who was quiet, competent, and eager to please.

But Tansy was not in a mood to be pleased.

"Not the green. The blue."

The abigail pulled the blue from the closet.

"Not that blue. The *other* blue." The girl pulled it into her arms and turned around halfway when Tansy said, "No, perhaps the pale green silk?"

"I think you'll look beautiful in any of them, miss," the poor abigail said desperately.

Tansy nearly stamped her foot.

"Tell me, Annie," she demanded. "Have you a beau?"

Annie blushed. "Aye, miss. He works in the stables."

Tansy softened, genuinely curious. "How lovely! Is he handsome, your beau?"

"Aye, if I do say so myself. His name is James. We're to be married, but—"

"Oh, *are* you to be married? How lovely!" She beamed.

Annie glowed. "Oh, it is, it is. And yet we must

wait, for we haven't enough money to set up housekeeping, you see. James would like to build a little house for us to live in, so we needn't always live-in, and . . . surely I shouldn't bore you with this, Miss Danforth," she said desperately.

"I'm not bored at all. It's terribly important to have a home of your own. I should like one, too, you see. For I haven't one anymore. Or a family, you see."

And in that moment the hopes and concerns of womanhood transcended their societal roles and bound them fast in a subtle accord.

"You've a home here and we'll look after you," Annie said firmly. "If ever you need anything, Miss Danforth."

"Thank you," she said, quite touched.

There was an awkward, warm little silence, and Tansy turned away again, toward the wardrobe.

She'd never worried so much about a ball gown. Along with every young woman in New York society, she had taken her ability to captivate utterly for granted, regardless of what she wore. This was why the sympathy calls had been shot through with a subtle, yet unmistakably morbid glee. The queen had at last been nudged from her throne. It had taken disaster to do it, but still.

The balls had gone on without her while she dealt with solicitors and the like. And only a very few of those young women ever called on her again.

Tansy hated to admit it, but her confidence was

not as ironclad as it once was. Though perhaps all it needed was a little exercise in the proper context. Such as a ballroom full of men.

"Now . . . think about it this way," she said. "If you were me, and you wanted your beau to look at you and forget that anyone else in the world existed, which dress would you wear?"

Annie looked captivated by this notion, then turned and perused the dresses hanging there. "The white with silver ribbon," she said decisively.

*Now* they were making progress.

"Why?" Tansy pressed.

"Because you'll look like an—"

"Please don't say angel!"

Annie smiled. "A pearl what stepped from an oyster. A mermaid. A nymph."

A pearl! A nymph! A mermaid! Tansy liked all of those. She held the dress beneath her chin and studied herself in the mirror. With her hair down about her shoulders, she supposed she *did* look a bit like a mythical creature. The silver ribbon reflected the silver blue of her eyes, the white made her skin glow nearly golden, and her lips were blush, the color of the inside of a shell.

It would do. She exhaled.

"You see, Annie, it's just that I've only the one chance to make a first impression. And it's been so very long since I've been to a party like this."

"I will make certain you'll be unforgettable, miss."

Tansy gave a short nod. "Thank you."

The white dress it was. She slid it over her head like a gambler choosing the card that would decide the game.

AT DINNER SHE was introduced to myriad Everseas.

Her first impression was of a forest of tall, darkly appealing men, all white smiles, magnificent cheekbones, and exquisite manners, with manly, very English names: Colin, Marcus, Charles. They were so clearly of a piece, variations on a theme begun by their parents, who were two very handsome people. All of the boys were taller, just a little, than their merry-eyed father. The mother had the same heart-shaped face as Genevieve.

If they'd been bonbons in a box, she thought she might have first selected the one called Colin, the tallest of them, the only one whose eyes, she could have sworn, were more green than they were blue. And they sparkled.

She smiled at him.

He smiled back, and almost, not quite, winked.

And then his body convulsed swiftly as if someone had stabbed him with a fork.

He frowned, and the frown wavered and became a smile aimed at the woman across from him.

Her coloring was striking, her hair black, her skin fair, her dark eyes enigmatic. She had the air of permanent confidence of one who knows she is loved, and she was wearing a little private smile for her husband.

His wife. Madeleine. The other wives were named Louisa and Rosalind.

For alas, every last one of the Everseas was married.

Everyone, apart, that was, from Olivia.

And at the first sight of Olivia Eversea, Tansy's confidence wavered just a bit.

It was easy to see why she'd inspired the men of greater Sussex and beyond to turn the house into a thicket of flowers. Where Genevieve's beauty was warm and calm, Olivia glittered, like a diamond or a shard. Her eyes were fiercely bright and she was thin, perhaps a bit too thin, but it suited her; there was no angle from which Olivia Eversea's face wasn't somehow fascinating. Tansy found herself admiring the way she held her shoulders, and how graceful her slim arms were when she reached for the salt cellar.

"How very interesting to have an American in our midst, Miss Danforth," she said. "You hail from New York?"

"I do. I was born here, and I remember it fondly. But I love New York." A wave of longing for her previous life crashed over her so suddenly that her hand stilled on her fork. She'd once sat around a dinner table with her own family, laughing and bickering, and had once taken it for granted.

She reapplied herself to her peas. She needed stamina for the evening ahead. She hoisted the fork up again.

"Now, the south of your country in particular is populated by slave owners, is it not, Miss Danforth?"

Tansy's fork froze on its way to her mouth.

Oh, Hell's teeth. It sounded like a trap.

And she strongly suspected Olivia Eversea was a reader of the sort that she and the duke were not.

"I suppose some might say that," she said very, very cautiously.

"Do you know anyone who—"

Olivia suddenly hopped a few inches out of her chair and squeaked.

"Mind the stockings," she muttered darkly.

Or at least that's what Tansy thought she'd said. Tansy frowned a little.

"Olivia works so hard for excellent causes." This came from the matriarch, Mrs. Eversea, and she managed to make it sound both like pride and a warning.

Ah, *that* was likely why Olivia hadn't yet married. Tansy couldn't imagine a man in the world who would tolerate that nonsense for long. Suddenly she was far more certain she'd be able to usurp Olivia's flower throne.

She smiled at Olivia, as a way of apologizing for that unworthy thought.

Olivia smiled back at her, as if she'd heard every word of that thought and wasn't the least bit worried about her supremacy.

"Where is your brother?" the matriarch, Mrs.

Eversea, asked the handsome Eversea next to her. Marcus?

Brother? She looked up the table at all those handsome faces. There were *more* of them?

Which one of these men was the balcony pagan? she wondered.

A surge of optimism swept through her. Perhaps men like the Everseas were commonplace here in England. Perhaps finding a beautiful titled husband would be as simple as shaking an apple from a tree.

"Last I saw of him he was out with Adam repairing a paddock fence or a roof or something somewhere," the one called Chase said. "And they'll be at the vicarage repairs for days."

The duke looked up and said dryly, "As a form of penance for his usual—"

His face contorted in a wince. She knew a ferocious twinge of pity. Possibly when one got to his age, which was forty at least, many things made you wince. Gout, heart flutters, capricious digestion.

"Our cousin Mr. Adam Sylvaine is the vicar here in Pennyroyal Green," Genevieve said to Tansy. "He's always helping the Sussex poor. We're so very proud of him."

"How lovely to have a vicar as part of the family. Have you another brother?"

"Aren't we fortunate to have such wonderful weather at this time of year?" This came from the duke, a question posed to the table at large, as if he hadn't heard her question at all. Perhaps he hadn't. Perhaps she'd underestimated his age and he was beginning to need an ear trumpet to hear voices over a distance of several feet.

"IT'S LOVELY. DO YOU NORMALLY HAVE INCLEMENT SPRINGS?"

She had a sudden impression of the whites of eyes as they all widened.

"Our springs are so beautiful, Miss Danforth. You'll love them," Olivia volunteered, softly, carefully, as if demonstrating the proper indoor tone.

"Have you another brother?" she tried, more softly, a bit suspicious now.

"What are your interests and pursuits, Miss Danforth?" This came from Colin. It was a subject change, but his eyes held a promising sparkle.

"Oh, I've become a bit of a wallflower, I'm afraid. I'm looking forward to learning what the natives of Sussex enjoy."

Colin recognized this as flirtation, she could tell. This one was a rogue, or once had been.

"Colin likes cows," Chase said abruptly, irritably. "Very, very much."

"Cows . . ." Tansy mused. "Well, I can think of few things more fulfilling than raising a bovine to adulthood," she said.

There was an astonished hush.

Colin looked as though he was torn between thinking this was balderdash and wondering whether he cared whether it was or not, since it was precisely what he wanted to hear.

"Miss Danforth, have you ever traveled to the East Indies?" Chase interjected. It sounded almost experimental.

She swiveled her head toward him. "I haven't had the pleasure yet, but I imagine working for the East India Company is so *dashing*. The two of you must be very talented. I hope you'll tell me more about it during my stay."

She beamed at them.

And everyone could see the moment when Colin and Chase surrendered to the big eyes and eyelashes and the smile and they glowed.

There was another almost palpable hush.

And then Chase and Colin began talking over each other about cows and the East India Company until the footman brought in the blanc-mange.

# Chapter 5

❧

"Wallflower my eye!" Olivia said to Genevieve after dinner. She perched at the edge of Genevieve's bed and rubbed her ankle. "So much kicking and poking going on beneath the table tonight! Will we need to edit our conversation forever while she's here? 'I can't think of anything more rewarding than raising a bovine to adulthood.' *Honestly!* And it's not like she won't *see* Ian at some point. We can't disguise his existence forever. She may not find him in the least appealing when she does. She's such a young thing, and Ian can be such a jade."

Genevieve hesitated. The ironic parting words of Tansy's paid chaperone, "Good *luck* yer Grace," echoed in her mind.

She judiciously decided not to share this with Olivia. Not yet, anyway.

"Well, we shan't be sharing every meal with her. I think she's charming. She's alone in the world and I think she's only trying to please. She's just as charming to everyone, including me, and she'll be that way to you, too, if you give her a chance."

Genevieve was magnanimous in happiness and love and prepared to be blinkered and loyal to a reminder of something her husband cherished from his past.

"We shall see," Olivia said to the mirror. Love had been less kind to her, and she would never trust easily again.

AFTER A BRIEF dash to her room to pinch her cheeks and bite her lips and shake out her dress after sitting for dinner, Tansy ventured toward the ballroom.

She arrived on the threshold just as an excellent orchestra launched into a reel. And suddenly it felt as though her heart had been lifted up and twirled.

Lively music was very close to perfect happiness. Her life for so long had been full of movement, none of it particularly pleasant, none of it her choice. Tonight she would love to lose herself in one dance after another, like a butterfly flitting from flower to flower.

She took another tentative step into the room.

It wasn't yet crowded. None of the faces she immediately saw were familiar. It was odd to think that by the end of the night they likely would be.

She took another step into the room. A bit like wading into cool water and becoming accustomed to it, bit by bit.

She took another step, smiling.

And then she froze.

Something terrible happened.

Her breath left her abruptly, as if she'd been dropped from a great height. Her vision spangled. She gave a half turn and peered over her shoulder, as if expecting to see the assailant who had taken a shovel to her head and utterly scrambled her senses.

She slowly, cautiously, turned her head again back toward ballroom. Toward that wall.

Alas, she already knew it wasn't a shovel assailant. It was much worse.

It was a man.

A disturbing, delicious heat rushed over her skin. The entire world amplified inexplicably. Suddenly everything seemed louder and brighter and she was terribly conscious of her limbs, as if they were all newly installed and she would have to relearn how to use them.

For heaven's sake. It wasn't as though she hadn't *seen* handsome men before. She'd routinely managed the affections of handsome men with the skill of a puppeteer. And it wasn't a result of being out of the game, as it were. Giancarlo, handsome as he was, had scarcely raised her pulse.

What on earth was the difference here, then? Was it the way he held himself, as though the world itself was his to command? The faintly amused, detached expression, as if he intended to use everything and everyone he saw in it as his plaything, and make them like it? The sleek fit of his flawlessly tailored, elegantly simple clothes, which only made her wonder, shockingly, about what he looked like under the clothes? The arrogant profile? His delicious, nearly intimidating height?

It was all of those things and none of them. All she knew for certain was that it was new, and suddenly she was as blank-minded as a newborn.

Conscious that she was gawking, she forced herself to look in some other direction, which turned out to be, for some reason, up.

The only thing of interest on the ceiling was the chandelier, so she feigned wonderstruck admiration.

When she looked down again, the man was watching her. Clearly puzzled.

Her heart kicked violently.

His mouth tilted slightly at the corner, his head inclined in a slight nod, polite, a little indulgent.

His gaze kept traveling across the room, idly.

He'd skimmed her. As if she'd been a chair or a chandelier, or, *unthinkably* . . . a plain girl.

For the second time in minutes she experienced the shovel sensation.

A horrifying thought occurred to her: what if she wasn't considered attractive in England? What if there was something about her features the English found comical? What if golden hair was considered passé? She felt as though the sword had suddenly been flipped from her hand.

She nearly leaped out of her slippers when someone touched her elbow. She'd forgotten there were other people in the world.

She whipped her head around again and found Genevieve next to her.

"Oh, there you are! Good heavens, don't you look beautiful! Do come with me, Tansy. We'll have your dance card filled in moments, I *assure* you." Genevieve looped her arm companionably through hers and pulled her determinedly away. "And please don't feel shy. Everyone will be delighted to meet you, I promise you."

Tansy allowed herself to be led away, far away, from that man, and as she did, she aimed a smile radiantly, recklessly, across the room, into the crowd. The young man who happened to be standing in the path of it went scarlet, and then his face suffused with yearning and she knew, she *felt*, him watching her walk away.

And as she and Genevieve wended through the ballroom, she sensed male heads turning, one by one, like a meadow full of flowers bending in a summer breeze.

Before the night was over, she'd make that man take notice, too.

GENEVIEVE LED HER through the crowd, making introductions to young men and young women. A gratifying number of eyes went wide; conversation was stammered; dances were begged. In short, everything was as it *should* be, and she began to relax and enjoy herself. Stingily, strategically, she gave away just one waltz to a randomly chosen young man, so that all of the others would wonder why she'd chosen him, before she told Genevieve, "All of this conversation has made me a bit thirsty. Do you think we can visit the punch bowl?"

She began heading in that direction before Genevieve could reply or effect another meeting.

The man was still standing alone against the wall, observing the ballroom at large. Time seemed to slow as she approached.

She watched as if in a dream he straightened, turned, and said, "Well, good evening, Genevieve. Where are you off to in such a hurry?"

He was on first name terms with the duchess!

Tansy's heart was now pounding so hard it sent the blood ringing into her ears.

Genevieve said, "Miss Danforth, I'd like you to meet my brother, Mr. Ian Eversea. Captain Eversea, since his promotion."

Her *brother*! The brother no one would expound upon!

*Ian. Ian. Ian Ian Ian.*

It wasn't Lancelot, but it would do.

His bow, which was graceful, seemed unduly fascinating. She suspected everything he did would be fascinating—yawning, scratching, flicking sand from the corners of his eyes when he woke up in the morning. She found it difficult to imagine him doing anything so very ordinary.

Up close his face was a bit harder, a bit scarier, and more beautiful. Cheekbones and jaw and brow united in an uncompromising, faceted, diamondlike symmetry. His mouth was elegantly sculpted. His eyes above cheekbones as steep and forbidding as castle walls were blue, amused, ever-so-slightly cynical. He was older than she'd originally thought. He was even larger than she'd originally thought. He had shoulders that went on for eons. And he was able to look at her without scarlet flooding his cheeks, unlike so many other young men.

All of the things she felt in his presence felt too large to contain, too new to name. And it was this, perhaps, she'd been waiting for her entire life.

Could *this* be the balcony man?

"It's a pleasure to meet you, Miss Danforth."

His voice was so baritone, resonant, she fancied she could feel it in the pit of her stomach, like a thunderclap. Aristocratic. Warm but not too enthusiastic. Good. Fawners could be tedious.

And she would see what she could to amplify that enthusiasm.

It occurred to her then she hadn't spoken yet. She steeled herself to dazzle.

"I hope you'll call me Tansy."

Funny. Her voice had emerged sounding surprisingly small.

He smiled faintly down at her. "Do you?"

The English all seemed to find this amusing.

To her shock, she could feel a fresh wave of heat

rushing into her cheeks. He was likely looking at a literally scarlet woman.

She tried a radiant smile. It felt unnatural, as though suddenly twice the usual number of teeth were wedged into her mouth.

What was the *matter* with her?

"My friends do. And I hope we will become friends."

"Any friend of my sister's is a friend of mine."

Said with pretty, impartial gravity.

And the faintest hint of what she suspected was, again, amusement.

Genevieve made a small sound in her throat. Tansy glanced at her curiously. It sounded almost like skepticism. Perhaps a warning.

"We're on a quest to fill Tansy's dance card with the most splendid dancers, Ian."

It sounded very like Genevieve didn't want to include Ian in that number.

"I've been a bit of a wallflower, I'm afraid."

Tansy lowered her gaze demurely. Which gave her a clear view of his hands. Big hands, long straight fingers. A prickle of interesting heat started up at the back of her neck. "I'd be honored if you would dance with me, Mr. Eversea."

Very, very bold of her. Quite inadvisable, and yet, she could blame it on American manners, and she knew no English gentleman would be able to refuse.

She suspected that hadn't been Genevieve's intention at all, for whatever reason, but even so.

She looked up again to find Ian exchanging an unreadable look with Genevieve and mouthing words. They looked like: *Must I?*

The. Nerve.

"It would be my honor and privilege if you would share a waltz with me," he said solemnly, but with a glint in his blue eyes, which he probably thought was devastating.

The fact that it *was* devastating was beside the point. So devastating she nearly forgot he'd just been insufferable.

As nearly as insufferable as she'd been.

"I shall look forward to it greatly, Mr. Eversea," she said just as gravely, as Genevieve towed her away again.

# Chapter 6

MISS DANFORTH WAS DANCING a quadrille with Simon. The young man looked dumbstruck by his luck, and frequently stumbled over his own feet. Ian would warrant young Simon had danced that particular reel a hundred times in his life if he'd danced it once. Miss Danforth smiled radiantly at him each time he stumbled, as if he'd done it on purpose for her entertainment.

Ian frowned faintly.

His sister appeared at his elbow.

"Good evening, again, Genevieve. Did the dancing exhaust your husband?"

She rolled her eyes. She was so confident of her husband's vigor that insults and jests regarding his age rolled off her. "He was pulled into an impromptu meeting. Something regarding an investment he'd like to make." She paused. "It's thoughtful of you to be . . . kind . . . to Miss Danforth, Ian."

He smiled a slow, grim smile. "So thoughtful of your husband to warn me not to corrupt her."

"Oh. Did he?" She didn't sound surprised, however. "You can see where he might be sensitive on the topic, however."

She was teasing him. Mostly. He tried to work up righteous indignation, but it was difficult to remain self-righteous when it came to Genevieve. Especially since she was so *happy* with the duke that she all but walked about glowing like a medieval saint.

And also because he wasn't exactly proud of cuckolding the man with his former fiancée.

He sighed. "I'm not a corrupter of *innocents*, Genevieve." The implication being that the duke's erstwhile fiancée had hardly been an innocent, and had been rather complicit in the whole episode.

Genevieve made a noncommittal sound.

And said nothing for a time.

And then, "She's very pretty, Miss Danforth," she said carefully.

He sighed. "I suppose she is. Then again, so many women are, to my everlasting gratitude."

And, he was certain, Miss Danforth was quite accustomed to being called pretty, quite taken with herself and quite accustomed to wielding her eyelashes and big eyes to get what she wanted from men. Yet she was the veriest child, for all of that. The blushing. The blinding smile. The awkward conversation. He had seen it before, a million times it seemed, and now it distantly amused him, and when he wasn't in the mood to humor it, it irritated him. It posed no challenge. He had no use for it.

"How very blasé you are, Ian."

"Yes," he said simply, not in the mood for a lecture.

He looked about for his brothers, or his cousin Adam or someone who could be persuaded to sneak up to the library to join him in draining his father's brandy decanters in order to make whatever dancing ensued more interesting for them. He didn't see any of them. He supposed he'd have to settle for ratafia in the short term.

"I wish you trusted me, Genevieve."

"I wish I did, too," she said lightly, with a playful little tap of her fan.

And it wasn't until then that Ian was certain that she didn't. Not really.

It stung a bit, but he supposed he ought not be surprised. He hadn't earned his reputation as a rogue by not applying himself to the task.

"Falconbridge is charged with finding a match for her," his sister said. "Preferably a titled or at least spectacularly wealthy one. Those were the terms of her father's will."

"Dukes are hardly thick on the ground, though, are they? Though the Duke de Neauville's heir is of age, and could use a wife, no doubt. As all heirs do. I've spoken to him at White's. Fine manners. Not too much of an ass. He's perfectly inoffensive."

Genevieve laughed. "I suppose one can do worse than perfectly inoffensive."

He shrugged. "My felicitations to Miss Danforth and the poor devil she *does* marry. Speaking of which, here comes *your* poor devil."

But Genevieve had stopped listening to him, because she'd already seen her husband moving across the crowded ballroom, aiming for her like a ship aims for shore.

HAVING ABRUPTLY ABANDONED Genevieve for the punch bowl, he gave a start when he saw a pair of eyes peering through a tall potted plant. He leaned closer.

"Oh, good evening, Miss Charing."

"Good evening, Captain Eversea." Miss Josephine Charing's china-blue eyes blinked. She was a pretty, garrulous young lady with a big heart and a brain comprised primarily of feathers and air. She was lately engaged to Simon Covington.

"Is aught amiss? It's not like you to hide in a corner."

"It's what *you* do, isn't it, Mr. Eversea? When too many girls want to dance with you."

"Er . . . I may have done, on occasion," he said carefully, a bit startled. "Sometimes one just likes to take a bit of a rest."

"It's challenging to be beautiful, isn't it?" she said with an air of wistful authority.

"I suppose it is." He was amused. And he was fairly certain Miss Charing had been at the ratafia a bit too enthusiastically. "Why are you behind the plant? Is something troubling you?" He regretted asking immediately. Confidences were the baili-wick of his cousin Adam Sylvaine, the vicar. But Adam wasn't here. Feminine confidence in par-ticular invariably panicked and baffled Ian. The things women fussed over!

"Is some*one* troubling you?" he added, almost hopefully. He could easily dispatch any rogues who might be a little too free with their hands or words. He almost hoped that was the case. He was feeling restless and irritable and wouldn't have minded taking it out on someone who de-served it.

"It's just . . . well, I'm afraid," she confessed on a whisper.

"Who are you afraid of?" He was instantly alert. He scanned a practiced eye over the ball-room but saw no one who appeared unduly men-acing. Unduly drunk, certainly.

"Have you seen Miss Danforth?"

He blinked again. "Yes. Are you afraid of Miss Danforth? She didn't appear to be armed when I saw her."

She hesitated.

"My Simon is dancing with Miss Danforth."

Ian peered in the direction she was looking. And so he still was. Serious Simon Covington, with his long sensitive face, who was so walking-on-clouds smitten with Miss Charing, was indeed dancing with Miss Danforth.

"Isn't she pretty?" Josephine said querulously.

Attempting to be magnanimous. But sounding panicked.

"Yes. But so are you."

"You are kind," she said distractedly, the second time he was accused of such a thing tonight, and neither time had been entirely sincere. It was a testament to how much in love she was with young Simon that she didn't even look at Ian when she said it, when he knew that in days of yore the compliment would have enslaved her.

"Whenever he dances with someone else, he always looks for me. Not rudely, mind you. Otherwise he might trip over his dancing partner. And he hasn't looked for me once since this waltz began. Not once," she repeated mournfully.

"To be fair, you're hiding behind a plant at the moment," he pointed out.

"It was an instinct, I fear, after he'd gone round and round with her and seemed to have forgotten I existed."

Ian turned to scrutinize the happily rotating couple. Miss Danforth was beaming up at Simon as though she'd never seen or heard anything quite so fascinating in her life. So convincing was it that even Ian wondered if perhaps Simon possessed hidden depths he'd so far failed to see.

He frowned thoughtfully.

"Don't worry, Miss Charing. You see, I'm given to understand that Miss Danforth is a bit timid.

And Simon is mad about you. If she should make eyes at him, I'll call her out."

Miss Charing laughed. "*I'm* not timid at all," she said, sounding relieved. "Simon says he's happy to let me do all the talking for the both of us. He says it's a relief."

"A match made in Heaven, surely."

"Thank you, Captain Eversea."

"At your service, Miss Charing. Will you step out from behind the plant now, so Simon *can* see you? Perhaps you ought to have a sandwich?" He reached behind him and surreptitiously shoved the punch bowl out of her vision to take her mind off it and gestured with his chin to the sandwiches.

"I do love sandwiches!"

As she busied herself with the selection of one, he took a look at Miss Danforth and Simon again.

He couldn't help but notice that Simon seemed to be doing all of the talking.

SIMON COVINGTON RETURNED Miss Danforth to the waiting cluster of friends, and like a shred of iron sucked into a magnet, immediately attached himself to Miss Charing's side. Ian couldn't help but notice he looked contemplative, however, and a bit wonderstruck, as though he'd just had a religious experience he was struggling to interpret.

What had *gone on* during that waltz?

He took a step toward them, tempted to investigate, when a flash of red at the corner of his eye spun him around with an unerring instinct.

A lush, dark-haired beauty appeared to be perusing the sandwiches.

He knew precisely what she was actually perusing.

He smiled, and as he spoke, aimed his gaze nonchalantly out over the ballroom.

"Good evening, Lady Carstairs. Are you looking for something to satisfy your appetite?"

He turned slightly, saw her swift little enigmatic smile without turning fully around to look at him. And she bent, just a little, to select a sandwich, which allowed him to admire the curve of her derriere outlined in garnet silk, which of course had been her intent. She was a widow and a friend of the family of the late Lady Fennimore, and she divided her time between Sussex and London.

"Presuming my appetite *can* be satisfied," she said lightly. "You see, I've a taste for the unusual."

"One need only make a special request to have it met," he said gravely. "I'd be honored if you'd discuss your unique appetites with me during your visit to Sussex."

And as she returned to her friends—without looking him in the eye—Ian reflected that it was a bit like five card loo.

If the Duke of Falconbridge was said to never lose at that game, Ian Eversea could be said to never lose at this one.

"MR. COVINGTON WAS telling me of the plans he has to build a house on the land near the . . . oh, what did you call it? The Academy of . . . the School for . . ." She paused, flustered, looking searchingly into his face, as though the answers to all of the world's troubles could be found there.

"Miss Marietta Endicott's Academy for Young Women," Simon completed breathlessly, as if she'd said something too adorable.

Upon the conclusion of the waltz, Simon had escorted Miss Danforth back to where Ian stood with Miss Charing, and now the two of them were reminiscing about it.

Miss Danforth beamed at him. She swung her head to include the gathering at large. "Is he often like that, Miss Charing? Does he finish sentences for you?"

"No!" Miss Charing said, with something like alarm.

"But he's so very clever! How *do* you keep up with him?"

Simon was scarlet with pleasure.

"I sometimes wonder myself," Miss Charing said, studying Simon as if he was a stranger who'd just donned a Simon costume.

"I enjoy all of Miss Charing's sentences so thoroughly I'm happy to let her do most of the talking," Simon maintained stoutly. Mollification transformed Miss Charing's features.

Momentarily.

"I must say, your gift for conversation must be contagious, Miss Charing, for I found Mr. Covington to be positively scintillating. I hesitated to say one word lest I miss one of his." Miss Danforth smiled at him.

Simon beamed and croaked quietly, gleefully, wonderingly, to the gathering at large, "I'm scintillating!" Like a drunken parrot.

"You see, I've been a bit of a wallflower for some time, and it's very helpful to me when someone guides the conversation along, for I fear I'm a bit out of practice." She lowered her eyelashes.

"You did very well!" Simon defended. "Very well, indeed! Isn't she doing well?" he demanded of the gathering at large again, swiveling his head to and fro.

"*Very* well," Ian said dryly.

Miss Charing darted a panicked glance at Ian.

Miss Danforth looked up at him, saw the frown, and that pink rushed into her cheeks again, and she jerked her head abruptly away toward the ballroom floor. Away from him. A peculiar little thing, given to blushes and gushing, it seemed, and thoroughly intimidated by him. Such a child! Where had she been kept before she was sent across the ocean to England? Surely she hadn't been raised in a convent?

Just then his sister Olivia, stunning in willow green silk, limped toward them, leaning on the arm of Lord Landsdowne, whose face was a picture of somber solicitousness, as if Olivia were breakable.

"What happened, Liv? Did you kick a ne'er-do-well a bit too hard?"

"So witty, Ian. It was a rather too enthusiastic turn in the reel, I fear. My ankle went one way and I went the other. I shall live to dance again. I simply need to rest it a bit. Which sadly leaves Lord Landsdowne partnerless for the next reel."

Landsdowne promptly said, "It will be my honor to sit by your side and *will* your ankle to recover. I can be very persuasive."

She smiled at Landsdowne.

And then Landsdowne turned slightly, seeming to remember his usually impeccable manners, and saw Tansy.

A moment of silence and stillness ensued as Landsdowne's eyes settled on her in a bemused way. Ian could almost read the man's thoughts: *Surely she can't be as pretty as all that.*

"I haven't yet had the pleasure," he said slowly to her. Landsdowne was a grown man and a fairly formidable one. He wouldn't goggle or stammer. No. He would mull. And plan.

"Forgive my manners," Olivia said immediately. "Viscount Landsdowne, this is our guest, Miss Titania Danforth, of America."

Miss Danforth's lashes lowered and she curtsied, slowly and gracefully, for all the world like a petal drifting from a tree.

And Ian watched Landsdowne's eyes follow her all the way down. And all the way up.

"How fascinating to have an American in our midst, Miss Danforth," he said.

Landsdowne hadn't yet blinked. Bemusement

had evolved into something like wonder. His tone had gone a bit drifty.

"Oh, I'm the one who's fascinated! To be among such esteemed company. You are the very first viscount I have ever met." She cast those eyelashes down again.

Landsdowne smiled at this, obviously disarmed.

"And I'm the very first baron you've ever met!" the formerly silent Simon declared, elbowing into the conversation.

She turned, happily. "Oh, *are* you a baron, Simon? How *very* delightful."

"Not yet, he isn't," Miss Charing said somewhat churlishly, which made Ian eye the level of the ratafia cup she held. "His father has to die first."

"Do you attend many balls and parties in America, Miss Danforth?" Landsdowne asked smoothly.

"Not so many lately. I fear I've been a bit of a wallflower." Those fluffy dark lashes went down again.

To his credit, Landsdowne looked somewhat skeptical. "Well, we certainly must remedy that, mustn't we? I assume a round of gaiety is planned in order to introduce Miss Danforth to Sussex society? This party is only a beginning, Miss Danforth."

"Miss Danforth has been taken under the Duke of Falconbridge's wing," Olivia explained, and Landsdowne hiked an impressed brow.

"I've not yet danced a reel this evening. I

wonder if I remember how! I should be so embarrassed to try it in front of all of these people after such a long time."

"I'm a patient teacher, I'm told, if you'll allow me," Landsdowne said. "Will you?"

"Oh . . ." Miss Dansforth cast her eyes down, then up again. "I don't know if I dare subject you to the caprices of my dancing."

There was an odd little silence, as if everyone thought Olivia's blessing needed to be bestowed.

"Please do dance with him, Miss Danforth," Olivia urged finally, graciously. "He dances beautifully and we oughtn't deprive the assembly of the pleasure of watching him."

This, though ironic, was positively gushy for Olivia, and Ian knew it.

Landsdowne looked wry. "Then of course I shall dance for Your Majesty's entertainment," he said with mock gravity, and bowed low, very low, one leg extended, to Olivia, who nodded regally, accepting the fealty as her due.

SIMON AND MISS Charing wandered off to the garden, where a kiss or two might be stolen, or Miss Charing might vomit. It could easily go either way, Ian thought.

"You ought to be dancing," Olivia said to him.

"I like sitting with you." Which was true enough. He was less fond of reels than of waltzes, and he recognized that it was more or less his duty as a single man to dance, but he'd decided that Olivia needed the company.

Olivia snorted.

They were watching Miss Danforth and Landsdowne dance the reel. For an alleged novice, she certainly learned the steps very quickly. She was light on her feet and danced with every evidence of joy.

"He looks almost . . . playful." She said the word as if it were foreign and she was uncertain of its pronunciation.

Ian laughed. "Is he normally a somber chap? He seems it. Though a good one," he added hurriedly. "I like him a good deal."

"No, he has wit. The quiet, dry sort, however. I quite like it. He *is* a good one," she said absently. "I like him."

There was a pause.

"You like him. How torrid."

She shot him a wry sideways glance. But didn't expound.

His sister was passionate about nearly everything. The abolishment of slavery. The protection of the poor. The preservation of cherished historical landmarks. The color of clothing. Her tastes in nearly everything were very specific and impassioned and cleverly, usually wittily, reasoned, which was part of her charm. She was challenging and often exhausting, but never dull.

She was very guarded about Landsdowne.

And he had never once heard her utter Lyon Redmond's name since he'd vanished. He had often thought there would always be only one man for Olivia. And that one man had disappeared more than three years ago.

Landsdowne threw back his head and laughed at something Miss Danforth, the wallflower, had said.

"What do you think of her?" Olivia asked.

"Very pretty and vapid and uninteresting. An awkward ingenue. Ought to excel at being a spoiled wife of a rich aristocrat. And no doubt will be given the opportunity to be one soon enough."

Olivia mulled this. "I might agree with all of those words save one. I'm less convinced of the 'uninteresting' part. I wonder if she's . . . strategic. The bit with the lashes. All of that."

"I think when one is presented with a cipher, one can assign all sorts of meaning. The way we try to see shapes of things in clouds."

"You're likely correct."

Another silence ensued. Miss Danforth was smiling. Her complexion was creamy, faintly gold in the chandelier light, a luxurious, pearl shade. She moved lithely, and it was strangely a pleasure to watch her hop and clap the steps of the reel. She danced as though the music was part of her, and Ian felt something in him lighten as he watched. As if joy was her native emotion.

Landsdowne laughed again when she crashed into someone and was forced to apologize profusely.

"I don't know whether he laughs a good deal when he's with me," Olivia said.

Ian wondered if his sister, accustomed to being the toast of all of Sussex, and London as well, was worried.

"He's probably too busy being fascinated by you, Olivia."

"That *must* be it." Olivia smiled at that.

# Chapter 7

❧

LANDSDOWNE RETURNED MISS DANFORTH to them at the end of the reel, both of them flushed and happy looking. Then he settled down next to Olivia; rather like a regal, faithful hound who would never leave his mistress's side, Ian thought.

Which left him with Miss Danforth. Who wasn't smiling, or fluttering her eyelashes, but who had suddenly gone still.

When the strains of the Sussex waltz started, he bowed, and extended his arm to a girl whose dress was so white and gossamer she might as well have written "I'm a virgin" across her forehead. Ian thought of the widow in red across the room and let his thoughts stray in her direction, half resenting the opportunity robbed from him by this little girl. He suppressed a sigh.

Miss Danforth gave her hand to him almost portentously, slowly, as if she were pulling the sword from a stone. Lucky me, to be presented with such a gift, he thought wryly.

He took it with a certain ironic gravity, and placed his hand against her waist.

He felt her breath hitch in the jump of her slight rib cage.

Suddenly, he wondered how long it had been since his touch had felt new, surprising, exciting, to a woman, and a little of that was communicated to him, too.

A rogue, fierce surge of protectiveness swept in, startling him, and then swept out again.

He looked down. Into eyes of such a singular crystalline silver-blue color he fancied he could see himself in them. The eyes of a woman who had no midnight trysts or any other stains of any sort on her conscience.

They *really* would have very little in common.

He eased them into the one, two, three of the other whirling waltzers the way he would ease his horse through the traffic on Bond Street.

She hadn't yet said a word. She was staring as though she was from one of those distant islands Miles Redmond wrote about and had never before seen an Englishman in the flesh.

He was tempted to lead off with *Boo*.

"How are you enjoying England, Miss Danforth?" he said instead.

"I like what I've seen of it so far very much indeed."

It was delivered with such fervor, he widened, then narrowed his eyes briefly. If he hadn't known better, if a different woman had issued the words, he would have considered that an innuendo. That, combined with the "I'd be honored to dance with you, Mr. Eversea" and the "I hope you'll call me Tansy." Perhaps all Americans were just a bit too forward.

But now she was looking up, gazing limpidly back at him. He was a connoisseur of women's mouths, and hers was a work of art, he was forced to concede. The bottom lip a shell-pink pillowy curve, the top shorter, with two gentle little peaks. A bit like a heart. Both whimsical and sensual, one was tempted to trace its contours with a finger.

Her face was rather heart-shaped, too, and the heat of the crowded ballroom and the vigor of dancing had made her rosy. It was the sort of color a good bout of lovemaking put into a woman's cheeks.

He contemplated telling her this, just to shock the living daylights out of her.

"Is something amusing, Mr. Eversea?" She said this with something like strained gaiety.

"Oh, something is always amusing. I suppose that's my motto, if one must have one. What is yours, Miss Danforth?"

"Never surrender," she said instantly.

He was a bit taken aback.

"That *is* a pity," he tried. Murmuring. Half-heartedly sending out the innuendo as a smuggler would send a signal with a lamp from the coast, but not expecting much by way of response.

Something did twitch across her cloudless brow. Irritation? Confusion? Indigestion?

"I beg your pardon?" she said politely.

He didn't expound. "That's a much better motto than the one for, oh, Leicestershire: 'Always the Same.'"

This elicited a burst of loud laughter from her that made him suppress, just barely, a wince.

She modulated it instantly, then fell abruptly silent. A moment later she cleared her throat.

"Then again, there's a measure of comfort in sameness," she said, to the man who thrived on risk and newness, especially new women. "Why did you mention Leicestershire? Is there something special about it?"

She seemed to be waiting with bated breath. As if *everything* hinged on the next thing he said.

"It's where Richard the Third was buried. Or so they say." That was nearly all he knew about Leicester. That, and the motto.

"Richard the Third? The kingdom for a horse king? The poor bent chap? Are you very interested in history, then?" It was a rush of barely contained eagerness.

"One and the same. Are you very interested in history, Miss Danforth?"

The answer was important. If it was affirmative, it would encourage him to avoid conversation with her altogether in the future. Not even an opportunity to play red flag to the Duke of Falconbridge's bull would tempt him to endure conversations about ancient history.

The present was so much safer than the past, as far as Ian was concerned, and the future was a concept he'd only begun contemplating with excitement. It would be his refuge, all those ports on that map of the world. He would run like a river, never stopping. He suspected, after all, it was his nature to keep moving.

He looked out over her head at the ballroom, and saw Olivia sail by in the arms of Lord Landsdowne, who looked possessive and proud. So she'd either walked off her sore ankle or decided she'd better dance with Landsdowne on the heels of his reel with Miss Danforth. Olivia looked . . . one never knew with Olivia. She'd perfected the art of appearing as though everything was perfect. And there was a certain defiance to her lately. As though she thought Lyon Redmond was actually looking on when she went walking with Landsdowne, and when she danced with him, and suffering over it.

"I'm interested in some periods of history. Perhaps I'll go to Leicester one day." Miss Danforth sounded a trifle desperate.

He returned his attention to her.

"Perhaps you will," he humored. And as if this entire conversation was rudderless and he could not be blamed if he failed to stay the course, he looked out over her head again . . . There she was. Lady Carstairs dancing with some other fortunate soul.

He knew her quick sultry smile and that little head toss were all for him, and he wondered which of the alcoves he ought to attempt to maneuver her into before the night was through. For at least a little more charged conversation.

*Now* that *was how one flirted, Miss Danforth*, he was tempted to instruct.

"Have you an occupation, Mr. Eversea?" Miss Danforth tried, a trifle sharply.

"I do. Primarily it's scandalizing decent people."

He had the grace to regret it. It was a terribly unfair thing to say. Glib and arrogant and more impulsive than he normally was. It was just that life suddenly seemed too short for waltzes like this one.

Color flooded her cheeks. Again. The girl blushed as regularly as the tides moving in and out. And he knew he'd neatly cornered her: asking him to expound would be tantamount to wanting to hear scandalous things, which would of course mean she was indecent.

She clearly hadn't the faintest idea what to say.

It was poor form to punish the girl for being innocent and sheltered and inexperienced, and uninteresting to him because of it.

"Why do people call you Tansy?" he said, as if he hadn't just been unthinkably rude.

"Well," she said thoughtfully, "nicknames are usually shortened names, are they not? For instance, if the diminutive derived from the first syllable of the name Jonathan is Johnny, what would my nickname logically be given my name is Titania?"

"Well I suppose one would call you Tit . . . sy."

An infinitesimal moment of horror passed.

He was halfway into the word before he fully realized what he was saying, and momentum carried him all the way through it.

He stared at her as if a mourning dove had just sunk fangs into his hand.

Had . . . had this delicate well-bred "wallflower" actually led him right into saying "Titsy" to her?

*Surely* that hadn't been her intent?

But now he was thinking about her breasts.

*Really* wondering about them.

He would be damned if he would look down at them.

Perhaps quite *literally* damned.

She gazed back at him evenly. He thought, though he could not be sure, he detected a glimmer of triumph or defiance there, but that may have just been the light of the chandelier glancing from her clear, innocent eyes.

"You see, one can hardly call me that, Mr. Eversea," she said somberly.

"I suppose not," he said shortly.

The final moments of the waltz were passed in utter silence between them.

And as he bowed farewell, he did look at them on his way down.

They were excellent, indeed.


TANSY RETURNED TO her chambers late, late, very late, quite foxed on ratafia, champagne, and compliments, both given and received.

She stood motionless for a moment in the center of the sea of carpet, riffling through memories and moments, smiling softly over each little triumph, each glance, each laugh won. Until she got to the only one that truly mattered.

And then her smile slowly dimmed.

She groaned and covered her face in her hands and rocked it to and fro.

She had been grace personified with everyone else. With him, she'd brayed like a mule with laughter and enthused over everything he'd said with the force of an animal released from a trap. Graceless and appalling. She'd watched it happening, as if she were floating over her body in the ballroom, and there was nothing, nothing at all, she could do to stop it. What was *wrong* with her? If this was love, it was dreadful.

The difference, primarily, was that she'd never before needed to really try for a man's attention. Or try *very* hard, anyway. More specifically: she'd never before wanted a man's attention the way she wanted his.

"Titsy!" she moaned. "I made him say Titsy!"

It wasn't as though he hadn't deserved it.

She yanked off one satin slipper and hurled it across the room. It bounced very unsatisfactorily off the thick carpet, soundlessly.

"He's a *boor*," she said aloud to the room and the great arrangement of flowers, now drooping.

So few good opportunities existed to use that word.

And then she yanked off her other slipper, looking about for something to throw it at.

She threw it at the wall.

She fancied she heard a grunt on the opposite side.

Excellent.

She exhaled at length, and then settled at her desk, stabbed a quill into some ink, unfolded her sheet of foolscap and carefully added to her list:

*Makes you feel like you're the only woman in the world when he's with you.*

It seemed a terrible character flaw. A terrible, terrible character flaw to look past her shoulder at a brunette who, while certainly pretty, was also getting on in years. But then, if she was a widow, that meant she possessed the freedom to do whatever she liked—including all of those things Giancarlo had suggested in Italian slang—with Ian Eversea. Who wasn't a duke, who would never be a duke, who did not even have a title, even if he had those blue blue blue eyes that made her breath snag . . .

Tansy flung herself backward on her bed. Just for a moment. Just for one, long, lovely moment. She would close her eyes for just a moment. Her feet were sore and it would be lovely to . . . lovely to . . .

# Chapter 8

*AARGH!*

The moment her eyes fluttered open, her hands flew up to cradle her head. Cannons were firing in there. Last night's champagne and ratafia seemed to have re-formed into a boiling ball of lead and situated itself behind one eye.

*BOOM. BOOM. BOOM. BOOM.*

She lay as still as she possibly could to avoid jarring anything overmuch. No effigy installed in Westminster Abbey had ever lain quite so motionless. She was fascinated by, and a little proud, of the gruesome pain. She felt very worldly. And nauseous.

She glanced down. She was still entirely dressed. Apart from her slippers. Where were her slippers?

But it was just about dawn . . .

Curiosity was stronger than nausea.

She slipped out of bed and very, very gingerly, as though her head was a grenade balanced atop her neck, carried herself to the window by following that beam like a tightrope. She gingerly parted the soft curtain.

*Aargh!*

Ghastly punishing light!

Even though the sun was just a suggestion on the horizon, like half of a peach rising from the water.

She recoiled and gripped her head.

But instinct forced her forward again, and she tentatively cracked her eyelids.

She was rewarded for enduring pain. The man was standing on the balcony!

The sun had just reached him, and he was part in shadow, partly gilded. A pagan harlequin.

For one merciful moment pain ceased.

All of her senses were marshalled to the job of seeing him, like spectators rushing a fence at a horse race. She breathed and she felt him everywhere, again. As though her entire body wanted to participate in his beauty.

But then even in her incapacitated state something about him . . .

Something about the height . . . something about the way her breath stopped . . .

*Could it be a certain insufferable in-love-with-himself Eversea?*

He arched backward again, thrusting sunburnished gorgeously muscled arms high into the air like an acrobat landing, and he roared—though this time the roar tapered off into what sounded suspiciously like a hungover groan.

And then he broke wind, scratched his chest, and ducked back into his room.

She snickered.

"Ow ow ow ow ow ow!" And was immediately punished by the return of the booted battalion in her head.

She stumbled and fell upon the servants bell-pull as a lifeline.

She would have happily traded all the blood in her veins at that moment for coffee.

"Have you any books on Richard the Third? Bent fellow, the kingdom-for-a-horse chap?"

It seemed a miracle to be ambulatory, but after her second well-sugared cup of coffee and two and a half fluffy scones, Tansy and a similarly for-tified Genevieve set out for a walk into town, on the theory that the fresh air and exercise would do them good and that Tansy would naturally like to get a closer look at Pennyroyal Green.

The fresh air *had* done them good. It smelled faintly of the sea and green things, and she liked it. She could scarcely remember anything about it, though she'd lived here as a child, but the land-scape of Sussex, as far as she could tell, was subtle. Modest. The hills were mild swells and the trees a humble height, unlike the arrogant, craggy-faced mountains and unruly forests of America. Sheep dotted the hills and clouds dotted the blue skies, like puffy white reflections of each other.

The church and the pub were opposite each

other, which surely must be good business for both, and she craned her head as they passed an intriguing shop called Postlethwaite's Emporium, which featured an enticing selection of bonnets and gloves in the window.

The dark of the bookshop was a blessing to her still faintly pounding head after the bright light. She enjoyed horrid novels, and she'd read a novel by a Miss Jane Austen which she'd quite liked, but lately she'd become fascinated by adventure stories. Specifically, stories of survival. Robinson Crusoe had lost everything—how had he managed to get on after that? That sort of thing. She'd acquired a tome written by a Mr. Miles Redmond, who had a series of adventures in the South Seas and was nearly eaten by cannibals. He'd lived to tell the tale. Surely she could prevail over the upending of her own life if others had triumphed over odds and humans who ate other humans.

The bookseller, a wiry older gentleman called Mr. Tingle, beamed approvingly at her and fidgeted with his spectacles, which was, she suspected, what he did when he flirted—the equivalent of a lash bat.

So she rewarded him with a lash bat.

"I aver, Mr. Tingle, this may be the finest bookshop I've ever set foot in! I've never *seen* such a fine selection. You must be very discerning, indeed."

Mr. Tingle's face suffused with happiness, and he did more fidgeting with his spectacles.

"We have the play of Richard the Third set forth in a collection of works by our own Mr. William Shakespeare. Perhaps you'd be interested in reading it? Or would you prefer to read a history of the man?"

"The latter, if you please."

"Ah, a *scholar*!" He clasped his hands with such glee she hated to disagree with him.

"*Are* you interested in history, Miss Danforth, er, Tansy?" Genevieve was perusing a biography of Leonardo da Vinci, rapt. Turning pages over, slowly, one by one.

She hesitated.

"A sudden fascination swept over me," she decided to say.

This much, at least, was true.

"I suppose new places can inspire new interests," Genevieve said.

"Truer words were never spoken," she agreed vehemently.

"Well, I'm delighted to be of service to such a fine mind," Mr. Tingle declared. "In fact, I'd like to make a present of this volume, Miss Danforth, as long as you choose another one to purchase."

"You are too, too kind, Mr. Tingle! You are a generous man, to be certain."

"Oh, bosh." Color moved into his cheeks. "It's a pleasure to do business with such an avid reader." Avid was a bit of a stretch, but she suspected he'd be mightily disappointed if she disabused him of the notion. "Can I interest you in another period of English history? Perhaps something about William the Conqueror?"

"Well, let me think . . . have you any books written by Mr. Miles Redmond?"

Mr. Tingle's hands froze on his spectacles. His eyes darted toward Genevieve and back again.

Tansy felt, rather than saw, Genevieve go motionless.

A bewildering, indecisive little silence followed.

At last Mr. Tingle cleared his throat. He lowered his voice. "We *do* have a selection of Mr. Redmond's books," he said, as carefully as if he were confessing to a collection of pornography.

"I enjoyed one of his books on his adventures in Lacao. I would love to read more about that particular journey."

Mr. Tingle lowered his voice to something like a discreet whisper.

"I'll just go and fetch the one that follows for you, will I?"

THEY'D EACH ACQUIRED a new book, each one very much representative of their own personal fascinations and who they were as people, though they didn't know that, and they clasped them to their bosoms as they walked. Genevieve reminded her of the Sussex landscape: subtle. She wasn't prone to chatter or untoward confidences, she was intelligent and measured, her wit quiet but quick. When she spoke. The emphasis was on the *quiet*. And Tansy felt a bit tethered. Her own personality, in general, was decidedly buoyant. A bit more impulsive.

"May I ask you a question, Genevieve?"

"Certainly."

"How long have you been married?"

"Nearly a year now."

There was silence, as they trod side by side, coming abreast of the ancient cemetery surrounding the squat little church. Tansy stopped, mesmerized by the stones. The newer ones were upright, the older ones reclining a bit, sagging, as everything is wont do with age. A huge willow rose up and sheltered most of it, like a hen fanning its wings out over her chicks.

The English all seemed very restrained, and she told herself she probably ought not ask the next question.

"How did you . . . know? About the duke, that is. Or . . ."

Or *did* you know? was what she wanted to know, but it seemed far too presumptuous. And given the looks she'd seen Genevieve exchange with the duke, she was certain the question was unnecessary. He'd said he was happy. She knew he was happy. But how did one know?

Genevieve smiled. "You'll know when it happens to you, if that's what you're worried about. There's really no mistaking it."

She did have a little of that married woman superiority Tansy generally found *infinitely* irritating.

"Did you by any chance ever lose your powers of speech around him?" she asked, half in jest.

Genevieve looked amused, yet puzzled. "I daresay I rather found my powers of speech when I met him."

Alas. Tansy suspected her own particular affliction might very well be unique. Ian Everseaitis.

He was unpleasant and rude and beautiful and scary, and she wondered hungrily if the book she held would somehow hold a key to him. How did an interest in Richard III reveal him, or would it? It was all she had at the moment, so she clutched it to herself like a map.

"Do you mind . . . do you mind if we walk through?" She gestured at the gravestones.

"Not at all."

She silently wove through the yard, which wasn't so much sad as it was peaceful and wistful. She rather liked the idea of the graveyard surrounding the church. Dead was dead; there was no getting around it, really. She of all people ought to know. Perhaps the location of the graveyard served as a reminder of those who were bored with attending church that it was all dust to dust, and they ought to see to their souls if they wanted to proceed through the pearly gates after a tombstone was erected on top of them.

She silently read the names on the stones as she strolled through.

"Quite a few Redmonds," she said. "And Everseas. Is Mr. Miles Redmond a part of the Redmonds of Pennyroyal Green?"

"He is, indeed," Genevieve said politely.

Interestingly, she didn't expound.

Tansy didn't press for more information. The Everseas were not as subtle as they thought they were. She would get to the bottom of that particular mystery in time, she knew.

And then she stopped and knelt near a particular stone. A certain Lady Elizabeth Stanton had passed a good thirty years ago at the age of twenty-one. Did Lady Elizabeth marry her title, or was she born with it? Why did she die so young? Was it childbirth or a fever or a fall from a horse or . . . ? Had she ever lost her powers of speech when a boorish man stared down at her as if he could read every thought in her head and found them criminally mundane?

She didn't have any flowers on her grave, but she was flanked by graves that were freshly adorned, and this struck Tansy as wholly unfair.

"There aren't any flowers on this one."

Genevieve sympathetically studied Lady Elizabeth Stanton's stone. "I suppose over the years families move away, or the last of them expires, and sometimes stones are forgotten."

"Well, they ought to have flowers, don't you think?" She felt urgent about this suddenly, as if she were the naked one, not the grave. "*Someone* ought to remember. We can't have flowers on some and not all."

It didn't sound remotely rational even to her, but Genevieve didn't appear to have an argument for this.

Tansy scanned the churchyard, and Eureka!

She found one little blue wildflower, poking through a fence.

"Sorry!" she whispered to it. "And thank you," and she gave a little yank.

She transported it to the grave and lay it gently down.

That was better.

"Blue is your color," she whispered to the late Lady Elizabeth, just to amuse herself.

Tansy turned to see if Genevieve was watching, but she was looking upward and waving at something.

There, at the very top of the vicarage, was Ian Eversea, hands on his hips, watching the two of them.

He was significantly smaller at that distance, but she still knew. Her body seemed able to sense him. She fancied she could feel his blue eyes from where she stood, like the beams of two little judgmental, cynical, gorgeous suns.

She could practically feel all of her native charm and polish evaporate the way sun evaporated rain. What *was* it about the man that made her feel so very gauche?

He lifted a hand—there appeared to be a hammer in it—in a sort of salute.

"He always was an excellent climber, my brother."

Genevieve sounded a bit ironic.

But Tansy barely registered this. Suddenly he was all she could see, delineated against a blue sky. And her heart had struck up a sharp beating, like a hammer against a dulcimer.

She stood abruptly, brushed her hands down her skirts and mutely followed Genevieve around the corner.

Only to abruptly encounter a cluster of men deep in conversation, gesticulating in that universal language men shared when something needed to be built or repaired. Each of them seemed to be clutching a tool of some sort—a spade or hammer or saw. *How* men loved tools, she thought.

Then turned abruptly when the ladies rounded the corner.

They stopped talking and gesticulating.

Their eyes rapidly tracked from Genevieve to Tansy and back again.

And they stalled on Tansy, as motionless as pointing hunting dogs.

She gave them a demure smile. And fluttered her lashes.

And then they all bowed, and when upright again, commenced variously gaping, toeing the ground, or fidgeting with their hair.

Which was just as well, because she couldn't speak, either. Because she'd watched Ian Eversea clamber down from the roof and now he was striding ever closer. For a moment he seemed to use the air she needed to breathe. Her lungs had stopped moving.

She tipped her head a little back, as if the air were clearer there, and took a long breath.

Genevieve made the introductions as Ian drew ever closer.

"Gentlemen, this is our guest, Miss Titania Danforth. Miss Danforth, this is my cousin Reverend Adam Sylvaine. You met Simon last night at the ball, Miss Danforth, and Lord Henry Thorpe has returned from abroad and is kindly helping with repairs to the vicarage."

Lord Henry was young enough to still have a few pink spots sprinkled on his cheeks. His hair was closely cropped.

The man leaning on his shovel found his voice first, and didn't wait for the niceties of introductions.

"Mr. Seamus Duggan at your service, Miss Danforth." He had curly black hair and green eyes and his Irish accent was a beautiful thing. It leaped and lilted like a jig. He bowed low, keeping one arm suavely slung around the shovel as if it were a spare lover. "I do mean that. If ever you need anything, and I do mean *any*—"

"We try to keep Seamus too busy to get into too much trouble," the vicar interjected pleasantly.

"Ha ha," Seamus laughed, in a hail-fellow-well-met way, but he shot a faintly aggrieved look in the direction of the very tall vicar.

The vicar was clearly from the Eversea mold of stunning men. He exuded an air of lovely calm and strength, and Tansy suspected it was the sort he'd earned the hard way. Because she knew a bit about learning things the hard way.

But she wasn't interested in "calm." She was

interested in that spiky, breathless, ground-is-shifting-beneath-her-feet feeling she'd only felt for the man who was . . . now right upon them.

IAN HAD AN unerring instinct for excellent examples of the female form; like a weathervane, he invariably spun toward it. He'd been pounding a nail into the roof when something made him pause, and slowly rise to his feet, and . . . watch. His breath suspended. Something purely carnal touched its fingertips to the back of his neck and communicated with his nether region. All of his senses had marshalled to witness whoever she was.

Two women had entered the churchyard, and the way she moved—it was intangible, really, something about the line of her spine, the subtle sway of her hips—issued a call, and his body responded. His heart picked up a beat or two in anticipation of discovering her identity.

He shaded his eyes.

One of them was Genevieve—he recognized the color of the ribbon she'd used to trim her favorite bonnet.

The other one then must be . . .

. . . could it be Miss Danforth?

Alas, he feared it was. *Titsy* Danforth.

He gave a short humorless laugh at his own expense.

Still, he shaded his eyes and watched. He did like the way she moved. He frowned faintly as she plucked a flower from between the fence posts and knelt and laid it on a grave. Genevieve looked up at him and gave a surreptitious shrug.

And then she waved her arm in a great arc of greeting.

His manners drove him down off the roof.

Unsurprisingly, he could *hear* Miss Danforth well before he was upon the group of men.

"I'll *definitely* keep you in mind, Mr. Duggan," Tansy was saying as he approached. A bit like an actress trying to reach the back of the house. Perhaps she was a bit hard of hearing? She *had* laughed rather more heartily than a lady ought to the other night when they'd danced. "Thank you *so* much for your kind offer."

What offer had Duggan made?

"Oh, please *do* keep me in mind, Miss Danforth," Seamus said gravely.

And she smiled at that, slowly, and with great satisfaction.

And despite himself, her smile had an interesting effect on Ian, too. He was tempted to look away, and yet it was as though she'd flung a handful of fairy dust at them. He'd seen similarly dumbstruck, biddable expressions on a man subjected to a mesmerist's pendulum.

"Good afternoon, ladies," he interrupted politely. "I assume all introductions have been made?"

"They've been made," Seamus affirmed fervently, "and I shall never forget this day for as long as I draw breath."

Miss Danforth rewarded this stream of blarney

with another dazzling smile. Not the least non-plussed.

She hadn't yet looked Ian in the eye.

He frowned again, then caught himself just in time and arranged his face in more neutral planes.

"Will you be attending the Sussex marksmanship competition, Miss Danforth?" Simon wanted to know. "And my lady," he hastily appended, including Genevieve as an afterthought. He'd known Genevieve his entire life. Calling her "my lady" had been a bit of an adjustment for everyone.

Genevieve shot Ian a wry glance.

"A marksmanship contest! How exciting! *May* we attend?" Miss Danforth clasped her hands beseechingly and turned to Genevieve. And then she swiveled back to the men. "Will all of you be shooting in it? You all *look* like marksmen. I'm absolutely certain each of you wield your tools with skill and precision."

Ian's eyes widened again and he intercepted a darted glance from Seamus Duggan, who was a dyed-in-the-wool rogue and a bit of a ruffian, and who could be counted on to hear that sentence precisely the same way he had.

"Of course. I think Ian is one of the judges this year," Genevieve said. "Aren't you, Ian?"

He gave a little grunt of confirmation and swiped a hand across his brow where perspiration had glued his hair to his forehead.

"It's archery *and* shooting," Genevieve volunteered. "And Adam took home the shooting trophy during the last competition."

Adam, the vicar, shrugged modestly.

"Good heavens! A shooting vicar!" Miss Danforth seemed awestruck. "How *very* impressive. Remarkable skill and control are required to properly aim a musket, isn't that so?" Her dark lashes flickered up and her blue eyes peered up at Adam through them.

"I suppose there is," Ian heard his usually brutally pragmatic, utterly unpretentious cousin say, after what could only be interpreted as a moment of dumbstruck admiration.

Ian shot him a look, and Adam gave his head a rough little shake and turned. "If you'll all excuse me, I need to finish writing a sermon. A pleasure to meet you, Miss Danforth. Good day, Genevieve."

Everyone else seemed to ignore the departure of the vicar.

"But I came in fourth in archery," Lord Henry hastened to brag. "And this year, I vow, I'll take home the prize."

She swiveled toward Lord Henry. "Oh, if there's something I admire more than a man who is confident about repairing things with his hands, it's a man who's competent with a bow and arrows. So elegant! So primal! It calls to mind Greek gods and that sort of thing, don't you think, Genevieve?"

Genevieve was startled to be called upon. She'd seemed bemused by the entire exchange.

"It wasn't the first thing that came to mind," she said, quite diplomatically. "But I suppose one might view it that way."

"There's nothing more impressive than men up on the vicarage roof for repairs," Ian tried. Just to amuse himself.

No one heard him.

They were all muttering "mmm-hmmm" and nodding vigorous agreement with Miss Danforth, though in all likelihood none of them would have been caught dead calling themselves Greek gods in any other circumstance.

"I *love* to shoot," Simon claimed wildly. "Guns, arrows, everything I can!"

Miss Danforth aimed the rays of her attention at him. "Oh, I often feel that nothing is more masculine than excellent aim. Such a useful skill." She gave a delighted little shiver. "I suspect you're very good at it."

If a man could be said to preen, Simon—quiet, levelheaded Simon—preened.

And the expression on the others immediately darkened, and shifted.

Suddenly they began speaking over one another all at once, describing their prowess with weaponry. And her head turned to and fro between them, shedding upon each of them in turn the radiant beam of her attention.

If he didn't know any better, Ian would have thought Miss Titania Danforth had played all of them as skillfully as an orchestra conductor.

And at last her eyes met his, and hers were as clear and innocent as ever.

Unless . . . well, surely that glint in them was just the sunlight.

"And how is *your* aim, Mr. Eversea?" she asked. Seemingly emboldened.

He met her gaze evenly.

And said nothing.

In seconds color crept slowly back into her tawny cheeks.

She cast her fluffy lashes down. And looked away from him.

He sighed.

"All right, back to work, gentlemen," he ordered in a brook-no-argument voice. "The roof and fence won't repair themselves, and I know some of you are going to need a few more points in your favor in order to get into Heaven . . . Seamus. Good day, ladies, and we'll see you at home this evening."

TANSY DID WHAT amounted to brooding on the way home. Genevieve attempted conversation once or twice and then fell politely silent, too.

At home they took two steps into the foyer and stopped short.

"Please tell me no one died!" Genevieve blurted at the footmen.

There were flowers *everywhere*. Or it appeared that way. Vases stuffed full of them were scattered about the foyer.

"I am pleased to tell you that everyone lives, Your

Grace, to my knowledge. Two of these arrangements are for Miss Olivia, and the other . . . three," and the footman smiled fondly, "are for Miss Danforth. The mantels of the house can scarcely accommodate *two* such popular young ladies. How you do brighten up the house. We haven't yet found places for all of them, and I thought Miss Danforth would like to see hers and decide where they should be placed."

Tansy circled them with awe.

Three different admirers! After only just one ball! Her heart began to take up a steady beating. Dare she hope that one of them was from . . . ?

But it was a foolish hope.

She perused the cards. From two young lords and another young man she could scarcely recall, to her slight embarrassment. Boys. They were all boys.

The copy of Richard III seemed to glow like a little coal in her hand.

"And the table is set for luncheon if you ladies would care to go through," the footman told them.

And when they did go through, Tansy found a small paper-wrapped, string-bound package next to her plate. She picked it up with delight and hefted it. "What could it be?"

She unwrapped it gleefully while everyone watched.

She laughed merrily and held her gift up to the assembled.

*The Dancing Master*, by John Playford.

She read aloud from the sheet of foolscap enclosed.

"'Please don't construe this as a criticism of your dancing, but I've an extensive library, and I could spare this one.'

"It's from Landsdowne. How very thoughtful of him! He did so graciously tolerate my clumsiness the other night."

"Yes," Olivia said politely and very carefully. "He is generally very thoughtful."

Her grip, Genevieve noted, was a bit white on her fork.

# Chapter 9

❧

Since he was already dirty from working on the vicarage roof and was too late to join everyone for a meal, Ian visited Mrs. deWitt in the kitchen for a chunk of bread and cheese, and decided to clean his old musket, the very first one he'd ever owned, an activity he found meditative. He thought about what manner of weapons he ought to bring with him on his journey, and the kinds of women he might encounter, and the opportunities to make money and friends, and he had the thing taken apart and was busy with oil and rags when Genevieve wandered in.

"Good afternoon, sister of mine. What do you want?"

"How did you know I . . . Never mind. Ian . . . what do you think of Miss Danforth?"

He paused mid-wipe. "Are you asking because of that interesting conversation outside the vicarage? Or because you're gauging whether I'm merely biding my time until I ravish her?"

"Conversation? The word 'conversation' implies

I was included. And if you wanted to ravish her, you'd have to plow through a thicket of other men."

Ian laughed. "Ahhhh, Genevieve. Are we jealous?"

"Hush. Of course not. It's just . . . does she seem to you . . . well, a trifle too . . . effusive?" She'd chosen the word delicately, Ian could tell, which amused him.

"Are you worried because not one of those men gave you a second glance, Genevieve, when usually they go misty-eyed at the mere sight of you? You've already landed *your* duke."

She gave him a playful push.

"I think she's a bit awkward, Genevieve. And young. And American. They seem a bit louder and brasher, Americans. But yes, pretty. She's just accustomed to attention, no doubt. And knows how to get it." He shrugged with one shoulder. "We're on the whole, simple creatures, men are, and some women discover this sooner rather than later."

Genevieve gaped at him. *"Awkward?* Are you mad? Are we discussing the same girl? She charmed Tingle at the bookshop—and you know what a skinflint he can be—into *giving* her *two* books for the price of one. I would wager poems celebrating her delicate grace and big eyes and the like will start arriving any day. She's a bit . . . I do *wonder* if . . . well, she talked to a flower today when she was pulling it. She apologized to it, and then thanked it."

"She apologized to the *flower*?"

"And then thanked it."

"Sounds downright pagan. Perhaps she *is* a witch, and she's casting a spell on all those men." He waggled all ten fingers in Genevieve's face like a conjurer. "One never knows what Americans get up to. Perhaps she wanted to visit the graveyard for a bit of graveyard dust, which I hear is useful in spells."

Genevieve snorted softly. "I don't think *magic* has anything much to do with it. Unless she can disorient men by batting her lashes and then— abracadabra!—transform them into glazed-eyed fools."

Ian was pensive. "I do wonder something . . . she might be a bit hard of hearing. She seems to lose control over the volume of her voice rather regularly for no discernible reason. And does she have a tic? She tips her head back at odd times."

"I've noticed the bit with the volume! Not with the head. Poor dear, to be so afflicted."

"Yes, let's pity the poor dear who has men eating out of her hand," he teased Genevieve. "That should make her more tolerable to you and all the other women."

She pushed him again.

"I knew a bloke like that at Cambridge who was subject to twitches and shouting. You'd be in the middle of a deep conversation, say, about economics or the Peloponnesian war, and all of a sudden his head would jerk violently to the left and he'd shout 'Bollocks!' Or something more profane than even *I* am comfortable saying aloud to you. All in all, a capital bloke, however. One got used to it. He said it was because he was dropped on the coal hod when he was a baby. But I doubt Miss Danforth is mad, or was dropped on the coal hod."

"Conversations with you are always so edifying, Ian."

"You're welcome," he said cheerily.

"Olivia doesn't like her."

"Olivia doesn't like anyone easily," Ian said shortly.

"Landsdowne sent Miss Danforth a book of country dances today."

Ian went silent and his hands stilled momentarily on his musket.

"Did he?" he said disinterestedly.

He pictured his sister watching Miss Danforth dance with Landsdowne, his proud, proud sister who would never grovel or maneuver her way into a waltz the way Tansy Danforth had, who had already lost enough, and something cold and hard that didn't bode well for Miss Danforth settled in his gut.

Ian was in fact considerably more skeptical of Miss Danforth than he was willing to reveal yet to Genevieve. Or to anyone. He was willing to watch and bide his time.

"And I know you aren't preparing to ravish her, Ian, because I'd never speak to you again, and I know you'll miss my conversation."

"Nonsense. You aren't *that* interesting," he said easily.

But temper tensed his muscles, tightened his grip on his musket. He had only himself to blame; he wasn't entitled to righteousness in that regard. He didn't like the reminder, however.

"Are you any closer to buying a house in Sussex?" he asked.

"Falconbridge is most interested in Lilymont. It was Miss Danforth's home as a girl, did you know? As charming a place as you'll ever see. Rather compact for a duke, however." She smiled.

He went still.

Lilymont. He knew the house. It *was* small. From its hill one could see the downs rippling outward and a generous silver wedge of the sea. Large windows and gracious simple lines, and weathered stone walls, amber in the sunlight. An ample, but not too ample, garden of fruited and flowering trees was enclosed by a high stone wall with wild vines of flowers growing up it. It would need a little taming, but only a little. He liked things a bit wild, a bit disheveled. He liked things to be themselves, when at all possible.

He'd never seen a more perfect house, in its way.

It was interesting to hear Tansy had once lived there. Oddly, he could picture her as a flaxen-haired girl little girl, performing pianoforte pieces for the guests or playing in the garden. He wondered if she missed it, or even remembered it.

"It's a wonderful house. It deserves an owner who loves it," he said.

"ARE YOU ENJOYING your stay, thus far, Miss Danforth?"

While Genevieve and Ian were chatting about her, the duke had called Tansy into the study for another chat, and they were sipping tea together.

"I'm having a lovely time, and everyone is so very kind and generous."

"I saw the flowers sent to you. I think your father would have been proud. And worried."

She smiled at that. "Oh, I'm certain it's nothing but generosity. The people of Sussex are just being kind."

The duke's eyebrows went up skeptically at that. "The male people."

This made Tansy laugh. "And the Everseas are such a lovely family. Everyone is so warm and kind. And charitable, it would seem."

She crossed her fingers in her lap over this little lie.

"Charitable?" This word bemused him.

"We stopped into town, and I met the vicar, Reverend Adam Sylvaine, and Mr. Ian Eversea was on the roof, hammering. It seemed a charitable pastime for a wealthy gentleman." She said this as innocently as she could muster.

"Was he." The duke had, rather quickly, gone so cold and remote it was like being thrust out of a warm cabin into a frigid winter. "I'm not surprised he was on the roof. Ian Eversea excels at climbing."

She wasn't certain what to say about this, but it definitely sounded ironic.

And hadn't Genevieve said something very similar in the churchyard?

"I was surprised to see him at work with the others . . . not of his station."

"I suppose it would be surprising."

She sensed their conversation would rapidly end if she continued her Ian Eversea fishing expedition. It was all *very* interesting.

"My brother was a soldier," she said.

The duke softened.

"As many of the Eversea men were. You must miss your brother."

"He was irritating and bossy and protective and quite funny."

"He sounds just about perfect."

She dug her nails into her palm and smiled.

She would *not* cry. She could feel the urge pressing at the back of her throat. She was tougher than she looked, and she would not. She simply nodded.

He seemed to know it. How she liked him, even though he still frightened her just a very little.

"After my first wife died, I was a bit . . ." He seemed to be searching for just the right word. ". . . lost."

He presented the word carefully. As if he was handing her something a bit delicate and dangerous.

It was a gift, she knew, this confidence of his. She was honored by it.

She knew precisely what he meant. But looking

at him now, it was nearly impossible to imagine it. He radiated power; he seemed so very certain of himself, so rooted to the earth, it was difficult to imagine him feeling the way she did frequently now, like a bit of flotsam floating on the air.

"I know what you mean." Her voice had gone a little hoarse. Close to a whisper.

"But I knew, because of my first wife, that I would make a good husband and a good father and that it was what I wanted to be. I didn't want to make my life a monument to loss. In some ways I think the losses make us better at knowing how to be happy. And at knowing how to make others happy."

It was a lovely way to put it, and she never would have expected it of him. Which hardly seemed a charitable thought, but there you had it.

"Do you think so?"

He smiled slightly. "I know so. And I think losses help you to understand who deserves your attention, too. For life is too short to spend the best of ourselves on, shall we say, people who will not appreciate it or return it in kind. People who do not deserve you."

The duke fixed her with a gaze that seemed benign enough.

Tansy returned his gaze innocently, though she wanted to narrow her eyes shrewdly and study him.

Ah, but she was clever. All of this talk of knowing who deserves whom, she was fairly certain, was an oblique reference to Ian Eversea and implied a certain intriguing . . . unworthiness. But why? Because of glances exchanged with a wanton widow?

Then again *everything* since she'd seen Ian Eversea felt like an oblique reference to him. He had become the story, and everything was a footnote for now. She didn't necessarily like it that way. But she would need to read it to the end.

"I shall remember that," she said solemnly. "Thank you."

He gave a short nod and turned toward the window, and she knew she was dismissed.

SHE DIDN'T SEE Ian again until evening, when most of the family gathered in the parlor after dinner.

His shirtsleeves were rolled up and he wore snug trousers and Hessians, and while she pretended to read her book about Richard III, she peered up at him and tried to imagine him without his shirt.

She looked down again quickly when warmth began to rush over the backs of her arms.

"Plan to stay in Sussex long, Ian?" This came from Olivia, who was stabbing a needle in and out of a hoop of cloth. Flowers were blooming in a violent profusion on it. As if there weren't enough flowers in the house already.

Genevieve sat next to her, feet tucked beneath her on the settee, a book fanned open in her hands. The duke had gone off on some matter of business, apparently.

"Bored with me already?" He said it abstractedly, however, as his eyes were on the chessboard.

"It's so very difficult to be bored when you're around, even if one tries."

The corner of his mouth lifted. He nudged a piece forward, and Colin, who had stopped in to borrow something from his father and was talked into a chess game, swore something beneath his breath.

"What did you ladies do in town today?" Olivia asked the two of them.

Tansy knew an opportunity when she heard one.

Her heart, absurdly, began to thud with something like portent.

"I've obtained a new book," she said. "You may be interested in it, Mr. Eversea."

All the Mr. Everseas present looked up, until it became clear she was looking at Ian. Too late, she remembered he was a captain now.

"Have you?" He glanced warily at the thing in her hand, as if to ascertain whether it was indeed a book.

"It's a fine history of Richard the Third."

His smile was small and polite. "Ah."

Not a conversation encourager, the word "Ah."

"You mentioned him the other night," she prompted. "Whilst we were dancing."

"Did I?" He looked bemused.

"He's buried in Leicestershire?" she pressed, a bit desperately.

"Ah, yes. I recall." His brow furrowed faintly

in something like concern, as if studying her for signs of witlessness.

Everyone seemed to have arrested what they were doing in order to hear this conversation.

The backs of her hands and her neck began to heat.

"It's fascinating. The book."

It wasn't. She'd read a chapter or two, gamely, but the author had contrived to make what was probably a fascinating or at least quite violent and bloody subject seem like a punishment.

"Are you about to tell us about it?" Ian said this pleasantly, but he sneaked a look at the clock over the mantel. And back at her. As if he were formulating an excuse to escape.

"What's this about Richard the Third?" Colin asked. "Ian hasn't willingly set foot in our library since he got in trouble for sneaking peeks at father's anatomy books. Ian enjoys climbing trees," he added, "and riding."

Ian flicked an amused warning look in his brother's direction before returning his gaze to her.

Another of those references to *climbing*.

Tansy felt her eyes burning with mortification. He could at least have the decency to look away while she flushed, slowly, to the roots of her hair, and while her face slowly caught on fire, or so it felt.

But no. Instead he watched, with mild dispassionate interest, much the way he might watch the sunset or the sunrise.

*Boor,* she reminded herself.

Still, she found herself saying, "You can have it, if you like."

"The . . . book?" He looked mystified.

She nodded, mutely. Slowly extended it.

His hands reached out. He took it gingerly.

"Thank you, Miss Danforth," he said gravely.

"You're welcome."

He stared at her a moment longer, and when it seemed she'd say nothing else, he returned his attention to the chessboard.

The alps. Ice skating. Snowbanks.

She tried to think of very cold things in the hopes that the flames in her cheeks would vanish.

Ian Eversea's heart.

Ah, how about that? That was working.

LATER, MUCH LATER, after everyone retired one by one and she had waited because she didn't like to be alone, Tansy returned to her bedroom and was startled by the sight of flowers in a vase.

*Ha, Ian Eversea! Take that!* Evidence that she was, indeed, appreciated. Desired, even! By not just one man, but by four! That she *did* possess grace and charm and *could* captivate. She stared at the flowers, waiting for a certain triumph to build.

She groaned and dropped her face into her hands and rocked it to and fro. It was no use. She relived the moment, as if it had stretched torturously in time: her hand stretching out the book to him and his baffled face as he took it. Indulging her, as if she were a foolish little girl.

She blew out a breath, and then yanked off her slippers. One at a time.

And then she hurled them at the wall.

*Wham.*

*Wham.*

"'You can have it if you like,'" she mimicked herself to herself. "Oh, good heavens, what a fool I am!"

But throwing the slippers had made her feel marginally better.

Then she stalked over to the desk and settled in.

She fanned out the sheet of foolscap and read it to herself as if it were a spell she could conjure right then and there.

How would *anyone* come to know her? To see her? To love her?

She dipped the quill into ink and wrote.

*Has known a loss or two.*

She'd begun to suspect it mattered.

# Chapter 10

&

SOME KIND OF THUMP made Ian struggle to the surface from sleep, choking like a half-drowned man, thrashing at his sheets as if he were digging out from an avalanche.

He lay still again.

His lungs sawed greedily for air as he fought his way to the surface of consciousness.

Bloody. Hell.

As he always did, he waited for his breathing to steady, for his heart to quit hammering away like an inmate beating on the bars of a cell.

He peeled the sweat-soaked sheets away from his torso, let the blessed cool air wash over his bare skin. He touched his fingers to the scar at his abdomen. It rather resembled the path that meandered to the Pig & Thistle from the Eversea house, right down to the way it was raised more at the end, like the little hill where the Marquess of Dryden had been shot not long ago. Chase had pointed out the resemblance to the road when they compared scars. Ian figured he could always follow it like a map back to the Eversea house if he drank a bit too much at the pub.

If he didn't stretch regularly and often enough, it drew all the muscles around it taut as a miser's purse strings and he could count on a day or so of agony, solvable only by hard liquor and a soft woman and a hot bath.

It had been dug there by a bayonet on the day of his greatest triumph and his greatest failure.

There were other scars, too, but this was the only one that liked to make its presence known, as surely as if it were another organ. His heart pumped blood, his lungs moved air in and out, and the scar's job was to never let him forget.

The room still felt too close—it was smaller than his own room, and the curtains were heavier—so he heaved his body out of bed and was at the window in a few strides. He shoved it open.

He peered out the window.

And one balcony over . . .

. . . well, damned if that wasn't Miss Danforth.

And how had no one noticed he was sleeping in the room next to *hers*? Surely the duke would have made sure one or the other of them had been removed to a room at the opposite side of the house posthaste.

He decided then and there, however, that he wouldn't request his room be moved. He would stay right where he was.

Lamplight poured out the open window, and she had brought a lamp with her onto the balcony.

Her chin was propped on her fists and she was gazing out over the Eversea grounds, which from her vantage point rolled almost as far as the eye could see. She looked smaller than usual, rather slumped in a manner that was almost defeated. For the first time it occurred to him that the sparkle she seemed to bring everywhere with her resulted from some effort, rather than some supernatural source of charm allotted to her in exchange for selling her soul to the devil.

She tipped her head back, like a bird gulping water. She seemed to be scanning the skies above, for a sign, perhaps, from Heaven. It *was* entirely possible she had some sort of nervous tic. She'd been doing that in the ballroom, too. Or perhaps she was subject to nosebleeds.

And then she lowered her head again, and her shoulders dropped, and her hands disappeared for a moment as she appeared to rummage around somewhere out of sight.

She produced a small pouch and propped it on the edge of the balcony.

And then she removed from the pouch a scrap of something.

What the devil . . . ?

It couldn't be.

Oh, but it was.

It was a *cigarette* paper.

He watched, fascinated and appalled as she expertly ran her tongue down it. Then she flattened it on the balcony edge, shook a little tobacco in a slim line down it. To his wondering eyes . . . she rolled it as adeptly as any soldier.

She held it beneath her nose, closed her eyes, and her shoulders rose and fell as she inhaled deeply.

*Holy* Mother of—

Ian gave a start when someone knocked on his chamber door. He swore under his breath and ducked back from the curtain.

Yanking the door open, he found a footman there, holding a tray bearing the brandy he'd rung earlier for, as well as a sheet of folded foolscap on a tray. "A message for you, Mr. Eversea."

He flipped it open so quickly he nearly sliced his fingers.

" 'I will in all likelihood take rooms at the Pig & Thistle whilst I'm in Sussex,' " he read aloud.

It was signed *LC*.

Who the devil was . . .

Lady Carstairs.

He'd nearly forgotten about Lady Carstairs.

Beautiful. Brunette. Unusual tastes.

"Yesthankyouverymuchgood-bye."

He shut the door in the startled footman's face and, message in his hand, bolted to the window and peered out.

Surely he'd dreamed that. But she was gone, and the wind was sweeping away a few stray flakes of tobacco.

IT WAS NO use. Just past midnight Tansy threw off her blankets with a long sigh, rolled from her bed and shoved her feet into her slippers. Then she knelt to fish about in one of her trunks and came up with a pair of painted tin soldiers that had once belonged to her brother. She held them gently, and smiled faintly. As much as she cherished the memory of playing soldiers with her brother, she was certain he would rather they saw active duty, so to speak, rather than languish an eternity as mementos. He would have teased her for her sentimentality, anyway.

Soldiers in hand, she seized a candle and progressed down the shadowy hallways to the kitchen.

It was time, if at all possible, to obtain a few answers, or she would likely never sleep a night through again.

Mrs. deWitt was sitting at the table, spectacles perched on her nose, poring over a book of what appeared to be accounts, muttering to herself. ". . . beef for Thursday . . ."

She looked up and shoved over a plate of scones, as if she'd been anticipating Tansy's arrival, and stood to put the kettle on.

Tansy settled in. "Are you going over the accounts?"

"Aye. 'Tis a fine bit of balancing, doin' the budget, though it's generous enough. What's that ye've got in yer 'and, there, Miss Danforth?"

"I thought Jordy might like to have these. They were my brother's."

She pushed the soldiers over to her.

Miss deWitt's eyes went wide with surprise and

then she beamed meltingly. "Ah, the boy ought to 'ave some toys. Ye've the heart of an angel, Miss Danforth, to think of a wee servant boy."

Tansy regally waved away the compliment, but she blushed with pleasure. "I did the accounts after my parents passed away."

"Did ye now?" Mrs. deWitt looked up, sympathy written all over her face.

"I liked it, I discovered."

" 'Tis a bit like a puzzle, isn't it? Deciding what you ought to buy and how much you'll need and so forth?"

"Oh, it is." She'd needed to pension off some of the servants and decide who would remain as a small crew to keep the house open. She'd held difficult conversation after difficult conversation. She'd expected to be overwhelmed, it had instead been a respite. The quiet moments in the kitchen, discussing the day-to-day running of the house with the small staff, was nearly meditative, and she'd found comfort in their voices and company.

"How are you getting on, Miss Danforth?"

"Everyone is quite wonderful." She said this with the same ceremony as she would have said "Amen." It was precisely what she ought to say, she knew.

This made Mrs. deWitt beam.

She bit into the scone. "Heaven on a plate, Mrs. deWitt! I could eat these every day of my life."

"Thank you, my dear. You know how to warm

an old soul's heart. Now, are you enjoying your time with the family?"

"Oh yes! They're all very charming. And there are so many of them and I'm still trying to remember everyone's names. Let me see. Now . . . Colin is married to Madeleine, yes? The lovely dark-haired woman?"

"He is indeed, and a dear girl she is, so clever and kind and quiet."

"And Marcus is married to Louisa? She's so pretty, isn't she?"

"Oh, my, yes, indeed! And two people more perfect for each other cannot be found anywhere on the face of this earth!"

"And there's Genevieve married to the duke . . ."

Mrs. deWitt sighed happily. "Such a love story, that one, and what a grand man."

"And then there's Ian and . . ."

Mrs. deWitt's gaze drifted. "Well, would you look at that time? We ought to be in bed, the two of us."

She stood up and began bustling about, pushing utensils and crockery around the kitchen rather aimlessly.

"And then there's *Ian and . . .*" Tansy repeated stubbornly.

Mrs. deWitt went still in the midst of shuffling.

And then at last she sighed heartily and turned, slowly, in resignation.

"Now, child, I can tell you this: ye dinna want your head turned by that one."

"Ha!" Tansy laughed unconvincingly. "Ha ha! My head turned! I ask you! My head is on straight, thank you very much. I was simply curious."

There was a long hesitation during which the cook regarded her shrewdly and Tansy reflected back nothing but bland innocence. She'd perfected the look when she was a little girl.

"God love 'im," the cook sighed at last. "The boy is trouble."

Tansy's heart stood still. This was going to be *good*.

Or awful.

"He's not a boy," she said thoughtfully, before she could think better of it.

Mrs. deWitt looked at her sharply.

"Aye, that he ain't. 'E's a man, and he's been to war and back, and to London and back, and men are shaped by the things they find in both places, aye? For good or for ill. I've seen it time and again. Ye've only to look at the lad, and . . . well, my own old heart turns over when he smiles, and that's the truth. He gets what he wants just that way. 'E's good at heart but 'e's a restless one, and any woman who pins her hopes to him is asking for heartbreak, or my name isn't Margaret deWitt."

Tansy suspected the cook's name really was Margaret deWitt.

She remembered again the look Ian had exchanged with the lovely dark-haired woman at the ball. All silent, understood innuendo, swift and expert and sophisticated, as if Tansy wasn't even there and didn't matter. And a hot little rock of some nameless but deeply unpleasant emotion took up residence in her stomach. Jealousy. Or shame. Definitely from the same family tree as those two emotions.

She didn't like to think of herself as one of legion.

She didn't like to think of Ian Eversea bedding and breaking the hearts of a legion.

Or of anyone, for that matter.

She didn't want to think of herself foolish enough, ordinary enough, to fall just like any other woman.

Nor had she ever in her life thought of herself as a fool.

She risked the question anyway, even though she didn't really want to hear the answer.

"*Has* any woman pinned her hopes . . . ?"

"Oh, a host of them, I daresay. Beginning with poor Theodosia Brackman back when the boy was just fifteen. Then there was—"

"A list won't be necessary," Tansy said hurriedly. Her imagination filled it in, anyway. She expected the list of names all began with *poor*. "Poor Theodosia Brackman, poor Jenny Smith, poor Tansy Danforth . . ."

She'd never been *anyone's* poor *anything*.

". . . and one hears things about—" Mrs. deWitt lowered her voice to a whisper. "—certain kinds of women in London."

She wasn't *that* sheltered. She was certain she knew what "certain kinds of women" meant.

Worse and worse.

Mrs. deWitt probably ought not say such things to her, but probably thought she needed a powerful warning.

It was unpleasant to hear, yet she indeed needed to hear it, the way she needed cod liver oil on occasion. It would do her good. Perhaps it would cure her of what was in all likelihood a passing condition, which, given that it made her charmless, stuttery, and given to blushes, had nothing at all to recommend it. And given that he was indifferent to her charms, was really rather a waste of time. And her talents.

Besides, she was destined for a duke, wasn't she?

She wanted a husband, a family and a home, and it was time to cease wasting her time on thoughts of Ian Eversea.

She returned to her bedchamber filled with scone and resolve, yet her legs and heart felt heavier, somehow, as if she were returning to walking on the ground after a little sojourn in the clouds.

SHE OPENED HER eyes just before dawn again, wondering, before memory set in, why she felt low-spirited.

Then she recalled her figurative dose of cod liver oil from the night before.

And sighed.

The little rosy strip of light lay where it usually did, beckoning her to walk it.

She debated breaking herself of the habit. It would be the mature and sane thing to do. But the gentle little sunbeam road lay there on the carpet, and she found herself sliding from the bed to follow it, the way an animal has no choice but to follow an intriguing scent. She gently parted the curtains.

He was already standing on the balcony. A moment later it occurred to her he was standing unusually still. Staring out over the strata of Sussex colors as she had, only he'd likely seen them countless times before. When he turned to look out over the morning, she thought she saw, but couldn't be sure, darker hollows beneath his eyes. Probably from staying up all night counting the women he'd seduced, the way other people counted sheep. He turned his head, and it seemed to her he was a trifle tense and white about the mouth. Perhaps he'd been at the Pig & Thistle until very late, or romping with a widow, and now his head was pounding.

And at last he stretched as he always did, bending backward, thrusting his arms into the air, and the beautiful line of him arching pulled something taut in her, too, like a bowstring drawn back. She could feel that pulling, tightening sensation inside her.

He began to roar, as she'd heard him do before in the morning, but stopped abruptly and winced.

Then he rested his hands on the edge of the balcony and breathed, his big shoulders moving slowly, deeply. As if something hurt and he was breathing through it.

She could vouch for how hangovers hurt. She wasn't utterly devoid of sophistication.

Perhaps all that heartbreaking he went about doing had worn the poor soul out.

Cod liver oil, she reminded herself. And gave a haughty sniff.

She backed away from the curtain.

# Chapter 11

❧

"ARE YOU SURE YOU wouldn't like to come along?" Genevieve hovered in the doorway, pulling on her gloves. "You could accompany Olivia to the meeting of the Society to Protect the Sussex Poor. They would love to have you, I'm certain."

Tansy very much doubted Olivia would love to have her. And besides, she had other plans, and they didn't include spending the day with the frighteningly beautiful Olivia Eversea, whom she had begun to think of as her competition, or, more specifically, the bar above which she planned to rise in Sussex. Because every woman needed a goal. Four bouquets and counting, she thought. And a book.

As if summoned by her thoughts, a footman appeared in the doorway, bearing a great vase full of pink and white flowers. "For you, Miss Danforth. Where would you like me to put them?"

More flowers! She clapped her hands together. "Thank you so very much! How delightful!"

She peered at the note attached and read it

aloud. "'Because their brightness and purity reminded me of you.' Henry Thorpe, Lord Lester."

*Purity*, was it, Lord Lester? What on earth had
given him that impression? Still, it was meant to
be a compliment and so she was pleased.

"That's five bouquets for you this morning, and
four for Olivia," Genevieve said, somewhat wickedly. "Good heavens, I never did think anyone
would give Olivia any bouquet competition."

"Oh, I would *never* dream of counting!" Tansy
said, staring down at her note. "What a generous
lot the young men of Sussex are."

"I suppose they are."

She turned to the footman. "Perhaps we can
distribute the flowers a little more widely? If you
would take a bouquet to Mrs. deWitt, and then
perhaps send one down to the vicarage for any-
body buried in the churchyard who might need a
flower or two?"

The footman was clearly enchanted, too. He
beamed at her. "Anything you like, Miss Danforth."

Genevieve watched the footman depart, the
corner of her mouth quirked wryly. "Will you
be all right on your own today, Tansy? We'll in
all likelihood be gone until this evening, at least.
With luck we'll be home before dinnertime."

Genevieve sounded genuinely worried. Tansy
reached impulsively for her hands.

"Oh, you're so very kind to invite me along
with the two of you, but I've so much correspon-
dence from home to attend to—a few matters of

business, you know—and it would be a wonderful opportunity to see to it. And tomorrow, with the marksmanship contest, will be so very social and lively. But perhaps I can persuade a groom to accompany me on a short ride? I do so love to ride!"

"What a wonderful idea! Of course! I'll have them saddle my mare for you! She's lovely. And the groom will be happy to accompany you."

Tansy also had no intention of taking a groom, and had every confidence she could concoct a story to convince the groom to stay put and not make a fuss. Why *should* she take someone? She rode like she was born to the saddle, which she nearly had been, and she was accustomed to riding alone over her property at home, or with her papa at her side. She wasn't going far. She could, in fact, see her destination, if she peered hard enough through her bedroom window. It wasn't as though she would be set upon by brigands. There was no place for them to hide in this mild little landscape, unless perhaps they dressed all in green and leaped out from the shrubberies. A brigand would get bored indeed waiting for someone to trundle by, and would likely fall asleep before someone did.

And she just didn't want anyone to witness what she wanted to do today. Not even a groom, who likely wouldn't say a word, given that servants were paid for their discretion.

She told the groom she was off to meet a friend

at the end of the drive and kicked the little mare into a trot before he could say anything.

She had her eye on the fluffy knot of woods beyond the stream and not far off the road she'd walked with Genevieve into town.

The air was delicious; both she and the mare gulped great winey draughts of it, and tossed their heads. She would love to have undone her bonnet and let her hair fly free.

She drew the mare to a halt.

A girl was sitting next to the stream, arms wrapped around her knees. A long apron covered a brown walking dress decorated only with a narrow band of lace at the sleeves.

"Oh. Good morning," Tansy said cautiously.

"Good morning," said the girl, just as cautiously. Very politely.

It seemed that no other conversation would be forthcoming. They continued to study each other.

Until the girl asked, "Are you Miss Danforth?"

"Why, yes, I am." In a small town, doubtless nothing remained a secret for long, and this girl probably knew everyone there was to know.

"How do you do, Miss Danforth. I'm Polly Hawthorne. My father owns the Pig & Thistle. The pub."

"Oh, of course! I've seen it. Seems a lovely place. I hope to visit while I'm in Sussex."

It was the right thing to say. Polly smiled. She was a pretty thing, almost elfin, small and slight with big dark eyes, a pointed chin, and black hair wound up in a braid.

The two wordlessly eyed each other a bit longer. Tansy sensed no one knew Polly was here, either. While at the same time, the girl doubtless knew that well-bred young ladies didn't ride alone, unless they were up to something.

"I just like to have a bit of a think here, when I get a moment away from the pub," Polly said by way of explanation. "About life, and the pub, and the Everseas, and the like."

Tansy shrugged, as if this went without saying. "It's hard not to think about the Everseas, I daresay. There are so many of them and they're everywhere you look. And admittedly they are easy on the eyes."

Polly grinned at that. "They do brighten up the Pig & Thistle. And to think so many of them almost died."

This was startling. "You don't say?"

"Well, I was just thinking about it this morning, you know, because I hear Captain Ian Eversea will be traveling again, and on a dangerous trip, for all of that. Master Colin, he nearly lost his life at the gallows, until there was an explosion and he disappeared. And Master Chase—the other Captain Eversea—his leg was injured. And Master Ian nearly lost his life in the war, I'm told. It's livelier at the pub when they're all home, and they do leave generous tips. And they're so kind. Sometimes I think Master Ian is kindest of all."

It was quite a fascinating litany. Colin had gone to the gallows? *Had* Ian nearly lost his life? Tansy's heart clutched at the thought. To think she might have never seen him from across a crowded ballroom and lost so many things: her ability to think, to speak, to charm.

And he was *leaving*?

When would that be?

Her gut felt hollow at the thought.

She tossed her head. It mattered not at all to her.

Well, so be it. She'd sworn off him, anyway, and it was so much more pleasant to be celebrated rather than ignored.

"It's a pleasant spot for a bit of a think. I was looking for one of my own," she said to Polly, tentatively.

"I won't keep you."

Tansy nearly laughed. She liked this strangely regal young girl, for no real reason except that she seemed utterly self-possessed. And she was convinced Polly wouldn't say a word about seeing her here.

"Perhaps I'll see you at the Pig & Thistle, then."

Polly nodded politely, and Tansy drew her horse around and set a course for the trees. And presumably Polly resumed pondering Everseas. Polly, who would likely live and die in Pennyroyal Green, and might never even see London, and so the Everseas, such as they were, comprised the weather of her days.

There was a lovely hush in this little wild portion of the woods; some of the trees seemed as old as time itself, through birches and hawthorn, over a little rise, until she saw a clearing.

It was small, mossy, surrounded by a number of large oaks and a horseshoe of shrubbery, but it would get enough light, and one day, perhaps next spring, anyone meandering by would think they'd stumbled across a fairy bower, if everything went according to plan.

She would have to hurry, as the sun was growing higher and she didn't want to perspire through her muslin.

She dismounted and tangled the reins in a hawthorn, then unwrapped a bundle of things she'd brought with her.

An hour or so of dirty, satisfying labor later her work was nearly done. She stood back, peeled off her work gloves, and surveyed her handiwork. Then sprinkled it all carefully with water from the two flasks she'd brought with her.

Then she led her horse over to the fallen tree and settled herself in the saddle again.

Polly was gone. Back at the Pig & Thistle, no doubt.

On the way home, Tansy indulged in loosening her bonnet and letting it dangle behind her so the breeze could run its fingers through her hair. Surely she wouldn't brown in just the few minutes it took to ride from the forest back.

She rode blithely back to the stables at Eversea House, confident no one would have witnessed a thing.

She was blissfully unaware of Ian Eversea standing at his window, frowning, watching her golden head bobbing like a guinea atop Gene-

vieve's mare, scandalously, well-nigh incriminat-
ingly, alone and looking a trifle disheveled.

SOME KIND OF thud in the wall had awakened
Ian from a perfectly satisfactory nap. It was the
second night in a row that such a thing had happened. Were the rodents brawling for territory in
the walls? Perhaps they ought to get a few cats.

He rolled from bed and was instantly, merci-
lessly, humbled by the fact that he was no longer
twenty years old and able to abuse his body in
all manner of ways without consequences. His
muscles had tightened after all that bending and
hammering on the vicarage roof. He needed to
stretch and bend all his limbs and have a good
scratch before he could move with any sort of
grace.

He settled in at his desk and bent again over
his map. He'd marked his ports of call with a neat
little star. China. India. Africa. South America.
America. He could keep moving just like this for
years, if he wanted to. And something in him
eased when he looked at that map. Whenever he
felt like a dammed river, whenever he felt caught
between Sussex and London, whenever Chase or
Colin said the word "wife" in a way that made
him want to kick both of them, he found the map
a great comfort. The day was coming when he
would set foot on the ship and it would move over
the ocean and not stop moving. It sounded perfect. He had no doubt about what and whom he

would miss. It was just that he suspected moving would feel like a relief, and that whatever dogged him might finally be left behind somewhere on the South Seas.

He looked down at the book on his desk. He hefted it in his hand, idly ruffled the pages, and quirked his mouth wryly. Why in God's name would Miss Danforth give him a bloody book? And blush scarlet while doing it? In all likelihood for the same reasons Landsdowne had given *her* one. Perhaps she had a cat's talent for crawling into the lap of the one person who could scarcely tolerate it. Miss Danforth was likely the sort who couldn't rest until everyone worshipped her. It was wearisome and irritating, yet admittedly faintly amusing.

All in all, however, the very notion of her made him tired. The girl wasn't quite who she wanted everyone to think she was, and that troubled him.

Still, the book had been a gift. And as he re-membered her face flushing scarlet, he laid it aside again with a certain tenderness he couldn't quite explain.

He looked up.

It was nearly twilight, and a stiff breeze was beginning to sidle in through his window, which was open a few inches.

He crossed to it to pull the curtains closed and peered out, then ducked back in, hiding behind the curtain.

Miss Danforth was out on the balcony, and

her blond hair down about her shoulders—good Lord, she had miles of it— almost created its own light, so brilliant was it beneath the half-moon. Soothing stuff. His hands flexed absently as he imagined drawing his fingers through it.

He watched, mystified, as she leaned slowly forward and assumed something like an awkward arabesque. Her night rail filled like a sail in a passing breeze, and he was treated to a glimpse of very fine white calf before it deflated. She tilted her head at an impossible angle, and her hair fell in a great sheet down her back. Soothing as watching a river move.

But what the devil was she *doing*? Perhaps it was some sort of interpretive dance? Was she bowing toward America the way Muslims bowed in the direction of Mecca?

He winced as she gracelessly righted herself again, her arms seesawing. He could rule out dancer.

She slumped again, propped her chin on her fists on the rail of the balcony and returned to gazing out at the black of the Sussex hills, as if she expected something to emerge from it, or something had vanished there. Perhaps expecting some beau to come and climb the balcony, à la Romeo Montague.

It was funny, but he'd done that more than once, too: stare off into the dark as if it were a crystal ball, as if the dark could reveal to him as much as it concealed.

And then she dropped her hands and rummaged about again at something he couldn't see. He held his breath, as he waited for the pouch of tobacco to appear.

She emerged with a bottle.

Of what appeared to be . . . Mother of God . . .

*Liquor.*

Surely not.

Surely he was *dreaming* this.

It was followed by a little glass, which she settled with a little clink on the edge of the balcony.

She yanked the cork and splashed just a drop or two into the bottom of it.

*Clear* liquor, which meant it was either gin or whisky.

Or water. Perhaps she found English water intolerable? Perhaps she'd imported American water.

But then she toasted the darkness and bolted it, and there was no mistaking the wince. God knows he'd winced just like that countless times in his life.

And like a diva leaving the stage after a second act, she backed into her room again.

# Chapter 12

❧

THE SUSSEX MARKSMANSHIP TROPHY gleamed on a little podium like a grail.

Which it was, for every man gathered. The contest would begin with archery, progress to shooting, and end with winner carrying away a tall silver cup, theirs to keep until the following year.

The row of targets were arrayed, waiting to have their hearts pierced with arrows.

The Everseas and Redmonds took turns hosting the contest, and this year the honor fell to the Everseas. Ian was the Master of Ceremonies, graciously bowing out of the competition, having taken home the cup twice in previous years.

Nearly everyone in Pennyroyal Green and Greater Sussex appeared to be present, including a few Gypsies and a regiment of soldiers, resplendent in red coats. The Pig & Thistle had been closed for the duration, and Ned was there with Polly.

Most years, the men would arrive and stand, eyes shaded, admiring the silver cups and fantasizing about victory, while exchanging advice and playful insults about prowess.

This year fully half of the men were gazing at another sort of grail.

Off on the sidelines, Miss Danforth, in a pale blue walking dress with a darker blue ribbon trimming it, had managed to find a place in the sun where the satin trim gleamed, setting her off like a beacon. She was surrounded by a crowd of admirers that ebbed and flowed a bit like the tide, according to whomever she was bestowing her attention upon. Lord Henry was among them, as was Simon Covington and Seamus Duggan, and Landsdowne was on the periphery, though he was at least proximate to Olivia. Ian saw his sisters, Genevieve and Olivia, Evie Sylvaine—his vicar cousin's wife—Josephine Charing, Amy Pitney, and a few other worthy ladies of the Society to Protect the Sussex Poor. But they stood in a knot that looked decidedly judgmental. A murder of crows, a pride of lions, a judgment of ladies, he amused himself by thinking. Still, he might need to revise it to a murder of ladies, given some of the expressions.

They were to take the competition in several sets; the contestants would have three shots each at different distances.

"Set one!" he called. "Take your places, please!"

The men filed onto the field, Simon among them, and he smiled and saluted in the direction of Miss Danforth.

"Good luck!" she called cheerily.

Seamus Duggan, who'd been too busy being poor and then a bit of a roustabout for most of his life, wasn't an archer, and so he was able to watch from the sidelines. Very close to Miss Danforth. He waved at Simon cheerily, ironically, too.

"READY!" Ian called.

The archers hoisted their bows and selected their arrows.

"AIM!"

The bowstrings were drawn back in near balletic unison, and targets were skewered with steely gazes.

And just then Seamus Duggan stepped in front of Miss Danforth and she reached out to touch his elbow, reflexively.

When Seamus Duggan turned to smile at her, Simon reflexively rotated toward the two of them as if he were helpless not to, as though it were a crime in progress he needed to arrest immediately.

And that's when he shot the arrow into the crowd.

Time seemed to slow as it whipped through the air toward the masses of people.

"RUN!" Somebody—many somebodies—screamed.

The crowd scattered in all directions like flushed birds, screaming for their lives, shedding handkerchiefs and bonnets and shoes in their haste to flee.

And when they had retreated and checked their persons for arrows, there was a murmur of relief and congratulations.

Which tapered off into a hush when it became clear one man remained behind.

Quite conspicuously behind.

Almost as though . . . he'd been skewered in place.

A brief ominous silence ensued as all eyes turned Lord Henry's way.

He was still upright.

He was white as a flag of surrender.

"I . . . think I've been shot," he said, bemused.

Alas, nobody disagreed.

The hush seemed to gather density, like a thunderstorm about to break.

"Yes, I do believe I've been shot." He said this louder.

Then louder, as shock gave way to clarity and, presumably, to pain. "*Help!* I've been shot! Help! Help! Murder! *Murder!* Murderer!" He pointed a quivering finger at Simon, who looked as though he wished the ground would swallow him.

There was a great murmuring in the crowd.

"Unless yer 'eart is in your arse, Henry, I think you'll live to see another day," someone shouted.

Henry whirled vainly trying to get a look, like a dog chasing its tail.

The arrow had entered his left buttock cheek. Everybody could see that except him.

"He shot me on purpose! *Scoundrel!*" He lunged

for Simon, just as Ian lunged for him, to seize his arm and pull him back.

"Calm yourself, lad. You oughtn't move overmuch."

The arrow was well and truly in there, piercing right through the nankeen.

"Aye, 'ave a rest, milord. Ye might not want to sit down to rest just yet, though," someone called, to general laughter.

"Don't laugh!" somebody else shouted. "'Tis a tragedy! He needs 'is arse for horse riding and sittin' at the pub chairs!"

"'E looks a bit like a weathervane, don't 'e, wi' that thing stickin' out o' 'im?"

"That's a fine tail feather ye got there, m'lord! Ye look like me prize rooster!"

"That there be a mighty funny-looking grouse ye've bagged there, Simon! Are you going to serve him up tonight?"

Simon was wretched and white-faced with shock. His hands were trembling. "Stop it!"

"Wot's it feel like, m'lord?" somebody asked the wounded Lord Henry.

"It hurts!" he said, sounding surprised and martyred. And a bit intrigued. "Quite a bit, actually." He was doing an admirable job of not weeping, though it certainly looked as though he wanted to. And Ian knew the look of a man who would faint at any moment.

"All right. That's enough," he barked. "Behave yourselves, gentlemen. And ladies," he added ironically with a swift and pointed look in Tansy Danforth's direction, whose gaze fled from his. Having been skewered before, though admittedly not with an arrow, Ian had a good deal of sympathy for it. "Is your father at home, Miss Pitney?" he called.

Miss Amy Pitney's father was the town doctor.

"The next town over, delivering a baby," she said regretfully.

Ian sighed. His shoulders slumped. "Very well. I need ten tall and preferably wide volunteers . . ."

AND THAT'S HOW, thanks to Miss Danforth, Ian found himself on his hands and knees carefully extracting an arrow from the large white hindquarter of a whimpering man.

He was laid out, facedown, on a blanket. Rather like a grouse at a banquet, in fact. Ian's volunteers surrounded poor Lord Henry in a circle, backs to him, shielding him from the crowd. Nankeen was trimmed away neatly with a knife. Ian thrust his flask at him and instructed him to drink. He was given a rag with which to muffle his screams. And when the arrow was extracted, he was bandaged adroitly, because Ian had needed to do it dozens of times before during the war.

Lord Henry didn't faint, but it was a near thing.

"See the doctor this evening, if you can," Ian instructed the unfortunate, punctured Henry.

Simon was white and wringing his hands, hovering on the outskirts of the circle. "I'm sorry. I'm so sorry, I'm so sorry, I'm so sorry. I didn't mean it, Henry, I'm so sorry."

"No hard feelings." Harry was clipped but magnanimous in martyrdom. "Do you intend to shoot Duggan next?"

Ian seized Simon by the elbow and pulled him aside.

"How in the bloody hell did that happen? You're a better shot than that, Simon. Not as good as I am, naturally, but . . ."

Ian knew how it had happened. Or why it had happened. He wanted to hear it from the man himself.

Simon drew in a long breath and exhaled miserably, thrusting his hands deep into his pockets.

"It's just . . . Ian, it's well . . . it's just . . . well, *look* at her," he said with muffled anguish. "I don't want to think the way I think, Ian. I really don't, but . . . *look* at her."

Miss Danforth was wringing her hands, and a small crowd of young men were jostling each other for the honor of comforting her. From where he stood he could see the sun glance off the tears glittering in the corners of her big eyes. Her lush lower lip was trembling. She looked convincingly distraught, for someone so skilled at fomenting mayhem.

Instantly, a half-dozen handkerchiefs were thrust out to her. She looked up, limpidly grateful.

"Oh, she's pretty, all right," Ian said grimly.

Behind them was a small knot of females, all of

whose mouths had gone hard and horizontal and whose arms were crossed across their chests. Ian was reminded of wasps about to swarm.

"Pretty? She's an *angel*!" Simon corrected, on an outraged hush. "So delicate and kind."

"I'm not certain 'flattery' and 'kindness' are synonymous, Simon."

"You can simply tell she has a heart of gold. Like her hair . . ." he said dreamily.

Ian snapped his fingers beneath his nose, and Simon looked surprised.

"You shot Lord Henry because she's an angel? I think you have your winged beings confused. It's *Cupid* who supposedly shoots arrows at people."

"It was an accident! I was distracted. She was . . . she did . . . she did something to distract me, let's just leave it at that. She said archery was her favorite sport of all. That no one looked more like a Greek god than with a bow and arrow. And . . ."

"And you . . . wanted to be a Greek god?"

"Of course! Wouldn't you?"

"But Cupid is the deity with arrows, and he's a fat little baby."

Simon sighed with exasperation. "I think you're missing my point, Captain Eversea. What *wouldn't* you do for a woman like that? I care for my Josephine with all my heart. And yet . . ."

Ian looked over there again, and found Miss Danforth looking his way, her eyes bright and silvery even from that distance. As if she wanted to see his opinion of her performance.

He raised his hand in a subtle, sardonic little salute.

She gave her head a little toss and graciously waved away the handkerchiefs thrust at her. Tilted her head up and offered up a tremulous smile to the crowd of men.

On the outskirts of which stood Josephine Charing and Amy Pitney, who looked very willing to shoot her with an arrow. Ian was confident their aims would be terrible, and confident Miss Danforth would somehow escape, because if ever there was a survivor, she was one.

It was an interesting question, however, that Simon had posed. Ian had done a lot to *get* a woman. Doing something foolhardy *for* a woman, in order to impress a woman, however, or earn her regard . . . never. Never had he made a fool of himself for a woman. Most of his family failed to recognize he had a pragmatic streak a mile wide. He'd never called anyone out and he'd never yet been called out, though the duke had cut it very fine. He'd never lost his mind over a woman, though he'd nearly lost his life over one and had certainly lost his dignity once.

He'd never lost his mind to the point where he'd shot anyone with an arrow over one, that much was certain.

"I think *you* need a drink, Simon. I think we all need a drink. And you best make sure Henry truly forgives you. Because the next competition is shooting, and I saw enough carnage during the war."

PERHAPS IT HAD been all the stiff drinking they'd done to settle rattled nerves after the arrow incident, or perhaps it was because not enough drinking had been done in the wake of the arrow incident, but otherwise skillful marksmen were shooting shamefully wide of the mark. Over and over and over.

And the mark target was an apple, glowing like a beacon at one hundred paces.

They stepped up, one by one.

Shot, one by one.

And missed, one by one, again and again and again.

The apple remained mockingly smooth and whole and gleamed improbably in the sunlight.

"I don't know what the trouble is," Ian muttered. "At this rate, if we all needed to shoot our food in order to survive, we'd starve."

He would have loved to shoot it. It was such an easy target, and he was such a skillful shot, and he felt trapped in a moment that was both dull and embarrassing. The apple needed shooting, for God's sake.

Yet another hapless contestant stepped up to fire, and missed.

"Oh, for heaven's *sake*," Tansy Danforth muttered.

He swiveled toward her in surprise.

Her eyes flew innocently wide. She bit her lush bottom lip. Which instantly made him wonder what it might be like to sink his own teeth gently into it.

Which surprised him, and made him frown more darkly than he intended.

She at least blinked at the frown. "May *I* . . . have a go?" She said it tentatively. Very shyly. The lashes went down.

He almost sighed.

This posed a bit of a dilemma, as within days of meeting her the men of Sussex had decided they wouldn't dream of depriving Miss Danforth of any whim.

The gentleman currently holding the musket turned to her.

"It's a very heavy gun," he apologized, as if he'd forged it himself and should have anticipated her need to shoot it.

"I'm sturdier than I look."

This brought a rustle of chuckles and the choked, helpless words, "Like gossamer," from somebody.

Ian rolled his eyes.

"Very well," the man said. "It's a bit unusual, but as you're a guest, perhaps we can make an exception for Miss Danforth . . . Captain Eversea? What say you? May we have a ruling?"

All the men in the crowd were nodding encouragingly.

Ian was torn between genuine concern that she would sneeze or topple beneath the weight of the musket and shoot someone in the crowd, and he was more or less fond of, or at least used to, everyone in that crowd, and wanting to see what would happen when she fired that thing.

Because he had a hunch about Miss Danforth.

"Nobody move, nobody say a word when she pulls the trigger, are we clear? I want no undue distractions. I want everyone to hold as still as they possibly can. Pretend it's the aftermath of Pompeii and you'll never move again. Are we clear?"

Heads bobbed up and down.

And then they dutifully froze.

After all, the truly undue distraction, Miss Danforth, would be the one holding the musket.

"Allow me." Ian took the musket from the previous shooter, who promptly froze into position. "Now, allow me to show you how to hold it, Miss Danforth."

She cleared her throat. "Oh. Good idea."

Suddenly Miss Danforth was blushing again. She untied the ribbons of her bonnet slowly, carefully, and something about that motion— the undoing of a ribbon, a sort of ceremonial undressing—again touched soft little carnal fingers to the back of his neck.

What the devil was it about her? There was just . . . something innately sensual about the girl. He remembered watching her emerge from the woods, her bonnet bobbing behind her, and wondered if this seeming innocent might have come by her sensuality by taking a secret lover. But no; everything else about her was virginal.

He realized he was staring, and she was staring back at him, her bonnet now dangling from her fingers. She lowered it gently to her feet.

He gave himself a shake.

"Very well, Miss Danforth. You heft the musket up to your shoulder just . . . so . . ."

He stood behind her, and heft it up just so. Her hands went up and expertly closed around the weapon.

He was close enough now to feel the heat from her body. She radiated warmth like a little sun. Close enough to see the little arc of pale nape, and the scattering of fine golden hairs there. The temptation was to brush a finger over them, or to apply a slow, hot kiss on that little secret strip of skin. He knew from experience it was a splendid way to get nipples to go erect.

He realized he hadn't moved in some time, mesmerized, in a bit of a reverie, and it might have been seconds or hours. He looked up. Everyone was still frozen in place. But some incredulous glares were aimed his way.

He cleared his throat.

"You hold it like this . . ." he said, then realized he'd already said that.

Ian braced himself as a good portion of the crowd tensed and bristled and stirred.

"I wager she shmells like rainbowsh," someone near him surmised on a murmur. Someone who had been at his flask all morning, from the sound of it.

She didn't. She smelled faintly of something floral, perhaps lavender, but he was no expert on flowers. The sweetness and tang of fine milled soap rose from her warmed skin. It was as if suddenly someone had flung open a door onto a sylvan meadow. He could feel a sort of delicious torpor stealing in, as if he could easily melt into her. Surely the temptation to close his arms around her and pull her into his body was nothing more than a reflex. That was what one *did* when women were just this close, after all.

When a beautiful woman was this close.

A beautiful woman who smelled like a meadow.

So he made sure she had it hoisted correctly and then stepped back abruptly and lifted his arms in the air, as though held at gunpoint or as if she were a hot stove, so the crowd wouldn't rush him with pitchforks and torches.

Interestingly, that musket nestled into her arms like a long lost pet.

Ian had a hunch they were looking at a ringer.

He folded his arms over his chest.

"Now, this thing has a bit of a recoil, Miss Danforth."

"I've been watching, thank you," she said primly. "I think I may be prepared."

The crowd obeyed their orders.

The silence was, in fact, so taut, Ian thought he could have bounced a guinea from it.

And just when it seemed no one could hold their breath any longer, she pulled the trigger.

She flew backward into Ian as the apple exploded.

He levered her upright. He felt his fingers linger on her shoulder blades. They were delicate, and there was another moment where her fragility caught him by surprise. That rogue surge of protectiveness swept in again. And swept out.

Such a joyous roar arose you would have thought she'd negotiated armistice after a long and bloody war.

She stood holding the musket, still aiming it, wearing a look of grim satisfaction, but, interestingly, not surprise.

She smiled modestly.

"A fluke, surely," she insisted demurely, again and again, as all the men surged forth to congratulate her. "Beginner's luck, of a certainty. Americans. We're born knowing how to shoot things, I suppose. All those bears and wolves and Indians from which we need to defend ourselves."

"I'll defend you, Miss Danforth!" came a voice from the crowd.

"I would *never* be afraid if I were protected by an army comprised of the men of Pennyroyal Green and Greater Sussex. I've never known such gallant, thoughtful men."

For God's *sake*. Surely at least Seamus Duggan, who was Irish, would recognize blarney for what it was.

And yet they all seemed like hounds, pushing their snouts into her hand for more strokes every time she said such things.

She was no beginner, he'd wager. At shooting, or at creating a mythology for himself, or at getting men to eat out of her hand.

Wallflower, his *eye*.

*He* ought to know. He conducted his own seductions with the finesse of a fine conductor.

"Well done, Miss Danforth," he said quite cynically.

She turned her gaze upon him. He felt himself brace against the impact of it, which surprised him. He blinked. There were times he forgot—or would like to forget—just how very pretty she was. He was accustomed to beauty. But hers was stealthy; his body reacted to it before his mind could dismiss it.

And for a moment he could have sworn he might have blushed.

It made him strangely angry; he felt tricked, somehow. He did not want to find a woman he distrusted so thoroughly appealing.

To his surprise, scarlet rushed into *her* cheeks again.

"Thank you, Captain Eversea. The compliment means a good deal coming from you."

"Does it?" he said so abruptly, so ironically, she blinked. "Why?"

One never knew whether she meant what she said.

She apparently had no answer for that—she stared wide-eyed up at him as if her wits had abandoned her, or as if he'd caught her in the midst of some heinous act. And that flush migrated into her tawny cheeks and spread down her collarbone, and he watched its progress.

And for a moment he found himself simply staring back, as if he'd been given an opportunity to observe a rare wild creature.

Their mutual stare was interrupted by two men chuffing over, ferrying the trophy between them.

"We've all between us decided you deserve the trophy this year, Miss Danforth."

"Oh, my goodness! Surely I don't warrant the trophy for shooting one little apple!"

"It would be our pleasure. What say you, Captain Eversea?"

Miss Danforth stared up at him, and her white teeth sank into her bottom lip.

He could have sworn she was holding her breath.

"Miss Danforth may have the trophy."

The trophy came nearly up to her hip.

And there was no shortage of volunteers to haul it back to the house for her.

# Chapter 13

❧

THE ENTIRE MARKSMANSHIP COMPETITION crowd migrated to Eversea House, thrown open for the purposes of a party, and happy villagers and competitors milled over the lawn—admittedly, some did more staggering than milling—as well as in and out of the larger parlor, and a long table had been dragged out to the green, covered with a cloth, and piled with an assortment of little cakes and fruit. Ned Hawthorne had been persuaded to part with a few kegs of his light and dark for a price ruthlessly haggled by Mrs. deWitt. An impromptu orchestra of sorts was recruited—really, two fiddles and an accordion. Dancing commenced on the lawn.

IAN WANDERED INTO the house and paused on the periphery of the parlor, studying the scene before him.

He gave a short laugh. The light loved Tansy. He would have sworn it deliberately sought her out like any other lovesick swain, and bathed her in glow.

It could, of course, be the other way around. She in all likelihood had a stage diva's knack for finding the best light in any given room. Regardless, it was easy to imagine her as the lamp in a room and all the young men as moths, circulating, moving in closer at their peril. Each of them secretly soldiers in the game of love, plotting strategies.

They hadn't a prayer. Titania Danforth was Napoleon.

She could possibly even outshoot Napoleon.

She held court on a settee, accepting a plate of cakes and a glass of ratafia from one swain, smiling up at another. Like the sun, the rays of her attention seemed to effortlessly include all of them while leaving each both convinced and uncertain whether he was her favorite. Or whether she had one.

It might have been more amusing—he might have admired the sheer mastery and showmanship—if one of the men circulating hadn't been Lord Landsdowne. Granted, Landsdowne wasn't quite as obvious as the younger men about it. But then, he wouldn't be. Ian watched him, as he'd watched him the other night, and recognized the look on his face. Not rapt, per se. But a certain inscrutable thoughtfulness. He was a patient man. Older. Wealthy. Titled. Utterly confident, quite solid. He'd courted Olivia in patient, persistent, inventive ways that kept her intrigued, and had lured his notoriously capricious sister into something close to an understanding. And that was by no means an unimpressive feat, given that no man in three years had come near to anything of the sort.

And the trouble was, he'd seen that look on Landsdowne's face when he'd looked at Olivia.

And when he thought of Olivia—his proud, difficult, brilliant, charming, beautiful sister—the idea of her sustaining yet another blow to her heart made him suck in his breath, as if he was sustaining that blow right now.

A cluster of women were arrayed opposite. One of them was Olivia, and she was pretending not to notice. And yet he was somehow certain she was suffering.

Suddenly Colin was next to him, a seed cake in one hand and a glass of something that looked like the Pig & Thistle's dark in the other.

He followed the line of Ian's gaze.

"So . . . what do you think of our Miss Danforth?"

"She's horrible." Ian presented the word absently, with a sort of reverent hush.

Colin's head jerked around to stare at him. "What on . . . Did you sustain a blow to the head? How on earth did you draw *that* conclusion?"

"It all began when she didn't blink at all when I said the word tits. And you just did, and you're a jaded roué. Or were, before you were married."

"Insults and blinking aside . . . I'm struggling to imagine the context in which one would say 'tits' to Miss Danforth."

"She dared me." Ian said this on an awestruck hush. "That . . . that . . . *wench* actually led me right to it. Or rather, she led me into saying 'Titsy,' but the difference is the same."

Colin was examining him thoughtfully, with concern, as though searching for signs of fever.

"Assuming this is true," he said, "and I'll allow that it's a trifle unusual, given her wealth and background and youth, and so forth . . . you didn't have to take that dare, now, did you?"

Ian launched an incredulous eyebrow. *How long have you known me?* "Furthermore she goes about collecting hearts as blithely as if she's picking blueberries, Colin. Without thought to the consequence."

"Hmm. Now, who does that remind me of?"

"She smokes and drinks! Hard liquor!" Ian insisted wildly.

Colin snorted. "I'm starting to think *you've* been smoking and drinking hard liquor."

Ian hesitated, and then presented his coup de grace on a hoarse whisper: "I think she may even have a secret *lover*."

It was quite an accusation, and he knew it.

This drew Colin up to his full height. He fixed his brother with a hard, searching stare. For one wild instant Ian wondered if he was about to be called out.

Then Colin's face cleared as if he'd clearly reached a conclusion.

"How long has it been since *you've* taken a lover? A good week or so? No wonder you're losing your mind."

Excellent sarcasm.

"I'm telling you, Colin, she's Beelzebub in a bonnet. Satan in Satin."

"The devil in damask?"

"*Precisely,*" Ian agreed fervently. Deliberately ignoring Colin's irony.

"Ian . . ." Colin's tone was placating. "I wonder if this isn't all wishful thinking on your part, because you know the duke will murder you sooner or later and Genevieve would never forgive you if you . . . shall we say . . . went near the girl. Or through her window, to be more specific."

"For God's sake, Colin, I'm not *mad*. You know me. I've never lost my mind over a woman in my life, and I see them all quite clearly, thank you very much. I'm only telling you the conclusions I've drawn upon observation. Just watch her."

As Colin was a good brother, he humored Ian and did just that.

"For heaven's sake, Ian . . . I mean . . . just look at her." His voice went a trifle drifty over the last three words.

Ian turned very, very slowly and glared at Colin. "And?" he said tightly.

"Ian . . . her eyes are so . . . may I tell you something?"

"Go on," Ian said sourly.

"You know I love Madeleine with all my heart. She *is* my heart. I would die for her, etcetera. I've never been happier."

"Very well."

"When I get to Heaven?"

"The 'when' presumes rather a lot."

"I think the color of the skies in Heaven are precisely the same shade as Miss Danforth's."

Ian stared at him. "Et tu?" he said sadly at last. "Et tu, Colin?"

He flung himself back against the wall and banged his head against it, slowly, rhythmically. Similar to the rhythm of a drum playing a man to the gallows.

"Have a drink, Ian, or have a woman. Surely you've one or two on the dangle. Just keep away from *that* one, if she troubles you so. How difficult can it be?"

Sage advice delivered, Colin gave him a thump on the back and peered out toward the garden. "Croquet!" he said happily. "What a splendid idea. Come out to the garden with me and Madeleine. I know hitting something with a mallet will make you feel better."

Ian shot him a weary, wry look. "In a moment."

"Suit yourself."

He watched Colin aim for Madeleine, who was sitting across the room in conversation with Marcus's wife, the way a man in a desert headed for an oasis. But then he always aimed for Madeleine that way.

"A FINE PAINTING I think you'll enjoy hangs in just the other room, and I've long wished to get a look at it. Would you care to accompany me? I'd be honored to hear your opinion."

Sergeant Sutton was dashing, though much of it had to do with the uniform, she was certain. And it was something about the uniform, something about the word "Sergeant" in front of his name, something about his gray eyes, that reminded her a bit of her brother. A bit. But she liked the look of him. He wasn't Ian Eversea handsome, of course— honestly, who was?—but he was handsome enough, and *certainly* considerably friendlier. They'd chatted quite easily about a number of things, and it was this easiness she found a balm after Ian Eversea's eyes on her—judging, searching, and . . . something else had been in his eyes, something darker and more confusing and a bit knowing. Something both thrilling and frightening.

Then again, there was something about being utterly unwilling to let any dare—and this felt a bit like that—go unaccepted.

So she followed Sergeant Sutton down the hallway—quite a ways, it seeemed—until they paused at a painting.

It was a painting of a horse. It struck her as unremarkable, though in all likelihood a fine one, if she had to guess, but she wasn't a student of art. She was fond of horses, and this one was lovely, but then again she couldn't think of a single reason why the Everseas might hang a homely horse on the wall.

"It's an excellent rendering," she decided to say. "It looks very much like a horse."

He didn't say anything. It had suddenly gotten

very quiet. So quiet she could hear Sergeant Sutton breathing unnaturally loudly.

"Miss Danforth . . . as you've no doubt concluded yourself, we have a spiritual accord."

This was startling information.

"Have we?" she said cautiously.

"Oh yes. Believe me. I have a sense for these things. I realized it when we both admired the painting. And do you know what must necessarily become of spiritual accords?"

Having never knowingly experienced a spiritual accord, Tansy answered truthfully, "No."

"They must find release in, shall we say, physical expression."

"Must they?" Damnation. She shot a surreptitious glance over her shoulder, to see if anyone was in the vicinity. Not a soul. She could no longer even hear the voices of the revelers. Blast.

She took a step backward. The click of her heel echoed ominously on the marble, as if to emphasize just how alone the two of them were.

"Oh yes. It is nature's law. And you're not a scofflaw, are you?" he teased.

"Not as of yet, I don't believe," she said cautiously. "Although if it's nature's *law*, as you say, I feel a little lawlessness coming on now."

"Oh, we can fight our desires all we wish, but nature always wins. Nature knows what's best. And why shouldn't we give it a little assistance? I *feel* that we should."

"*Our* desires, Sergeant Sutton?" He'd stepped

closer. She stepped back. "I *feel* you should have used a different preposition."

He laughed at that.

She took another step back. Another step or two and she would be able to make a reasonably graceful escape without lifting her skirts in her hands and running for it.

But that's when he reached out a hand and closed it around her wrist, brought her hand up to his mouth and pressed a hot kiss into her palm.

"Did you feel that down to your toes, Miss Danforth?"

"Truthfully, I felt it more in the pit of my stomach."

"That's excitement," he reassured her.

"That's revulsion," she corrected, and pulled back on her wrist.

He held fast. "It takes a moment for the effect to take hold. Sometimes it takes more than one kiss to get the job done."

He used her own arm as a lever to pull her closer, and even though she dug in her heels, her slippers slid across the marble as if she were on skis. The dark little caverns of his nostrils loomed and time seemed to slow as the dark maw slowly opened in preparation to latch over hers. The stench of cheap tobacco smoke permeating his coat stunned her senses, and she was just about to spit on him when—

"Unhand her."

The voice was lazy. Offhand. Quiet.

But something about it stood all the hair on the back of her neck on end.

She'd never heard anything more menacing in her life.

Sergeant Sutton dropped her arm as if it were a snake and spun around.

"Captain Eversea!"

Ian Eversea was indeed standing there, towering, his posture gracefully indolent. But his face was granite, apart from the faint curve of a very unpleasant smile.

Tansy reclaimed her wrist jealously and rubbed at it.

She wondered if she could get away with kicking Sutton now that his attention was diverted. She eyed the back of his trousers.

Ian Eversea took her in with a glance, ascertaining that nothing more than her dignity was hurt, and warned her against violence with the slightest shake of his head.

And he said nothing to her.

" 'Physical accord'? 'Spiritual accord'?" His voice was still nearly a drawl, as if he couldn't be bothered to raise it over a toad like Sutton. But his scorn made each word crack like a whip. "I have never heard such a steaming load of shite. Get out of here, Sutton. Go. Before I make it impossible for you to move. And if you ever bother Miss Danforth again, I will make certain she's the last female you ever bother."

Sutton's jaw was tense. A swallow moved in his throat.

The air crackled with suppressed violence, like the prelude to a thunderstorm.

For the first time in a very long time, a surge of genuine fear swept her.

"And you'd know a bit about killing, wouldn't you, sir?" Sutton finally said. It sounded a bit like an insinuation.

Ian smiled at this. Swiftly. It was like watching a saber being unsheathed.

His voice went silky. The voice a cobra might use, Tansy thought, to mesmerize its prey.

"Enough so that one more wouldn't make a damn bit of difference to me, Sergeant."

And before her eyes, Sergeant Sutton blanched. She'd never actually seen someone do precisely that before.

Sutton stared at Ian a moment longer, then muttered some oath under his breath and spun on his heel.

They watched him until he walked down the hallway and disappeared back into the party.

She cleared her throat. "Thank you," she managed, with a certain amount of dignity. Her voice was a bit frayed.

He said nothing. He was staring at her as if he couldn't quite decide whether she deserved killing, too.

"Killing?" she queried. "Done a lot of it?" she said, just to interrupt the stare.

The stare continued.

He still said nothing. He just studied her with those blue eyes, and she felt them on her like cinders.

"May I ask you a question, Miss Danforth?" His voice was still quiet, almost lazy.

She nodded permission.

"What the bloody hell are you playing at?"

Ah. Suspicions confirmed. He *was* angry.

She bit her lip a moment. "You don't have to curse."

Good God. Even she thought that was inane.

She could see he *almost* laughed.

"Oh, my *stars*. I do apologize for my rough ways."

She almost laughed at that. She sensed that would be unwise indeed, because he hadn't yet blinked. There was the sense about him of a coiled spring. Or a primed musket. Whatever anger he'd felt at Sutton—or at her—hadn't yet entirely spent itself. And here she was alone with him.

"Answer me, please."

He was probably a bloody good captain, if she had to guess. Scared the life out of his soldiers by just talking in a quiet voice.

"I'm not sure what you mean," she hedged, though she was pretty certain that she did.

"Flirting with men, encouraging their attentions with wild, insincere, yet strangely effective flattery, generally causing an uproar, all so you can have all of them eating out of your hand, and then recklessly finding yourself in a compromising, even dangerous, position as a result."

Oh. That.

*You noticed!* she was tempted to say.

"All of them except for you," she pointed out.

She couldn't *believe* she'd said it.

It was fairly clear this had brought him up short. He was staring at her with something like amazement now.

"Or perhaps you're . . . jealous?" she suggested hopefully, weakly. Half jesting.

Her own recklessness amazed her. But in for a penny, in for a pound.

And she wanted to jar a way past that stare.

She was sorry she'd said it when the next expression to take up occupation on his face was incredulity.

He shook his head slowly to and fro.

"I've watched you, Miss Danforth . . . in the midst of your games. And it's so very clear you know little to nothing of the . . . shall we say, matters between men and women. I would wager my entire inheritance on it. And I find game playing combined with ignorance tedious. I'm not a boy."

She was badly stung.

"The matters between men and women! Do you mean sex?"

A heartbeat of utter silence followed.

"I suppose you think you're being very bold," he said quietly.

She was fairly certain she had succeeded in shocking him.

Perhaps even rattling him.

She said nothing, because she'd shocked herself by saying it and needed a moment to recover.

"Have you ever even been kissed before, Miss Danforth?"

She contemplated which answer would incriminate her the least and impress him the most, though why she should want to do the latter eluded her. She *had* been kissed, but it hadn't caused a single unusual physical response.

Whereas simply looking at Ian Eversea seemed to cause her senses to riot.

"Perhaps."

She wouldn't have blamed him if he rolled his eyes.

Perhaps mercifully, the incredulity was simply amplified a bit.

"It's a risky game you play, *Tansy*. Why do you do it?"

She was angry now. "Because. I. *Can*. And because they like it."

"I suspect you mean because they like *you* when you do it."

This brought her up short. A tense little silence followed.

"Why do *you* do it?" she countered. *Ha!*

His eyes flared in surprise, then anger swiftly kindled in them.

Splendid. She was certain she'd at least startled him. *Yes, Captain Eversea, I know about your alleged exploits.* She imagined saying that aloud. She discovered she wasn't *that* brave.

But he ignored the question.

"I won't always be lurking around corners

when you face the consequences of your actions, Tansy. Not every soldier is born a gentleman, and not every gentleman understands the word no. Men are fundamentally brutes. Some just wear better clothes and have more money. You ought to be more afraid."

He was undoubtedly correct. She *ought* to be.

"Come now, Captain Eversea, surely you of all people know that a little risk makes life less dull, altogether."

He gave a short laugh. She suspected she'd surprised it from him.

"*My* risks are calculated, Miss Danforth. And informed by experience."

"And you can't possibly know that I know *nothing* about, as you say, 'such matters.'"

He inhaled deeply, exhaled at length, sounding oh-so-long-suffering. "Oh, you know how to make them yearn, I grant you. You know how to get *attention*. There's a look experienced women have, that's all. A demeanor. And you haven't the look."

This was news. How on earth would an experienced woman look? Shocked? Tired? Wicked? Reflexively, she tried an expression that she thought might incorporate all three.

He laughed again, genuinely. "I've seen that expression on one of Colin's cows, after she'd eaten something she ought not."

Torn between laughing and scowling, she frowned.

"You don't *need* the look. It isn't something to aspire to, Miss Danforth. You're going to marry someone with a title and all the money you'll ever need, isn't that so? Aren't you destined for a duke or something of the sort? So don't even think about practicing. Like I said, I won't always be around to rescue you."

"I imagine you've benefited from that 'look' any number of times, haven't you, Captan Eversea?"

She was out of her depth with him, which made her even more reckless than usual. She was like a kitten with tiny sharp claws crawling up his trouser leg. She suspected he would indulge her only so long before he shook her off abruptly.

"Miss Danforth," he said patiently. "It's clear you want to goad me into saying scandalous things to you that you can take back to your room and savor, pore over at night like found treasure. You want my attention. You don't want the consequences of that attention. You don't even know what the consequences *are.* And for me, it's just . . . it's well, just rather dull," he added with an attempt at kindness, and an intolerably condescending lift of one shoulder. "And in some circumstances, it might even be hurtful. And if someone I care about might be hurt as a result of whatever game you're playing . . . I simply can't allow you to do it."

*Dull!*

Someone he *cared about*!

Oh, the *infuriating* humiliation. Her eyes burned.

For some reason all of this hurt mortally.

"You don't know me at all," she said, her voice a rasp, her face hot. She could only assume it was a scorching, unflattering red.

"I know you some," he said easily, sounding bored. "And some is enough."

He leaned back against the wall of the terrace, struck a flint against the box and lit a cheroot without asking whether she minded. He sent the smoke up into the air and aimed his gaze out over the landscape he likely knew the way he knew his own face in the mirror.

His own damned handsome, unforgettable face.

"Well, I suppose you're right," she said. "But you ought to know, isn't that true, Captain Eversea? Because you of all people know it's all about the *getting* of someone or of something. Everything you do. Everything else is a waste of time. God forbid a woman should evince an interest in you first. I'll wager you'll run like a frightened little girl."

She couldn't seem to control what came out of her mouth when she was around him. Surely this was inadvisable.

He turned his head sharply then, eyes wide in surprise, then hot with a real fleeting anger. She took a step back, as though he'd lunged at her with a lit torch.

Then something speculative settled into his gaze. He studied her long enough for her heart to flop hard in her chest, painfully, like an obsequious mongrel. Eager to be patted or kicked, whatever he preferred. And she was angry that she was so very inexperienced that she couldn't stop her heart from doing otherwise.

At least she felt *seen* by him for the first time.

Oh, how she wished she knew what he saw.

"Know a bit about being a frightened little girl, do you, Tansy?" he said softly.

*Oh.*

She felt pinned like a butterfly to a board.

How, how, *how* she wished she had something to throw.

She opened her mouth. But she couldn't speak. Her voice had congealed.

She simply turned and . . .

Well, she didn't precisely run.

But she walked rather more swiftly than she might have done.

And as her footsteps echoed, making her feel as though she was chasing herself, he called after her, dryly, "You're welcome."

# Chapter 14

❧

HIS TEMPER STILL ON the boil, Ian found himself charging in the opposite direction from the festivities.

As it turned out he was on his way to the kitchen, which he hadn't realized until he arrived. By the time he did, a certain fascination had begun to edge its way into his rather complicated anger, which flared bright and fresh every time he pictured Sutton's hand closed around Tansy Danforth's wrist as she struggled to pull it away. His gut knotted. What a pleasure it would have been to flatten Sutton. She could have been hurt. Or at the very least, quite inexpertly kissed against her will, and no woman should endure that.

How dare the girl put herself at risk like that? How stupid did one have to *be*?

He stopped abruptly and pulled in a long deep breath. He was fair enough to realize his anger seemed all out of proportion to the circumstances.

*Is that why you do it?*

Ah. And there he had it. What in God's name had the girl heard about him? Or had that just been a guess aimed as skillfully as she'd aimed that musket?

This, perversely, amused him.

And at this thought he could feel something else sneaking in on the heels of his indignation. Something that felt a bit like . . . could it be . . . admiration?

Very, very reluctant admiration.

She *was* quick. He'd give her that.

When she wasn't trying so bloody hard.

He paused in the kitchen. It was mercifully dimly lit and peaceful at the moment. Much to his delight, arrayed on a tray like the crown jewels as if awaiting his arrival, was a solitary fluffy, golden scone. Just the thing for his mood. Surely it was fate.

He reached for it.

From out of nowhere a blur appeared and spanked his hand lightly.

He yelped.

It turned out to be Mrs. deWitt.

"Ow! Why the beating? You hurt my feelings gravely, Mrs. deWitt."

She laughed softly. "As if anyone could ever do that! Ach, dinna touch that, Master Ian. That there be for Miss Danforth."

Even *scones* were held in thrall for the girl?

"That *particular* scone is for Miss Danforth? *Why*, pray tell?"

"Yes, 'tis 'er favorite, and one does like to spoil 'er a bit, now, ye see."

"One *does*," he said, but Mrs. deWitt missed the irony. "Surely, then, there's another very similar scone for me."

"Not until after the baking this afternoon."

"I'll give you a shilling for this one," he said childishly.

She snorted. " 'Ave some cheese."

"I want a scone. I want *that* scone."

"Ah, now, Master Ian, and will *ye* be marryin' a duke, now, or some such, someday? Are ye all alone in the world now? Did ye win a trophy today?"

"Probably not, no and no," he conceded.

"Well then," she said, as if this decided everything.

Imagine that. Defeated by the cook. He wasn't child enough to snatch it from her anyway, though he was sorely tempted.

"Let me find ye a lovely piece of cheese, Master Ian," she pacified.

"Very well." He'd decided to be gracious in defeat. He settled at the table and irritably shoved aside a vase full of flowers.

"Those be for Miss Danforth," the cook said proudly, as if it were her own accomplishment.

"Shocking," Ian said.

He eyed them critically. They were from someone who possessed a hothouse, which could be nearly anyone with money in Sussex.

He was irritated suddenly, wondering precisely who it was.

"But she gave them to me, sweet girl she is. And she had the rest taken down to the churchyard. And she gave toy soldiers to little Jordy! She has a heart of gold, she does."

It was all Ian could do not to choke.

Then again, he didn't suppose he'd given much thought to Tansy Danforth's heart. Or hearts, as he should say, given that she'd gone on a campaign to steal them from nearly every man she encountered, including possibly the one he would not allow her to have, and that was Landsdowne's.

What went on in her heart? She *could* be hurt, that much he knew. She'd reacted like a wild thing prodded with a spear when he insinuated she might be hurting someone he loved.

He felt a little minute jab in the region of his solar plexus then. Sympathy, or guilt, he wasn't sure. Suddenly he wished he could unsay it. He found the notion that he might have hurt her feelings surprisingly distasteful.

Mrs. deWitt slid cheese and a slab of bread slathered in honey in front of him. The honey was a peace offering.

"How did you know this scone was Miss Danforth's favorite?" he asked.

"We have a visit of nights, and we've a bit of a bite to eat when we talk."

He nearly choked. "You . . . 'have a visit'?" He

was bemused. "Of *nights*? You and Miss Danforth?"

"Aye, Master Ian, she's but a young woman still and I think she's a wee bit lonely. We chat a bit in the kitchen sometimes at night. Not every night. Sometimes very late. I leave one out for her, and if it's gone in the morning I know she had trouble sleeping. She's a young girl alone in the world. And here you all be, a big comfortable noisy family, and you know everyone you see and all the land, too. She's a bit lonesome, aye?"

"She's lonely because she's alienated all the women in Sussex and bewitched all the men into injuring themselves and each other on her behalf."

Mrs. deWitt laughed indulgently. "Ah, now, surely you exaggerate Master Ian, and wouldn't that be just like you."

"No, I mean it!"

Mrs. deWitt just chuckled some more at what she likely suspected were his antics. "Ah, ye always did have a fine wit, Master Ian. Think of it. "

"Lonesome? Her constitution is made of iron. If she'd been born another gender, she'd give Napoleon a run for his money in terms of campaigns. She's shameless."

But even as he said it he could feel doubt encroaching.

"Of *course* her constitution is iron, Master Ian. She's alone in the world, what choice has the girl? I dinna ken about shameless. I for one believe she's as sweet as an—"

"Don't say angel!"

"Oh, I suppose she's just not for the likes of you, Master Ian. Ye never did take to the angels."

But she winked at him with great affection.

Ian sighed. "No, I never did."

*Lonesome.* He recalled her expression when he'd asked her whether she knew a bit about being a frightened little girl. As if he'd seized the collar of her dress and yanked it clean off. Stripping her of some critical disguise.

And yet it had all been for her own good, of that he was certain.

Why, then, did he feel a sudden uncomfortable urge to apologize?

His curiosity got the better of him.

"But what do you *talk* about?"

"Aye, just a bi' of talk between women, right? Budgets and cooking and the like. It wouldna interest ye in the *least.*" She said this quite inscrutably.

Just a day ago she would have been absolutely correct.

TANSY MANAGED TO convincingly sparkle through the rest of the afternoon.

But the day had gone on too long, and the supreme effort it took to charm had given her a headache, as if she'd drunk too much champagne, which she hadn't. She suspected it was a bit of a spiritual hangover, which had rather a lot to do with Ian Eversea's brutally accurate summary and dismissal of her.

She sat down hard, propped her chin in her hands and tried hard to hate him, but all she could muster was a sort of resigned, honest misery. She felt rather like a shoddy magician whose secrets had been exposed. She couldn't fault him, not really. She in truth rather admired it, which added a bit to her misery, given that she was fairly certain he now didn't like her at *all*, if he'd liked her just a little before.

But . . . though there had been a moment when he helped her shoulder the gun, where the air seemed to go soft and dense as velvet, and she could have sworn their breathing had begun to sway at the same rhythm, like two rivers joining, and she'd strangely never felt safer or more peculiarly imperiled. And she'd wanted time to stop then, to freeze the two of them the way the entire crowd had frozen, so she could lean against him, because that's where she'd always belonged, or so it seemed. And to just see what that moment was all about.

And at the recoil he had pushed her upright as if she'd been something aflame.

She thought about this. And decided she unnerved him, too. At least a little.

It cheered her, but it made her uneasy as well.

*You mean because they like you when you do it?*

*Aargh.* Her cheeks went hot again.

*Know a bit about being a frightened little girl, Tansy?*

She dropped her hot cheeks into her hands. But then she raised her head slowly and took a long steadying breath. Because regardless of what he thought of her, it was strangely a relief to be *known*.

Oddly, she wasn't tempted to throw her slippers at the wall this time.

The thing was, there were things she now knew about Ian Eversea that he probably didn't even know he'd revealed. That he might not even know about himself. There was a certain advantage to being underestimated, at least for a time, and the advantage was that she could surprise him into a flare of anger—disconcerting as it had been to be in the path of those blazing eyes—because she'd prodded some sore place in him. She took no pleasure in hurting him, but there was still a little bit of a thrill.

And despite her resolve, she found that the hunger to know him had in no way diminished.

He might not have the slightest interest in Richard III, but she'd found a way into Ian Eversea, anyway, quite inadvertently.

Tansy gazed at the wall.

She unfolded her sheet of foolscap and spread it out neatly and read it to herself. And then, because she was fundamentally honest, she added to the bottom:

*Fiercely loyal to those he loves.*

THE NEXT AFTERNOON Ian stopped in at the Pig & Thistle for a pint of the dark, which he'd been dreaming about for the last hour as he hammered nails into a decrepit paddock fence. Surely he'd purchased his way into Heaven with all of this work lately. Though his cousin the vicar assured him it didn't work quite that way.

He pushed open the door of the pub and saw Landsdowne sitting by himself, enjoying what appeared to be a steak and kidney pie and a pint of the light. Landsdowne looked up, saw Ian and beckoned him over.

Ian pulled out a chair and reflexively raised a hand. When Polly didn't appear in a heartbeat, he swiveled his head to look for her.

He didn't see her, but Ned noticed him and without asking brought Ian a pint of the dark.

"I give Polly a bit of time off during the day, Captain Eversea. She goes off for a bit, but she should have returned by now."

"I'm certain she'll be here any minute, Ned. She's a good girl."

Ned brightened. "Aye, that she is. That she is."

Polly Hawthorne was quite simply Ned's heart, Ian knew. And he reflected again on the dangers of loving. *Anyone.* The thing that allegedly made life worthwhile quite had the power to destroy you, too. Interesting irony, that the thing that made you strongest was also what made you weakest. Altogether more dangerous than war, love was.

"How goes it, Eversea?" Landsdowne offered laconically.

"It goes quite sweatily. But we're close to having a new roof on the vicarage."

"Admirable. Every building deserves a roof."

Ian gave a short laugh.

There was a silence between them. Ian drummed his fingers, wondering how to begin.

"What else is on your mind?" Landsdowne said politely, with a certain dry amusement.

"My sister . . ." He hoped Landsdowne would pick up the thread.

". . . is magnificent." Landsdowne completed this almost grimly.

Ian launched his brows and waited for more.

It wasn't forthcoming.

So he decided to be blunt. "Do you still think so?"

Landsdowne gave a soft laugh. "Ah. Did you come here to ascertain my intentions, Eversea? I should have thought my intentions are quite clear by now."

"And your intentions remain . . . unaltered in their course? Despite recent gifts sent to another young woman?"

"Are you perchance alluding to a certain blond angel who has lately alit upon Sussex?"

Good God, even Landsdowne talked like a fool about her.

Angel, my left hindquarter, he thought. He had enough of the gentleman left in him that he thought he would leave it unsaid, and he wasn't about to enumerate what he considered her secret vices.

Unbidden came an image of that bare, vulnerable little crescent of fair skin between the collar of her walking gown and her bonnet, and the delicate blades of her shoulders, and her clear eyes staring back at him, wide and as shocked as if he'd struck her when he demanded the reason his opinion meant anything at all to her.

That peculiar impulse toward protection rushed at him again. Fierce and quite irrational.

He understood then that she was only truly awkward around *him*.

No. He would keep her secrets. Though he could not say quite why.

Landsdowne sighed. "It was merely a friendly gift, Eversea. I meant nothing by it, truly, other than hoping to make her feel more welcome in Pennyroyal Green. But . . ." He leaned back in his chair. ". . . can you imagine what your life would be like, Eversea, if you awoke to her every morning? To eyes full of admiration instead of challenge? To simplicity and charm and innocence and that restful beauty?"

Ian nearly choked. This, however, was too much. Simplicity? *Restful?*

It was a moment before he could speak.

"If you intend to divert your attentions from Olivia in order to court Miss Danforth, you may find yourself part of a stampede," was all he said. Very carefully.

Landsdowne smiled a little. "I'm aware." He sounded entirely unaffected. After all, he was the man who had found a way into Olivia Eversea's seemingly impenetrable good graces and turned the ton's betting world on its ear. "And *you* don't intend to join the throng?"

Ian gave a short humorless laugh. "Ah, no. I'll be sailing soon for a half-dozen exotic ports of call. I can think of very few women who'll consent to be dragged along on a journey like that."

"Well, then. What would you do if I did tell you I intend to abandon my suit? To throw over Olivia for Miss Danforth? Will you call me out? What would that accomplish?"

"It would accomplish," Ian said thoughtfully, "the setting of an example. For if I shot you, odds are very good no one would throw over Olivia again."

Landsdowne grinned swiftly at that. "You're likely right."

A brief little silence felled, during which Ian silently compelled Landsdowne to explain himself. He certainly wasn't obliged to do it, but he was a man of honor.

"Here is the thing." Landsdowne sighed. And then his mouth quirked humorlessly. "I don't know if Olivia will ever love me. And yet . . . the more time I spend with her the more I can't do without her."

Lyon Redmond was indeed fortunate he'd disappeared, Ian thought. Because he would have strangled him on the spot had he reappeared just now. He'd left so much unhappiness in his wake, and the unhappiness rippled out to include people like Landsdowne, who didn't deserve it.

"And yet . . . I often think I would be happy to settle for simply her . . . esteem. To live with only that for the rest of my born days. For her. Olivia Eversea's mere esteem is worth more than the love and devotion of a dozen women. I cannot currently imagine a day without her. And it isn't my intention—I give you my word of honor—to pursue Miss Danforth. Does that answer your concerns with regards to your sister?"

He said it flatly.

It was as raw a declaration of love as Ian could imagine, and he felt a brief twinge of shame for cornering Landsdowne into it. He nearly pitied the man. He knew a brief surge of anger for his stubborn, prideful sister. He was a good man, a worthy man, and he deserved better than esteem. Olivia's pride had surely caused at least some of her own unhappiness.

But Ian's loyalty was to his sister.

He nodded shortly. "Thank you, Landsdowne, for telling me. Rest assured you have my utter discretion. And my apologies if I seemed intrusive. But I imagine you understand."

"I do. I, too, have sisters."

"I hear Miss Danforth is all but promised to de Neauville's heir, anyway."

It was a lie.

Because he'd just decided right then to write to the Duke de Neauville's heir to tell him about Miss

Danforth. He was young, a good shooter, handled the ribbons well even if he drove a bit recklessly, wanted the best of everything, was an otherwise inoffensively uninteresting young man, and the de Neauvilles owned property in Sussex. Surely if anything could turn Miss Danforth's head and *keep* it turned, it was a handsome, fledgling about-to-be-a-duke. And that was the sort of marriage she was destined for, anyway, wasn't it? He would be doing everyone a good turn in writing to the duke's son.

"Far be it for me to intrude upon another man's territory," Landsdowne said wryly.

Which was when Ian noticed his ale still hadn't arrived.

And it looked as though ales hadn't arrived at many of the tables. Woebegone faces were craning toward the bar, gesturing with empty tankards. Murmurs were beginning.

Ned rushed over to him.

"Captain Eversea, I'm worried now. Polly would never leave for this long without asking or without telling me where she's gone. I'm afraid something's amiss."

"Do you want me to help you look for her? Do you have someone to mind the pub?"

"I've been meaning to hire someone for some time, but things are so busy I just haven't yet gotten round to it. Jemmy can do it in a pinch, but he's a bit slow. We'll have a riot on our hands if we're gone long."

Perhaps an exaggeration, but not by much. They looked around at the yearning faces of the men in the pub, all very unused to being denied Ned's light or dark when they wanted it.

"We best hurry, then. Far be it for me to cause a riot."

# Chapter 15

⦻

It HAD BEEN DAYS before she was able ride out on her own again, but Tansy had seized the opportunity the minute the duke and Genevieve departed to inspect another property available for purchase, a good two hours carriage drive away. A little too far for Genevieve's preference, and just far enough from the Everseas, as far as the duke was concerned, and this was a source of more or less good-natured bickering.

Tansy had charmed the groom—who surely knew better, but had just as much trouble refusing her anything she wanted as nearly every other man in Pennyroyal Green—into saddling her mare and allowing her to ride off alone again, since it was to be such a very short ride on such a beautiful day.

She wanted to take a look at her handiwork.

She was parallel to the stream when she pulled her horse to a halt.

Someone was staggering toward her—a woman, she saw, when the wind whipped out a long dark skirt—who then dropped again to her knees with a squeak.

Tansy's heart lurched.

"Polly!"

She trotted over, scrambled almost gracelessly down from her horse, dashed over and knelt next to her, placing a hand on her arm.

"What's happened? Are you hurt?"

Polly seemed a bit embarrassed.

"Oh, I'm sound enough, except me ankle . . . oh, blast, but I've twisted it, Miss Danforth, in a blessed vole hole, I believe. I can't seem to get far. And oh, my dress! I've dirtied it! My papa is going to *kill* me."

Tansy understood full well the distress of dirtying a dress and worrying a father.

"If only I could find a stick to help with the walking . . ." Polly fussed. She furrowed her brow and looked toward the Pig & Thistle, as if she could will herself back into the pub.

"A stick! What nonsense. You'll wait here and I'll fetch help if we need it. But first, may I have a look? Here, let us take off your shoe, just . . . so."

Polly extended her leg without question, and Tansy carefully unlaced the worn, serviceable walking boot and handed it to Polly to hold.

"Oh, it's swollen! You poor thing. Now, if only we had something to wrap it . . . you see, I've done this before! My brother and I used to play together, and I would run after him. I never could catch up. He was older and his legs were longer and I tripped in holes in the pasture."

Polly laughed at that. "I always wished I had a brother."

"Mine was both wonderful and a great trial to me. He died late in the War of 1812."

"I'm so sorry, Miss Danforth. The men do love to go and be soldiers, and leave us at home missing them and worrying."

"Please do call me Tansy."

She wondered which Eversea in particular Polly had missed and worried over.

"Tansy. Thank you, Tansy. Papa will be so worried. I'm all he has, you know, and I only have the few memories of Mama. And I canna serve at the Pig & Thistle with a limp. How could I be so *foolish*?"

"Oh, we're all foolish at one time or another. We'll worry about that later. Let me see if this will help . . ."

Tansy fished out a handkerchief and was able to wrap it around Polly's slim ankle twice and tie it neatly. She bounded to her feet and hauled Polly gently upward.

Polly tried to put a little weight on it, leaning heavily on Tansy. She brightened. "Oh! It's a bit better." She tried another step and yelped. "Bloody *aitch*, Tansy! I'm afraid I can't do it all the way back to the Pig & Thistle like this. Oh, my papa will be so upset with me!"

"Well, he will be at first, but if I know papas, he'll be happier to see you alive than he will be angry that you hurt yourself. Here, lean on me and we'll settle you back down again. I'll go and fetch help straightaway."

Tansy managed to get herself into the saddle, which was a bit of a struggle, and she was afraid she'd showed Polly her stockings and part of her chemise in the process. Then she kicked her horse into a decidedly unladylike gallop and tore across the downs in the direction of town.

She was shamelessly enjoying the excuse to ride at breakneck speed when she saw two men riding toward her across the green.

She pulled her mare to a halt and stared. Then threw a glance over her shoulder at the woods. She really was quite in the middle of things and didn't see any refuge.

Ah. She wondered if this was the sort of thing she ought to have considered before she rode out alone.

She wasn't armed, more's the pity, for goodness knows she could have shot either of them from horseback where she sat.

If they wanted to abduct her and sell her into slavery on a pirate ship, she would put up a struggle, but there really was no doubt about who would eventually win.

She watched, and said a little prayer, and a moment later . . . something about one of the men . . .

. . . something simply about the way he occupied space . . .

She knew it was Ian Eversea.

Her relief seesawed with alarm for a moment before nerves settled in to stay.

Nerves and guilt.

And her heart, of course, took up that disorienting jig it normally did in his presence. Even when he was still at a distance.

He sat a horse so beautifully, her breath snagged in her throat. She decided to try to take pleasure in that before the berating began.

She saw the moment he recognized her, because he drew to an abrupt halt, too.

He kneed his horse into a canter and was beside her in seconds.

"Miss Danforth," he drawled, sweeping his hat from his head. "*Imagine* seeing you where you shouldn't be. And alone, too, which you also shouldn't be. Or are you?"

"And good day to you, Captain Eversea. I was riding into town to fetch Mr. Hawthorne. Polly Hawthorne was . . . out for a walk . . . and has twisted her ankle and she can't put her weight on it. I discovered her."

He transformed before her eyes. His face went brilliant with relief and joy. "*You* found Polly? Where is she?" He turned to shout over his shoulder. "Ned! We've found Polly!" He turned back to Tansy. "Is she otherwise sound?"

He sounded so worried, she found herself soothing him. "She's fine. She's turned her ankle and can't put her weight on it but she's otherwise well and cheerful enough. And worried about her father worrying about her."

"Ned! Polly turned her ankle but she's sound otherwise."

Ned's head dropped to his chest in relief and he kicked his horse into a trot.

"Where is she?"

"Follow me," Tansy said. Enjoying the opportunity to order him about.

"Miss Dan—"

She tugged her horse around and kicked it into a gallop again.

*Catch me if you can, Captain Eversea.*

POLLY'S LITTLE ELFIN face lit when they galloped into view.

Ned all but threw himself down from his horse and ran to her, then turned to Ian, wordlessly, who was next to them in a moment. Tansy watched as Ian scooped Polly up as if she were weightless. Together he and Ned gently situated her in the saddle of Ned's horse.

And if I were Polly, Tansy thought, I would never forget the feel of his arms around me, and how it felt to be lifted gently, as though I were precious. Almost worth turning an ankle over.

With a tip of his hat to Ian and Tansy and a heartfelt, "My thanks," to both of them, Ned Hawthorne urged his horse forward again. From the sound of things, Ned was clearly fussing and berating, and Polly protesting and placating.

She smiled. Lucky Polly, to be so missed.

She turned toward Ian.

He was smiling, too, at the two of them as they retreated.

Tansy's heart squeezed. It was a beautiful smile.

Warm, wholly satisfied and relieved, utterly unguarded. It made him look very young.

*That's* what he looks like when he cares about
people, she thought, wistfully.

That smile faded when it turned her way, alas.

"How did you happen to find her, Miss Danforth?"

He could have at *least* congratulated her. Or
thanked her.

She hesitated.

"I've seen her near . . . here. Whilst I was riding.
It's a lovely spot, isn't it? Very quiet by this stream."

"What were *you* doing here by *yourself*? Burying bodies? Meeting a lover?"

She pressed her lips firmly closed.

And when he refused to blink, she sighed.

"Nothing remotely as interesting. Would you
please, please, please stop being so bloody curious
and overprotective? I said please. *Three* times."

He studied her a moment, clearly fighting a
smile.

"No need to curse," he said mildly. "Are you
going to stamp your foot? You've that look about
you."

"Are you giving me permission to do it?"

He did grin again, and the grin evolved into a
laugh. He had a beautiful smile, even more beautiful when he aimed it at her.

A little silence followed, and he swiped a hand
over his hair, almost self-consciously.

"You ride very well," he volunteered. "Then

again, why wouldn't you? Every 'wallflower' rides like a hellion."

"Of course I ride well. This soft little country is nothing compared to rugged American terrain. I frequently rode by myself. And I have to dodge Indians and bears and the like when I do it."

Judging from the look on his face, he was thoroughly enjoying this bald-faced lie.

"Miss Danforth, I'm not ignorant of geography, you know. I'm familiar with your part of New York."

*Oh.*

"But doubtless you need to gallop hard to elude your suitors and incensed women," he added.

"I leave all of them in the dust," she said gravely, her hand over her heart.

And he laughed again, sounding delighted, and the laugh evolved into a happy sigh, as if she were part of something amusing being performed on Drury Lane.

Could it be that they were actually *enjoying* each other?

If she thought about it too much she would likely revert to gawking and stammering.

There was a silence that threatened to become awkward.

"Is that where you learned to shoot?" he asked. "Like a bloody marksman?"

"My father and brother taught me. I rather took to it. I don't very much like to shoot animals, however."

"But you have no compunctions over murdering apples."

She laughed. "That apple deserved to die. I know how to *load* a musket, too, you know. I should one day like to shoot a rifle."

"I have an excellent rifle," he said. "A Baker. Shot it during the war."

He stopped short of volunteering to allow her to shoot it, she noticed. And it seemed like those silent words filled the little pause that followed.

"From when you were in the army," she prompted.

"Yes."

He didn't expound. She imagined he'd shot a good deal when he was in the army, and seen a good deal, and suddenly she didn't want to remind him.

"You don't really like Richard the Third, do you?"

He looked startled. "I don't dislike him. I would have to say I have no powerful feelings about Richard the Third. Have . . . *you*?" He said it with great trepidation.

"No. I like stories of people surviving things. I'm rather fond of Robinson Crusoe."

He looked a bit taken aback by that. "Robinson Crusoe is a marvelous story," he said on a hush. "*Quite* tolerable for a novel."

"Isn't it?" she said eagerly. "I've also quite enjoyed the books by Miles Redmond about his South Seas Travels."

Amazement flickered across his face. "Mr.

Miles Redmond's stories have inspired me to take an ocean voyage around the world."

"You might be eaten by a cannibal," she warned.

"They'd have to catch me," he said soberly. "And I'm an excellent shot. Not as good as *you*, of course. Apple killer."

They regarded each other in another peculiar little silence. Somewhat alarmed by their accord. And by the fact that they appeared to be very much enjoying a conversation.

With each *other*.

She suddenly wondered if Ian Eversea—who allegedly was so expert and blasé about women—felt a trifle awkward around *her*.

His horse snorted encouragingly into the silence. Growing a little restive.

And yet he didn't suggest they leave yet.

"Do you miss your home in America, Miss Danforth?"

The question sounded almost tentative coming from him. As if he thought it were a delicate question, or was afraid it would result in a torrent of unwanted information. Men could be so amusing.

Then again, he could actually be trying to know her.

"Yes," she said, mimicking his taciturn answer of a moment ago.

The corner of his mouth lifted, appreciating this.

"Genevieve said you used to live at Lilymont."

She inhaled sharply in surprise. It was a bit like hearing the name of a loved one out of the blue.

She turned away, reflexively; she didn't quite realize it, but she'd aimed her body in the general direction of Lilymont. "I did."

"A charming house. I remember how much I liked the garden when I saw it last."

"I loved the garden. My mother planted so many of the flowers there. I had such a wonderful time helping her. And my brother would chase me around it, pretending he was a British soldier and I was an American. The joke was on both of us when we went to live in America and we couldn't decide who would be the enemy."

Ian laughed. "Brothers are experts at torment."

"I suppose you would know. You're fortunate to have so many."

"I suppose I am. Did you know Lilymont is for sale?"

"*Oh.*" It was a syllable of pure yearning. "How fortunate the new owners will be. I wonder if you can still see my name on the wall where I scratched it there with a little knife. Underneath the ivy in the corner next to my mother's favorite apple tree."

Ian was quiet. His hat remained in his hand, and the wind ruffled the hair away from his forehead. He had the eyes of a rifleman, she thought.

And there was a look of contemplative assessment in them, the same look her mother would get when poring over the kitchen budget looking for errors. As if he'd needed to erase an impression of her and start over at the beginning.

Suddenly his eyes focused at some point on the top of her head, flicked to and fro.

Where they stopped.

And then he slowly grinned.

"*Now* why are you grinning at me? It can't mean anything good."

He seemed to love it when she was riled. He did it very easily, riling her.

"It's . . . well, you should see your hair. It's every which way."

"*No!*" Her hands flew up to her head, aghast. "Is it? Well, I'm certain it's nothing compared to yours."

He gave her a look of pity. "Good try. As if I mind what my hair looks like."

"You *should*," she muttered darkly.

She could see him struggling mightily not to laugh again. "And where the devil is your bonnet? I assume you went out wearing one."

She felt around the back of her neck but already knew it was gone. "Bloody—that is, *drat*."

"Left it behind, did you, while you were burying victims, eh? Or trysting?"

She rolled her eyes. "I *thought* I felt it fly off. It was such a pleasure, you know, to ride like that, and I suppose I didn't . . ."

He craned his head behind them. "I don't see

it. Perhaps you left it . . . wherever you were. Why don't we go and fetch it?"

She rolled her eyes at him again. "Good try. But . . . I'll need to repair my hair before I return." She was fussing now. "I can't go home looking like I've been ravished."

She slid him a tentatively minxlike sidelong look.

He just shook his head slowly.

"Leave it be, Miss Danforth. I like it this way. It makes you look as wild and disreputable as you truly are."

"At least you like *something* about me."

A curious silence ensued.

He looked a bit taken aback. And thoughtful.

If she'd hoped he'd launch into a list of all the things he liked about her, she was sorely disappointed. He remained quiet, watching her, with a look that started a little ballet of butterflies in the pit of her stomach. She sensed there *were* other things he liked about her, but he couldn't say them aloud. At least not to her.

"I wish I had a mirror," she said finally.

He appeared to give serious consideration to her dilemma.

"Perhaps you can see yourself in my eyes."

She blinked.

And then went very, very still.

The words had been issued oh so offhandedly.

She had no doubt he would see the impact immediately, because he was watching her.

It was a dare. Suddenly, out of nowhere, without warning . . .

Was Ian Eversea at last flirting with her?

Or . . . testing her?

Or some interesting combination of both?

# Chapter 16

❧

She pondered this conundrum.

He maintained a neutral expression.

How many times had he said this sort of thing to other women?

Surely *she* of all people would be able to call his bluff.

"Perhaps I *can* see myself in your eyes," she said cautiously.

She took a step toward him.

And then another.

And another.

She saw his mouth begin to curl at the corners at her cautious progress.

At last she was close enough to catch just a whiff of what she suspected was bay rum and starch. Her head swam. Her heart lurched.

And then she subtly squared her shoulders and tipped her head back and looked into his eyes.

It was only marginally less difficult than looking into the sun, for different reasons.

His eyes were so blue she felt them like an ache

inside her, and she felt her fingers curl into fists, withstanding the impact. It seemed such an intimate thing to know about a person, that a darker ring of blue surrounded the lake of his iris, that his eyelashes were black but burnished a sort of russet at the tips, that his pupils had gone large and dark and his breath seemed to have stopped and—

Her nerve failed.

She exhaled, which is how she knew she'd stopped breathing, in a long shuddery breath, and ducked her head. And took a step backward.

He was deep water, and she was in over her head, as he never tired of pointing out.

She thought she could hear him breathing. How very still he'd gone. There was a suppressed energy about him. She was reminded of a fox patiently waiting for just the right time to pounce on a vole. She did indeed feel like the only woman in the world just then.

"No. I can't see myself very well in them," she said, her voice gone small.

On the contrary, she saw herself there very well indeed.

A peculiar prickling started up at the back of her neck. The butterflies were now performing a vigorous reel.

As he'd implied before, she didn't know quite what to do about it.

Which made her feel young and gauche again.

And a little angry. He never seemed to tire of

pointing out her naive inadequacy to her in all manner of ways.

There was an odd little silence as they perused each other from a safe distance.

He cleared his throat.

"Ah. Well, there's a stream, nearby, Narcissus." His voice had gone gruff. "I think you can see yourself reflected in it. Have a look, if you must."

They rode over to a likely place, and he dismounted, produced a handkerchief, and spread it out along the ground at the bank, which was mercifully not too damp. He gestured with a flourish for her to kneel.

Just like Sir Walter Raleigh. Well, almost like Sir Walter Raleigh.

Like an empress, her nose exaggeratedly in the air for effect and just to make him smile, she strode over and gracefully knelt, and bent to see if she could indeed use the surface of the stream as a mirror.

She could. And he was right. If they were going to reference the Greek myths, she would have to go with Medusa.

She set about pulling out the pins which were askew. A swift run of her hand over her head told her she'd lost a few of them. She thrust her fingers up through it and gave it a good raking, an attempt to tame it.

She was so preoccupied with the reconstruction of her hair it took her a moment to realize he'd been absolutely silent for quite some time.

She turned to make sure he hadn't disappeared.

An expression she couldn't decipher fled from his face as she did.

She might have called it "rapt," but it was gone far too quickly for her to be sure. Perhaps it had just been gas.

"What are you doing?" she asked.

"Just engaging in the time-honored pastime of suffering the loss of precious minutes of my life for the sake of a woman's vanity."

"Oh, you poor thing, to be so very ill-used. You're fortunate you're passable looking, Captain Eversea. Because if you actually possess any of that vaunted charm, I've yet to witness it."

This, as she'd suspected, just made him laugh. "Hurry," he said ungraciously, just to prove her point.

She managed to twist and tame her hair and jab pins into it, and she was satisfied with the result.

"How did I do?"

He studied her, wearing a faint frown, so long and in such a way that it suddenly became a bit more difficult to breathe.

"Less interesting, but more presentable," was his cryptic verdict.

She eyed him suspiciously for signs of mockery. None was evident.

He looked a little preoccupied himself, in fact.

He hadn't blinked in quite some time. Unnerving.

She felt a bit like prey.

And again, she wasn't quite certain what to do about it. The butterflies did a slow orbit in her stomach. This is why I oughtn't ride alone, she thought.

She stood without his assistance, plucked up his handkerchief, and he took two steps toward her horse in preparation for hoisting her up again.

And then—

Later, she would find it ironic that she hadn't actually thought to feign a stumble before then.

All she knew was that she was upright one moment and on her way down the next. She saw the ground coming at her and thrust her hands out with a muffled shriek and—

She hit what felt like a wall.

Which turned out to be Ian, who had lunged for her with lightning speed. Her head thumped his chest, and her hands latched into his shirt and pulled as he levered her smoothly upright again, as if they were performing some sort of awkward tango.

When she'd oriented herself again she realized she'd managed to yank open his shirt and her hand had slipped between the buttons.

It was a moment before she realized:

She was touching his *skin*.

Instantly she felt the leap and tension of his muscles.

She stopped breathing.

Judging from the tension in him, so had he.

The moment seemed suspended in time.

Her fingers fanned out, tentatively, just a little.

She just couldn't help it. She wanted to touch a little more of it, while the opportunity presented itself. She wanted to imagine the rest of him unfurling from just that spot.

And a beat of held-breath silence ticked by before he spoke.

"Don't," he said gruffly.

It was too late. She couldn't have moved her hand if he'd aimed a pistol at her.

His skin was hot and silken over a chest that was frighteningly, fascinatingly, hard. She was a little afraid now, but she could not have pulled away if she tried. "Tansy . . ." His voice was a soft warning.

He didn't pull away from her, either.

Time suddenly seemed to slow, to thicken, to soften, like . . . like . . .

Lava.

His voice was softer now. The edges husked. It stroked over her senses like rough velvet.

"You try too hard, Tansy. Do you know what you remind me of?"

"A dream come true?" she whispered it. *I'm touching Ian Eversea's skin I'm touching Ian Eversea's skin.*

"Someone who always grabs the soap too enthusiastically, and finds it flying out of her grasp over and over."

"Imagining me in the bath, are you?"

He laughed. Shortly, though. A distracted laugh. Somewhat pained.

"I think you come at everyone before they can come after you, Tansy. You're afraid to be—"

He stopped abruptly.

*Vulnerable,* she completed silently in her head, astonished. Certain that's what he meant.

It was astonishing for a number of reasons.

Because it was true.

Because he'd been unnervingly insightful.

And because she realized he'd stopped because . . .

He'd been talking about himself.

She didn't dare say *that* out loud.

She turned her face up to him.

He must have seen the wondering realization in her face, because his eyes almost *literally* shuttered. Cool, inscrutable. If it was a color in an artist's palette, she would have called it "Warning Blue." She'd have to be a masochist to want to breach that defense. He'd immolate her with a few drawled words.

"What happened to you?" she whispered, before she could stop herself.

Because after her parents died, she'd stopped knowing when to be afraid.

*Something* had made him the way he was. Just as something had made her the way she was.

Somewhat distantly she was aware of his heartbeat quickening beneath her palm. A glorious feeling. How incongruously soft and warm his skin was in contrast to those cold, guarded eyes. Her imagination wandered. Would his skin be like this everywhere on his body? Would she find different textures, curling hair, more muscle . . . his hands were on her thighs.

*His hands were on her thighs!*

She'd been so distracted by her own reverie, she hadn't noticed, and now it was too late. They'd landed softly, stealthily. And now he was drawing his fingertips up along them, up over the curve of her hips, lightly and achingly slowly, as if pointing out to her precisely how female she was, how he saw her, how ensnared she was.

Because she certainly was.

The hairs stirred upright at the back of her neck and over her arms; her nipples were suddenly almost painfully alert, and his dragging fingertips over the fine, fragile muslin sent rivulets of flame fanning out through her body. It was so exquisite and fascinating, she forgot to draw breath.

In seconds he'd knit a net for her out of her own desire.

Then, with the speed of a wolf seizing a hare, he scooped his palms beneath her buttocks and pulled her hard against him. And held her. He looked down into her eyes, his pupils large, black. He waited, it seemed, just long enough for her to feel the beginning of what would undoubtedly prove to be a very fine erection. For her body to soften, to yield, to fit to him. For her hands to slip around his neck and clasp him.

What followed wasn't a kiss so much as a siege. When his lips landed against hers—magically,

her head was already tipped back to receive
them—she tensed. An instant later it seemed the
rightest thing in the world, the fit of his mouth
over hers. Suddenly, it was the answer to everything. Ah, and too late she understood, *here* was
the danger of which he spoke. Firm, warm, sinu-
ously clever, he brushed his lips over hers, introducing her to the universe of pleasure that could
be had from her lips alone.

Before he plundered.

Her mouth parted beneath his with a sensual knowledge as old as time and stronger than
sense. Her hands slid down and she clutched at
his shirt for balance as layer upon layer of new
pleasure was revealed to her in the stroke, the
dive, the twining of his tongue with hers. And
somehow what began as a proving kiss of near
violence evolved into something different. Something sensual, depthless, heady, drugging. She
could feel him slow, his body ease. She was spiraling in some place where gravity didn't apply. She
would fall forever if she didn't hold on to him; the
kiss was her world now.

She moaned softly, her pleasure, wonder, spill-
ing into sound. His body tensed as he pulled her
more tightly. She could feel the outline of his hard
cock at the crook of her legs, and a shocking pleasure cleaved her. She pressed herself closer still,
and he ground himself against her, and it hurt,
and it felt wonderful. She wanted to disappear
into him.

"Tansy," he breathed hoarsely. "God."

And suddenly she knew that he could take her right here, right now, and she would not have minded. She wanted something from him with a savagery she'd never known. His hands moved up over her back, slid upward to cradle her head, to hold her at her mercy as his mouth took and hers gave, and he hoarsely whispered, *"Sweet."*

He gently dragged his fingertips over the bare skin of her throat, leaving fine little fiery rivulets of sensation that traveled, shockingly, boldly to her breasts. Lightly, one of his fingers hooked into her bodice and he dragged it roughly over her nipple.

It was exquisite and terrifying.

*"Ian."* A raw gasp. She wanted more. And she was afraid.

He tore his mouth from hers, dropped his forehead against hers. His breath was hot, swift, ragged, against her face. And like that they breathed together, her breath so tattered it sounded nearly like sobs.

She would never be the same, she was certain.

And then he abruptly released her and stepped back.

Which seemed an unthinkable cruelty.

The two of them stood and stared and breathed like pugilists backing into their own corners again.

Her senses were in utter ruins. She would be ages collecting them again. Perhaps she'd never get them back in the proper order.

It could have been an eternity or seconds later when he spoke again.

"Many, many men wouldn't have stopped, Miss Danforth." He said it quietly.

Ah. So this was yet another lesson. Or at least that was what he wanted to pretend. How altruistic of him.

She gave a short, bitter little laugh.

And still she couldn't speak. She'd once possessed the skill, she was certain of it.

*He* could.

"Please stop playing at things you don't fully understand, Tansy. It will be the undoing of you. It's so very, very easy to lose yourself this way."

She still couldn't breathe or think properly. She was furious that she needed to leave one hand against him to steady herself. She was furious at him for being right. And for being so bloody *self-righteous*.

*And* for being steady on his feet as he regarded her.

And then she realized he was trembling. She could feel it beneath her palm.

He was a seasoned rogue, and that kiss had shaken him.

Suddenly this unnerved her more than the kiss itself.

"Is that why *you* do it?" she asked softly. Ironically. "To lose yourself?"

Swift anger kindled in his eyes again. "Have a care."

So he didn't care for having *his* secrets unraveled, did he?

She took her hand away from him finally, slowly, as if he were a rabid dog and would lunge at her if she made any sudden moves. She was steady on her feet now. Her breathing had nearly resumed its usual cadence. She couldn't yet back away; he maintained a peculiar gravitational pull. She could still feel the warmth of his body on her skin. She wondered distantly if she always would. As if she'd been branded.

"What if I want to be lost?" she whispered.

Something wild and dangerous flared in his eyes. An almost incinerating longing. It was there and gone.

"You don't know what you're saying."

His hair had fallen down over his brow, and he looked faintly ridiculous, and never more beautiful.

Despite the fact that his face was suddenly granite.

"I know one thing. I know that you want me."

She didn't say, *As much as I want you.*

His head went back sharply. And then he froze. He was utterly motionless apart from the spirals of hair the wind was lifting. Did he look like this when he took aim at a target with a rifle? She suspected he did.

She would love to wind her finger in one of his spirals, let it unfurl.

At last he ducked his head into his chest and

dropped his shoulders. Then he spun on his heel and strode to her horse. He wordlessly held the stirrup for her, and with a jerk of his chin beckoned her over.

He helped hoist her up as if she were a sack of flour, and not a woman he'd just kissed witless. Then he mounted his horse and stared down at her, wearing a faint frown.

He gave his head a rough shake. "It's time we get back."

He wheeled his horse around and urged it forward.

She thought she heard him mutter a single bemused word under his breath.

She wasn't certain, but it may have been "devil."

# Chapter 17

❧

Ian closed his eyes.

Two birds were calling a leisurely, liquid sounding duet to each other across the enclosed garden. The hush had a waiting quality, perhaps because the plants had been allowed to flourish with abandon and muffled any sounds that might want to enter or escape.

He opened his eyes again, and slowly—the sound of his footsteps almost an intrusion—followed the inlaid stone path, which was tufted with grass and determined flowery weeds in some places and completely overgrown in others. The loosely serpentine walkway meandered through birches and oaks, walnut and apple and cherry trees, old and solid now, leafed out and healthy. A few lucky flies buzzed over fruit that had plopped to the ground.

The flowers were clearly planted according to a plan, but now every variety had run amuck, brilliant and fighting for room, like a crush at a ball. He didn't mind it, really. He liked a little chaos.

In the corner, the ivy was dense and inches thick. A peculiar sort of anticipation ramped in him as he approached it. He hefted it like a curtain and it released its grip reluctantly, its dry little fingers scraping against the wall.

He peered.

And there, ambered in the morning light, laboriously scratched into the stone, was one word: *Tansy*.

He put his finger on the word, tracing each letter. It had taken determination and a *knife* to do that. He gave a short laugh. A "wallflower" who wasn't afraid of guns and knives or riding at breakneck speed.

He wasn't certain why he'd wanted to come here today. It had something about how she'd looked when he said "Lilymont." Something brilliant and raw and very real had suffused her face, and then she'd tamped it. She'd uttered the word "Oh" with the rawest yearning he'd ever heard when he told her the home was for sale.

In so many ways she remained a walking question mark.

But this was real to her.

And he supposed he wanted to see why.

Because he thought he had tasted all of those things when he kissed her. Desperation and abandon, an unnerving, thrilling, recklessness, a fierce joy, a devastating depthless sensuality. She tasted of endless, endless pleasure and possibility.

It had shocked him badly.

And so he had taken refuge from it all by couching that kiss as a lesson. A dexterous bit of reasoning on his part, he thought.

And it *had* been a lesson.

For him, anyway.

After that kiss, he wasn't certain he'd ever truly kissed anyone before in his life.

*Is that why* you *do it?*

He hadn't fooled her.

She knew that he wanted her. Had likely known it before he did; the want of her stealthy, creeping into his blood over a series of days.

It infuriated him to be seen through, to the point where a red haze nearly crept over his eyes. It was fury, primarily at himself, for becoming ensnared.

And it also filled him with a sort of helpless, reluctant, very amused admiration.

He sucked in a long breath, held it in for a punishingly long time. Released it slowly, as if she'd been opium he'd inhaled into his lungs and he could expel her.

She would be better served by indignation and hurt pride and by at least attempting to believe that he'd meant to teach her a lesson, and by staying far, far away from him.

He'd been doing his part and avoiding her rather successfully ever since by rising very early and disappearing into good, wholesome, consuming physical work with hammers and boards and the like and taking his meals at the pub and lingering there over the chessboard with Culpepper and Cooke and retiring to his rooms very late at night, too late to peer out his window and catch Miss Danforth in the act of some new vice. He'd managed to allow an *entire* week to go by in just this fashion. He hadn't thought about her at all.

And yet here he was at Lilymont, as if he'd been driven there with no choice in the matter.

He did want her.

But that was neither here nor there. And while he normally got what he wanted when it came to women, he was sensible enough to know that the danger here wasn't in the getting of the woman but in the woman herself.

He dropped the ivy, watched her name vanish behind it.

Symbolically dropping the curtain on the entire episode.

The sun was higher now, and he could feel it on the back of his neck.

He wasn't certain whether it was this that made him turn suddenly. Only that something about the hush in the garden seemed to have shifted slightly, as if to accommodate another presence.

When he swiveled.

The Duke of Falconbridge was standing at the entrance.

There was an absurd moment when he actually wondered whether his conscience had spoken aloud and summoned the duke. Or perhaps he was dreaming, for dreams certainly had a way with presenting one with the worst scenarios possible. He ought to know.

The two of them froze and stared at each from across the silent, woolly garden.

And Ian, as he always did when he saw Falconbridge, felt a certain amount of shame. They had both shamed each other, on that fateful night, and really, it was hardly conversation kindling.

"Good morning," Ian said politely.

"Good morning."

Their voices echoed absurdly in the cool morning air.

A silence. Ian supposed it would be just a little too ironic if he scrambled up a fruit tree and clambered over a wall instead of walking past the duke, back to where he'd tethered his horse.

"Interested in Lilymont, Eversea?" The duke asked it idly.

"Yes," Ian said simply.

"Why?"

A presumptuous question.

It deserved a curt answer. "Curiosity."

The duke looked around at the trees. He strolled deeper into the garden, and Ian took a subtle step away from the ivy-covered wall, as if it would incriminate him. "I thought I'd stop by to have another look around. Genevieve likes it. It's a bit on the small side. Needs a good deal of work."

*And it's a bit too close to where the rest of our family lives, no doubt.*

"I can see why she likes it," Ian said instead.

Another silence. Not even a bird obliged them with a song. They were all collectively holding their little avian breaths, apparently.

"This was Miss Danforth's childhood home," the duke volunteered casually. He strolled deeper still into the garden, but not toward Ian. He took a sideways route, as if the apple trees and cherry trees were of critical importance to his decision whether to buy the house.

"It has a good deal of charm."

The duke turned to look at him. "You aren't interested in purchasing the property, too." More of a statement than a question.

"No. I'm departing for a long ocean voyage in a matter of weeks. Every penny of my savings will be devoted to that."

The duke nodded politely, as if none of this was of any true interest to him. "Ah. Yes. I recall. Your trip around the world." He paused. "Sometimes movement is precisely what a man needs."

Ian stared at him. He imagined the duke would be delighted that in a matter of weeks he would be moving inexorably farther and farther away from him. And given the caprices of sea travel, not to mention foreign cultures and food, could very well never return.

The duke simply turned, reached out, gripped a fine branch and pulled it down as if to inspect it. "And sometimes what he needs is someplace and someone who feels like home."

Ian fought a frown. Why was Falconbridge philosophizing about what a man needed? The duke knew nothing at all about him, apart from what he looked like naked and in the dark, and the fact that he was an excellent climber.

"I imagine you're right on both counts," Ian said politely.

The duke paused in front of a cherry tree, his profile to Ian, who could see the deep lines at the corners of his eyes.

*My sister loves this man.*

And suddenly he knew a moment of regret. A wish that he could turn back time and know him, too, to see in him the things Genevieve valued in him.

"I'll be off then, Falconbridge. My cousin expects me at the vicarage. Repairs, you know."

"Of course. Good day, then." The duke nodded, but didn't quite look at Ian.

They subtly skirted each other at a safe distance, like tomcats too conscious of each other's strengths to make even a token fuss about territory. Falconbridge going deeper into the garden, and Ian heading for the arched gate.

Once he'd seen the hem of Ian's coat whipping around the corner, the duke moved swiftly toward the ivy in the corner. He'd been watching Ian a little longer than Ian knew.

He lifted up the ivy and shaded his eyes. It was a moment before he saw the word.

*Tansy.*

He went still.

Ian Eversea had caressed that word with something like . . .

The duke could only describe it as reverence.

He pivoted slowly and shaded his eyes, stood listening thoughtfully, grimly, as the hoofbeats of Ian's horse tore away, like a man trying to escape something.

THIS AFTERNOON THE duke had asked Tansy to pour during their visit, and she was delighted with the ritual and the comforting sounds: The *tinks* of cubes of sugar dropped against porcelain, the bell-like music of the tiny silver spoons against sloped sides as they stirred.

"I've had word Lord Stanhope will be visiting his properties here soon. He's the Duke de Neauville's heir."

*A duke!*

The word jolted her pleasurably, and a bit of tea splashed into the saucer.

She couldn't help it. Duchess Titania de Neauville. She tried on the sound of it in her head. Good heavens, it was almost the only time the name Titania seemed appropriate.

Clearly she was *born* to be a duchess.

Would he be handsome? Clever?

Would he try to kiss her until she forgot her name?

Would he try to pretend it was all her fault that he'd kissed her, and that it had been a lesson, then dodge her for a week, when she knew better?

*Oh*, how she knew better.

She bit down on her back teeth against a little surge of righteous anger.

And to squelch the sensation again, which she found, both to her delight and dismay, she could conjure at will, of his fingertips trailing her throat then sliding into her bodice.

She looked down into the tea and remembered the hot demanding sweetness of his mouth, and a wave of weakness swamped her. And she didn't dare look up at the duke.

Ian Eversea was infinitely more sensible than she had credited. For he had made himself scarce after that kiss. Then again, she was not eligible for a complete seduction, unlike a certain attractive widow, for instance, and what use was she to him in that regard?

Although she suspected the reason for his absence was quite different, she couldn't help but regret his wisdom in keeping his distance.

Her face was heating, and she looked up, to find the duke's eyes on her speculatively. Perhaps he thought she'd gone rosy over the idea of a fledgling duke. The notion of whom had been introduced not a moment too soon.

"I thought *you* were the only duke."

He smiled faintly, indulging her. "We're a small club, to be certain. His son is a decent fellow. Pleasant, well-bred, educated, not a shred of controversy associated with his name. I daresay even handsome, and possessed of a certain amount of moral turpitude."

"Kind of you to remember my list."

He smiled again. "And wealthy. Very wealthy."

She hadn't listed wealth, oddly enough, because she would possess her own once she married. She certainly had nothing at all against it. She imagined the carriages, the gowns, the servants, the parties, the horses.

The home. The family. The children.

"He has a beautiful home here in Sussex," the duke added, when she didn't speak. "About twice the size of Lilymont."

The word, as it always did, made her stop breathing for just a moment.

"Lilymont always struck me as a very good size," she said. "But then, I was very small when I lived there. It's for sale, I understand," she added tentatively.

"Genevieve is interested in it. But we haven't yet made a decision about it."

A ferocious, rogue little surge of envy took her, and then she tamped it.

"How lovely it would be to keep it in the family." It would be lovely to know she would be welcome there, at the very least.

She did like saying the word "family." It occurred to her then that she was glad they were her family: the duke and his wife.

"The gardens were quite lovely, then, when you were a little girl. You used to run about there with your brother."

"I did," Tansy said faintly, smiling. "We used

to play at being soldiers. And then he went off to be one."

She didn't say, *And didn't come back*. The duke knew that.

"So often the ones that return . . . never really leave war behind. In so many ways. War changes a man irrevocably. There's a roughness and a recklessness that can . . . sink in, become integral to his character."

She regarded him guilelessly.

Or what she hoped was guilelessly.

"But doesn't life change you, too?" she asked. "Rather inevitably? One can hardly predict what will happen, isn't that right?"

The duke hesitated, then slowly nodded in concession, raising a brow.

"But I think sometimes it's like setting a broken arm," he said. "If it isn't done quite right, by someone very skillful and knowledgeable, it fuses in a particular shape and can never be quite right again."

Tansy fought to keep from narrowing her eyes. She suspected she was being warned in some fashion. Again. About Ian Eversea.

"Sometimes things are broken in such a way to fit with other things, are they not? Like the pieces of a puzzle or of stained glass?"

The duke drummed his fingers on the desk. A silence drifted by, and it lasted so long that the chink of a melting sugar cube against the side of a teacup was startlingly loud.

"You certainly are your father's daughter," he finally said.

GENEVIEVE WAS ALREADY in bed, reading, her hair roped into a dark braid, when he slid in and wordlessly reached for her.

She abandoned her book and went willingly, sighed while nestling into his chest as he burrowed his face into her hair. They lay in silence for a time, humbled by how fortunate they were, humbled by the miracle of loving and being loved and by how vigorous lovemaking really seemed never to lose its novelty.

"I've heard from the Duke de Neauville," he said. "His heir is arriving in Sussex to visit."

"Ah. I imagine you'd like to introduce him to Miss Danforth."

"How restful to know that I need never speak again, since you read my mind so perfectly."

She laughed.

He loved the feel of her laugh vibrating against his chest.

"Miss Danforth's brother was a soldier. Decorated. Lost in the war. Bayonet got him, I recall."

"Ah," Genevieve said softly. "Poor Tansy. Ian was decorated, too. For valor, I believe. He'd saved a life. He has quite a terrible bayonet scar."

"I've seen it," the duke said simply.

The two of them were silent at that, because Genevieve knew full well when the duke had seen it.

She nestled a little closer into her husband. Both because she knew he didn't like to remember that, and because she was grateful that whatever happened had ultimately brought the duke to her.

"Is he really leaving on a long sea voyage?" he asked.

"Ian?" Genevieve said sleepily. "Sometimes I feel like he's already on it. But yes. He is."

"Good," the duke said.

# Chapter 18

❧

A STEAMING BATH HAD CHEERED Ian immensely after a long, long day of physical labor, and Ned had to nearly push him out of the door of the Pig & Thistle, but he was sober enough by the time he arrived home.

He paused in the middle of his room. The bath, the pleasure of it, had made him unduly aware of his skin and his body and his muscles and his senses, and what a glorious pleasure it was to possess them. To be alive. To be able to feel and taste and . . .

And now his muscles tensed again. He slowly flattened a hand against his still warm, damp chest.

How . . . new . . . her hand had felt against his skin, the tentative unfurling of her fingers, that discovery of him, brave and reckless and innocent and yet somehow not.

She didn't kiss like a virgin. She kissed like she was born to do only that, with only him.

He wanted to touch her again.

He wanted to feel his skin against hers again.

He wanted to taste her. Everywhere.

And the need he'd been holding at quite sensible bay for over a week rushed over him like a bonfire.

He'd avoided his window for a week. He would not go to it now. He would not.

He told himself this all the way to the window.

When he got there, he peered out. A wedge of light emerged from her windows. His heart gave a lurch. For there she was, out on the balcony, doing . . .

What in God's name *was* she doing?

She was leaning far out over the balcony edge, one leg out behind her, and her arms had begun windmilling. His heart shot into his throat until she seemed to find a certain balance. Still, she remained in a precarious position.

Ian bolted from his room and flung open her chamber door, which mercifully wasn't locked, and was out on the balcony in a few steps.

He managed to keep his voice calm. "What the bloody hell are you doing? Everyone was speaking euphemistically when they refer to you as an angel. You haven't any wings, Miss Danforth. You'll hit the ground with a thud when you fall. And you will fall, if you maintain that angle."

She froze. There was a heartbeat of silence before she spoke.

"Oh, good evening, Ian. Aren't you funny."

"Step back from the balcony, Miss Danforth. I'm not worth jumping over, believe me."

"Ha. Believe it or not, I don't spend every waking minute thinking about you."

"Just most of them?"

She merely slowly, gracefully, straightened again, stepped back from the edge of the balcony, turned and looked up at him. It wasn't with reproach, necessarily, but she didn't say a word.

And suddenly he didn't think that was very funny, either.

"Then we're back to my original question—what the bloody hell are you doing?" He lowered his voice.

She hesitated. Her lips worried over each other.

And then she heaved a defeated sigh.

"It's just . . . well, I can't find the stars I need." She sounded abashed.

"The . . . stars you need? Are you an astrologer? Is that why you can read into my soul? Or perhaps you intend to use them to navigate a ship all the way back to America?"

"No, and I know you'd pine yourself right into the grave if I did navigate all the way back to America. I'm looking for the Seven Sisters. Or whatever it is you might call them in this country."

He was already smiling, damn the girl, and it was suddenly very clear to him, alarmingly clear, that her presence made everything better, colors brighter, the air more effervescent, and her absence over the last week had muted his experience of life altogether. It was like breathing air again after being trapped in a box.

Very, very alarming.

"Ah. The Pleiades. You can just see them from this side of the house if you crane your head . . . so. No need to risk life and limb by leaning over the balcony. See that very bright star there?"

"Where?" She leaned backward, far enough that her shoulder blades brushed his chest.

He suspected it was calculated.

He ought to move away.

He really, really ought to move.

He didn't move away.

"Oh! I see it! I see them! Or part of them." She sounded so delighted and relieved, he gave a short laugh.

She startled Ian by settling back against him as if it where the most natural thing in the world and stared up at the sky. And the thing was, it felt natural. In his weary state, the faint lavender sweetness and soft warmth of her made him dizzy. And he suddenly thought he might know what it would be like to be a planet, endlessly, gracefully spinning through the solar system. He couldn't, for a moment, think of why he hadn't held her just like this before.

"Why the Seven Sisters?" his voice had emerged somewhat huskily.

Hers was soft, too, when she replied. "My mother used to tell me a story about how they got up in the sky when I was a little girl. I loved it. It changed a bit, each telling." She gave a soft laugh. "That's why I liked it so much. She used to say to look for her in the sky when she was . . . gone. She said she'd be at a tea party with the Seven Sisters. And I guess I never thought she . . ." She hesitated. ". . . well, do you know how gone 'gone' is, Ian?"

He was struck dumb by the hollowness in her voice. He knew that sound. It came from the absence of someone you loved.

And oddly, he knew exactly what she meant. All the talk of living forever in Heaven wouldn't change the fact of *gone*.

"I do know," he said gently. "It's as though . . . death is merely a sort of theory, until it takes someone you know. Let alone someone you love. I was a soldier. 'Gone' was my daily way of life there, for a time. One never, never really gets used to it."

He'd never said anything of the sort to anyone else before.

"My brother was a soldier," Tansy confided. "And he died in the War of 1812. Bayonet got him."

Gone. Everything she'd been a part of was gone. And the enormity of that left him speechless. There really were no words to describe it. The simple ones would have to do.

"I'm sorry."

She knew he meant them. It was in his voice.

They didn't speak for a time. She leaned gently against him, and he allowed it, and silently they thought about "gone" and each other.

"My sister Olivia," he began, "she won't say anything about it, truly, but I believe—we all believe—she was in love with Lyon Redmond. He's heir to the Redmond family, and Mr. Miles Redmond's brother. And he disappeared a few years ago. I don't know what's worse. Knowing for certain whether someone is gone forever, or always wondering what became of them."

He felt her go still as she took this information in thoughtfully.

And then she sighed and moved a little away from him, just shy but not quite of touching him, as if she'd only just realized she was leaning into him for comfort, and was uncertain of her welcome.

His regret was a little too powerful.

Which was when he realized he'd been taking comfort in her, too.

"Forever," she drawled disdainfully, softly. "I hate the word 'forever.' It's hard to really imagine the concept isn't it? And then you *know*. When someone is gone forever, you finally understand what it means."

"I don't much care for the word, either. Especially with regards to matrimony, and staying in one place, and the like."

She laughed at that and turned around, and . . .

She might as well have aimed a weapon at him.

Her night rail would have been demure if it didn't drape the gorgeous lines of her so lovingly, so nearly tauntingly. The bands of muscles across his stomach tensed in an effort to withstand the impact of the sight. Her hair was plaited in a large, messy, golden rope slung over her shoulder and pouring down the front of her.

And an absurdly large, girlish bow closed the neckline.

He couldn't help but smile at that.

"Why are you grinning?" She sounded irritable.

"You look like a gift, tied up with a bow."

"Like the gifts you give to your mistresses?"

"Like the *what*?"

"Shhhh! Lower your voice!" She was clearly delighted, stifling a laugh. She'd achieved precisely the effect she'd wanted.

"I haven't 'mistresses,' for God's sake. There aren't a *host* of them. And I certainly don't buy them gifts."

"All those experienced women wearing experienced expressions. What do you call them?"

"There aren't 'all those' . . . It's not as though I . . . You make it sound as though I've a harem."

The woman was maddening. It was like jousting with a weathervane. And what in God's name *had* she heard about him?

Clearly, enough that was close to the truth. Or she was an excellent guesser?

"Poor women, who never get gifts," she mourned wickedly.

"Tansy . . ." he warned.

"It might be interesting to be part of a harem," she said wistfully, softly. "Never knowing whether one might get a visit from the maharajah . . . the anticipation . . . it would be . . ."

He held his breath, waiting on absurd tenter-hooks for what she thought it might be.

". . . delicious," she finally said thoughtfully.

*Oh, God. Oh God Oh God.* She was going to be the death of him.

He couldn't speak for a time. They were teetering on a precipice here more dangerous than her balcony arabesque of a moment ago.

"What if . . ." His voice was hoarse. He cleared his throat. "What if the maharajah never comes?" His voice was hoarse.

"With all those wives? I'm certain he comes often."

He stared at her. Had she *really* said that? Did she know what it *meant*?

He gave a short astonished laugh.

*"Shhhh!"* she said again.

"You would *hate* being part of a harem, Tansy. All those other women competing for a bit of attention. *Just* imagine."

"But it wouldn't be lonely."

The words startled him into momentary speechlessness. And he remembered what Mrs. deWitt had said.

How was it he hadn't realized before that she might be lonely? She was so *effervescent*; she could attract company the way a bloom attracted bees.

But he supposed it wasn't the same as belonging to someone. Or to somewhere.

But she *was* alone. He felt utterly chagrined that

he was only now realizing it. He'd been quite an ass, in many ways.

Then again, she wasn't entirely without fault in the matter. Captivating all the men in the town was one way to ensure that the women wouldn't thrill to your company.

"And I would be the favorite wife in no time," she hastened to add, before he could think about it any longer.

"If the maharajah didn't kill you first. I hear they use scimitars when their wives irritate them." He drew a finger across his throat.

She laughed at that. The throaty, delighted sound landed on his heightened, roused senses like fingernails gently dragged down his back.

And that's when he knew: he'd waited too long. He'd somehow missed the moment when he could have, and really should have, made a sensible retreat. The night rail, the night, the girl, the lavender, the laugh—he was now in thrall to his senses. *Everything* served to titillate them. He was theirs to command. And anything that happened next was a foregone conclusion.

And something would happen. Oh, something would.

"Do you know something, Tansy?" he said softly.

"Mmmm?" She'd been watching his face in the dark, as if she were searching for a particular constellation there, too.

"It's always been deucedly difficult for me to resist unwrapping gifts."

Her breath hitched in surprise.

She wasn't the only one who could be a devil.

Anticipation. It was the whetstone against which desire was honed. No one knew this better than he did.

The earth turned, the stars twinkled, the shadows swayed, as he waited to hear what she would say, which in the moment seemed the most important words he'd ever hear in his life.

"Is that so?" She'd tried for "casual"; instead she sounded breathless.

"It is, indeed," he said softly, as solemnly as a judge.

Anticipation could be delicious. It could also be torture. Often the two were one and the same.

He simply waited, and allowed her to anticipate.

He couldn't quite read her eyes in the dark, which he liked, too, because risk was part of the thrill. The risk of defeat. Was she deciding whether to flee?

Perhaps *he* should take this opportunity to flee.

It was silent, apart from the sound of her breathing, growing ever swifter.

And when he could have plucked the tension between them like a harp string, he watched, as if in a dream, his hand, so very, very inadvisably, slowly reach across the foot or so of safe distance between them and grasp the end of the ribbon.

That catch in her breath was one of the most carnal sounds he'd ever heard.

And then, tormenting the two of them, he

pulled the satin through his fingers and watched the bow unravel very, very slowly.

"There's the bow undone," he whispered.

And then he wound the ribbon in his fist and tugged her gently forward, until she stood just shy of touching his chest.

And for a space the shock of being close silenced both of them.

And then:

"I'm not a mule to be tugged about by reins," she whispered against his chin. With unconvincing indignation.

"True enough. A mule would have bolted away before I could have captured it. That is, unless the mule *wanted* to be captured."

She gave a short, nervous laugh. Her breath was uneven now. Excitement, or fear, or both.

He waited.

Anticipation. The seducer's best friend.

Or so he told himself.

He released the ribbon, and slowly, gently, pushed aside the folds of her robe.

He suppressed a groan of delight. She was nude beneath that robe, and he'd known she would be.

He slid his palms around her waist, took his fingertips on a leisurely slide along her rib cage, felt her belly leap. She was trembling. Her breath was hot and ragged on the vee of skin exposed by his open collar. Her skin was a silky miracle. He glided his hands across her belly, heard her softly breathed, helpless, "Oh," as delicious sensation coursed over and through her, and savored the decadent pleasure of knowing he was likely the first man to touch her like this.

He should stop. He should stop. This was madness.

He could feel the blood in his veins heat and thicken as if she was a drug, a powerful liquor. He filled his hands with her breasts. The full, silky give of them made him groan softly. He could hear his own breath now, a soft roar in his ears. And the tiny catch and stutter of her breath, and then the ragged intake of air as he caressed them.

Her head went back at the pleasure of it.

He drew his thumbs leisurely over her nipples. They were already ruched into hard knots.

She arched into his touch as though lightning struck.

He did it again. Harder. He wanted to take one into his mouth.

How quickly this had escalated.

"Ian," she whispered. Half afraid, half drugged with yearning, half plea. "It's . . ."

"I know," he said. "I know so many things, Tansy. So very, very many things about you, and how you feel, and what you want . . ."

He ducked and gently, just a little, flicked his tongue over her nipple.

He realized then he was playing roulette with his own desire. It was time to back away before he was too deep in. Just this taste of pleasure for her now, and then he could leave. He was always the one to leave women, anyway; like an actor who followed an excellent script, he'd always known precisely when to do it. Self-preservation was an instinct.

Why then, did he say: "I can make you see stars, Tansy." On a whisper.

She looked up into his face as if he were the universe.

He *had* to kiss her then.

Her mouth was as yielding as a feather bed; he sank into it with a sigh, a moan, that made him realize what a relief kissing her again was. That every moment he'd spent up until now not kissing her had been a shameful waste. And it began just that way, languid and wondering, a slow exploration, each of them taking unguarded pleasure in the textures and taste and perfect fit of each other. She gave and took in that kiss with a sensual grace and abandon that made him want to shout hallelujah, that nearly dropped him to his knees.

But he only took that kiss deeper, and his tongue dove and stroked, her hands clutched as they slid up over his chest and latched around his neck for balance, and she opened herself to him.

His fingers trailed her bare thighs, up to delicate, sheltered skin between them, up to the silky vee of curls. She ducked her head and buried it against his chest; her breath gusted hot and rapid on his collarbone.

The want of her shook him; his limbs felt stiff and clumsy. He could taste lust, peculiarly electric, in the back of his throat. His cock strained against his trouser buttons.

He skated his fingers between her thighs and found her slick and hot. Wet. So ready for the taking.

Her breath caught on the word *"Oh."*

He did it again. A tease, a feathery slide of one finger, and she jerked. "Ian . . ."

He did it again, harder.

She arched into it on a choked gasp, circled her hips against him, her hands clutching his shirt. How he wanted her hands on his skin. Her breath had begun to come in shallow little gusts against his throat.

He did it again slowly, tantalizingly.

He stopped. Testing.

"No," she begged softly on a whisper. "No, please don't stop . . ."

"Keep your eyes on my face, Tansy."

He wanted to witness her pleasure.

And so he was able to watch her eyes go heavy-lidded, and her head tip backward, and the cords of her throat go taut, and her head thrash forward again, and the air come shredded between her parted lips as he played with her desire like an orchestra conductor. And this was how he knew when to stroke harder, when to circle and tease, when to slide a finger deeper into her so that she moaned softly, gutturally, against his chest. A sound that nearly made him come right there and then.

With hands clumsy and shaking he unbuttoned his trousers, and his cock, thick and erect, sprang free, and he lifted her thigh with one hand, as high as his waist, and slid his cock against her wetness, tormenting himself, tormenting her. Once . . . twice. Three times. A dangerous, dangerous game, the most dangerous he'd ever played, when in one thrust he could be inside her and chasing his own pleasure, his own release, and he knew it would be explosive. His every cell cried out for it.

And yet the two of them did seem to seek risk. They would take it too far, he knew that now. It was inevitable. Perhaps not now, perhaps not tonight.

"Ian . . . I'm . . . *help me* . . . I'm . . .

He pressed his palm hard against her and circled, and she choked a sound of bliss, and her body bucked.

He pressed her head into his chest just in time to muffle her scream. And he held her close and felt triumph as he felt her body shake like a rag, over and over with what was likely her first ever release.

Silence apart from the ragged tide of breathing. Cool air over heated skin.

She shuddered.

He pulled her night rail around her, wrapped her in his arms and pulled her close. A little closer than his erection would have preferred. He felt quite martyred, in a way, and blessed in another.

He waited for her breathing to regain normal rhythm.

"*Shooting* stars." The words were muffled against his chest.

He gave a short, almost pained laugh. "I'm a man of my word."

He was afraid now. In a way he'd never before been. He didn't know how to extricate himself from this. Because he knew another woman couldn't possibly be the answer; nor was avoiding Tansy altogether. For this was a different kind of want. It wasn't mere sensual hunger. He knew how to sate that kind of hunger. He suspected the correct word for it was "need." There was a first taste of opium, or gin, for every addict, after all. This strange, wild, reckless, beautiful girl could very well be the end of him. He might as well throw himself off the balcony now.

How very ironic. The duke would finally have his revenge then.

He could feel her heart beating.

He savored it, as if the heartbeats ticked off the minutes they had left together.

She tipped her head back and looked up at him. For a long time, in silence. "Are you going to lecture me now? About how very dangerous all of this is, and so forth?"

How strangely fragile she felt now in his arms. His arms went over her shoulder blades. Suddenly it seemed to him that it did feel as though wings could sprout there.

"No," he said softly. "I think you know. This can't happen again, Tansy."

Her head jerked back and she looked up at him. He heard her breath catch.

And so the words had landed hard.

He'd meant it to sound like an order. It was difficult to shake the habit of issuing orders.

Knowing her, he suspected she'd interpreted it as a dare.

God help him if she did.

And it really was a prayer to God for help. If she dared him again, it would be all or nothing.

He looked down at her, and traced her lips with a single finger the way he had traced her name on the wall of Lilymont.

He dropped his hands abruptly from her.

"Go inside before you take a chill."

He suspected his tone had already gotten the chill started, which was just as well.

He backed away from her and didn't turn around until he was in his room again, the door closed behind him, the window firmly locked, and yet he knew he was hardly safe.

SHE DIDN'T EXPECT to sleep, but she finally tumbled over the edge into a deep, black dreamless one.

She was disappointed about the dreamless part. Her senses had just been thoroughly, properly used for the first time ever, and until she slept they'd reverberated like a thoroughly strummed instrument. She'd lain there and felt her body humming a hallelujah chorus. She wouldn't have minded reliving the evening again and again and again in her sleep.

For, as he'd said, it couldn't happen again. Not in waking life.

So that's what bodies were for, she'd thought, drifting back into the house from the balcony, realizing her feet were chilled. And that's what lips, and fingertips, and breasts, and nipples, and skin, and arms, and cocks, were for. And that's what men were for, and women were for. Suddenly, as bliss echoed all through her, everything else humans were capable of seemed superfluous.

*I know so many, many things.*

He *would* say that and then go on to say it couldn't happen again.

He was right, of course.

And when she awoke in the daylight, she had the sense to feel a certain reprieve. As though she'd escaped something. Daylight was slightly less conducive to madness, and she did not intend to be among the legion of women Ian Eversea had seduced and abandoned. A woman ruined because of a weakness for a beautiful man with a legendary way about him, and therefore useless to anyone, and a disgrace to the duke and his family, not to mention her own family.

She found the notion of that unbearable.

And yet . . . he kissed her as though he . . . *needed* her.

*Only* her.

As though he was searching for something and finding it . . . some solace, some ease, some answer. She'd felt his kiss in the soles of her feet, the palms of her hands, from the top of her head on down.

Through every part of her. He'd trembled when he kissed her, and his hands had been skilled and reverent, and she knew he'd been . . . lost.

Seducer. Seduction. She knew he was known for this, and the words implied calculation, process. It might have begun a bit like a chess game, but it had taken on its own momentum, and owned both of them.

It made her want to give and give. She had never thought of herself as an inherently generous person. But it worried her that she wanted to give him anything he wanted when he kissed her.

She would not believe he kissed every woman that way. He would have been worn to a nub by now.

Then again, how ever would she know? Perhaps it was all part of his magic.

And what if . . . well, he certainly wasn't a duke. He didn't even have a title. What would it be like to be married to Ian Eversea? Surely there was no harm in imagining it . . . surely a man like him would take a wife *one* day . . . She woke in time to find the stripe of light leading to the window. How would he look this morning? Any different than he had? How did she look?

She followed the little light road and peeked out.

But he wasn't there.

She waited a bit, the speed of her heartbeat ratcheting up a bit.

And he didn't appear.

And when the light was finally high enough, she knew he wasn't going to, which, she supposed, was all for the best.

Deflated, resigned, feeling quite martyred and mature, she flung the braided rope of her hair over her shoulder and settled in at her desk. She smoothed out the foolscap, and decided she would need to write smaller if she wanted to confine her list to a single page. She reached for her quill and wrote:

*Kisses me as though his very life depends upon it.*

# Chapter 19

&

"WE SET SAIL IN a little less than a month, Captain Eversea. Will you be on board? We could use a man like you. Pirates, you know. Le Chat is still sailing, or so rumor has it."

"I thought I was embarking on a pleasure jaunt, and you intend to put me to work?"

"Men like yourself live for it," the captain said dryly.

Ian couldn't argue with that.

He inhaled deeply. They were so close and yet so far from the sea in Sussex, and here the smell of it was primordial and thrilling. A heaving glassine green-blue stretching for as far as the eye could see. The ship seemed a behemoth at the dock but would be a speck on the chest of the sea. They would be at its mercy. He found the notion peculiarly soothing.

"I'll be aboard."

He thought of Tansy Danforth standing on deck, her bright eyes reflecting the seas and skies. She'd probably enjoyed that voyage, the risk, the danger, the newness. And how fun it would be to banter with her, to share the sights, to protect her from the goggling men on board and to watch her attempt to rein in those flirtatious urges.

And at night . . . in a narrow little bunk . . .

Something tightened in his gut again. He wanted her with a ferocity that bordered on fury. And it was this he needed to outrun, too.

He remembered the archery competition, and he thought sometimes he was like that: ever since the war he was like a bowstring pulled too far back for the arrow to do anything but overshoot every target. What he wanted and needed was to keep moving, until somehow his restlessness had run its course.

He watched the ship and dock activity idly a moment. The crew was working ceaselessly, repairing sails, scrubbing and sanding decks, bringing on cargo and supplies, checking the manifests as they grew person by person.

He'd apologized to his cousin Adam and begged leave for a day or two in London so he could put a deposit down to hold his place on this particular ship. It would sail as far as Africa, but he could step off in any port he chose along the way, or take another ship bound for anywhere. Anywhere at all. As long as his money lasted. And he'd saved enough money to keep moving for years, if he so chose.

"Eversea!"

A delighted voice spun him around.

"Caldwell!"

It was Major Caldwell who had suggested him for the East India Company promotion.

"A pity you won't be working for the company here in London, Eversea. Not only would we have a splendid time, we could use a clever sort."

"I'm flattered you'll miss me, sir, but this is something I've long wanted to do. Before I'm too decrepit to do it, mind you."

"Well, make your fortune and gather a few stories and bed a few brown maidens and return to us full of enviable stories, if you must."

"I must."

He said.

Meaning it.


HE RETURNED LATE enough that the entire house was asleep, and so he stripped off his clothes and flung himself, smelling of horse and the sea, into his bed, and fell too quickly asleep.

And in moments, it seemed, he could feel Jeremiah Cutler's little body tucked beneath his arm, plump and squirmy, vibrating with sobs. But he couldn't hear him over the screams of horses, the ceaseless roar of artillery, the guttural cries of men cut down. He handed Jeremiah back into the safety of his father's arms. He turned and lunged, dodging through chaos. He had only seconds to get to—

Ian broke through to consciousness with a gasp and a hoarse inarticulate cry.

He sat bolt upright, breathing as though he'd actually been running. He dropped his face into his hands and breathed through them.

The dream was potent; it was as if he'd lived it all over again.

He lifted his head at last.

Tansy was sitting at the foot of his bed, knees tucked under her chin, arms wrapped tightly around them, watching him.

He nearly yelped.

"What the bloody . . . *how* did you . . ."

"I think you were having a terrible dream," she said somberly.

"Am I *still* dreaming?" he asked wildly. "This isn't usually part of it. But if it is, I should warn you, it never ends very well for women."

He fell back against the pillow, hard.

Bloody hell. He threw a beleaguered arm over his eyes and sighed a sigh of despair.

Tansy slid from the bed, walked across his room to his bureau and sniffed the pitcher suspiciously. She poured some water into a glass, brought it back and held it out to him.

Ian reflexively took it and gulped it down. "Thank you."

"You're welcome."

He wiped the back of his hand across his mouth and clunked the glass down on his night table.

"How did you know I was home?"

"I saw your light."

A horrible suspicion struck.

"Wait . . . How did you get in here, Tansy?"

"Your window was open. Just a little."

"My wind— Oh God. Tell me you didn't climb from your balcony onto mine. *Tell me you didn't climb from your balcony onto mine!*"

"It was easier to do than I thought."

He opened his mouth. Only a dry squeak emerged. He tried again. "You can't *do* that. Mother of God. Do you want to die? You're going to marry a title and a fortune, remember? And live happily ever after." His words were still frayed. "Finding your broken body on the ground below my balcony would ruin my morning view."

"Shhhh," she said soothingly.

He closed his eyes. His breathing seemed deafening in the room, now that he had an audience.

He felt the mattress sink next to him and opened one eye.

She'd stretched out along the length of the bed, dangerously close to him but not touching, close enough that he could smell the sweetness of her, and now she was nestling her head into his other pillow.

Then she reached over and gently lifted his hand from his chest. Slowly, gently, carefully, as if stealing a bird egg from a nest.

"What are you doing, Tansy?"

"Comforting you."

He snorted softly.

She took the hand back with her to her side of the bed and held it companionably.

And because he couldn't think of a reason to pull away, he allowed it.

And it *was* comforting, strangely enough. He couldn't remember the last time he'd held anyone's hand.

They lay side by side, flat on their backs, in silence.

"I couldn't sleep, either," she said, after what seemed a long time.

He gave another short humorless laugh. "Bad dreams?"

"Sometimes. And very disturbing good dreams, too, about the man in the room next to mine."

He half smiled. "Tansy." A drowsy warning.

He could almost *hear* her smile.

They were silent again.

"Ian?"

"Mmm?"

"What was your dream about?"

He stiffened.

The thing was, he'd never told a soul. Oh, he'd told the story behind the dreams. It was part of the war stories men shared with each other. But he'd never confessed to being haunted by it at night.

And while he waited and said nothing, the fire said quite a bit. It popped and crackled and a log flopped over.

"Did you hear me say anything in my sleep?"

He'd always wondered. He dreaded the answer.

"It sounded like 'Justine.' "

Ah, bloody hell.

He sighed a long sigh of resignation and swiped his free hand over his face. "I wish you hadn't heard that."

"I've heard worse. I heard you break wind the other day on the balcony. Just a little."

"You *what*?" He was *not* going to blush.

And now she was laughing.

"Leave. Leave now. Or I'll do it again." But now he was laughing, too, and bit his lip to stop it. "Lower your voice, for God's sake."

But he didn't let go of her hand so she *could* leave.

"Have you been *spying* on me, Tansy?"

Though he was aware any indignation was hypocritical, given that he'd essentially spied on her, too.

"I wasn't *certain* it was you, until only recently. I just thought it was a man with a beautiful torso."

The words ambushed him. Beautiful torso?

He'd truthfully never been so disarmed by a woman in his entire life. She was one of a kind.

*Don't leave yourself so open to hurt, Tansy,* he wanted to tell her. *You shouldn't say those sorts of things to me.* He knew the power of words and flattery, because he'd used them strategically. And so did she, for that matter. But she was so *sincere.*

What was the matter with him when sincerity unnerved him completely?

He could tell her that he thought she was beautiful, too. That her lips were paradise. That her hair was a symphony of color. That her skin . . . oh, her skin.

But he wouldn't, because words like that bound another to you. Everyone wants to know how much they matter. He never used them lightly.

And in the wake of those words, he considered it might be sensible to drop her hand.

Perhaps . . . perhaps not just yet.

"Who is Justine?" she wanted to know.

"A bit of the war that won't let me leave it behind, I'm afraid. That's all."

"Were you in love with her?"

He made an exasperated sound. "God. Women and *that word*. They bandy it about so freely and I doubt half of them know what it means."

"In other words . . . no?"

He sighed, pretending extreme exasperation, which made her smile again. "Very well. Since you're relentless. Justine was . . . she was someone for whom I felt responsible, and she died in the war. I was too late to stop it. And I suppose I regret it every day."

He glanced over to find her clear eyes not on him but on the ceiling.

He smiled. She always seemed to be looking up.

His smile faded when he remembered she looked up for her mother.

"I'm sorry," she said softly, at last. As if she'd pictured the entire episode and genuinely mourned it along with him.

She knew what it was to mourn, too.

And strangely, there was a sudden easing in him, as if someone had finally played a note that harmonized with the one he sounded every day.

So as the words came for the first time, he aimed them at the ceiling, too, his voice abstracted.

"She was the wife of my commanding officer. Pretty, vivacious, very kind. I was close to both of them. We tried as best we could to keep women away from the battlefield but she traveled with our regiment and she wanted to be near her husband. She was intrepid as well as foolish, I suppose. But none of that matters. I was able to get to her child in time, but I couldn't get back to her—I took a bayonet in the gut, which rather slowed me down—and she got caught in cannon fire. I saw it. I never knew whether he would have preferred to have his wife or child alive because I spent the rest of the war recovering in a farmhouse in Flanders."

Her grip on his hand grew tighter and tighter as he talked. As if she walked the whole thing through with him.

"Oh, yes. I've medals and the like," he said dryly. "I'm brave as brave can be, so they said. I just wasn't fast enough to get back to her without getting myself skewered. And so I saved her child, but watched her die. And I get to watch her die in my dreams on occasion, too."

Tansy was quiet for a long while, taking this in.

"Well, as long as you have medals," she said thoughtfully.

He threw back his head and laughed, and had to bite his lip to stifle it.

And she laughed, too.

It was the *perfect* thing to say. *Well, you did your best,* or *It wasn't your fault*—it didn't matter how true those things were. It didn't matter how you tried to rationalize it away. The dreams would come anyway.

She knew it.

"Do you know . . . what's coincidental about that, Ian? My parents wished *I'd* died, instead of my brother."

It was such a ghastly thing to hear, his mind blanked for a moment. It was almost as though she'd confessed to murder.

He almost stammered. "Surely you're mistaken—"

"I heard them say it." She said this matter-of-factly, but he heard the steeled nerve in her voice. "Overheard them, I should say. My mother said, right after my brother died, 'If only it had been the girl.'"

It was like someone had punched him in the heart.

He was shocked by how literally painful the words were.

And a sort of furious flailing helplessness followed. As if he'd been once again one second too late to prevent someone from being cut in two by cannon fire.

"People say terrible, misguided things when they're in pain, Tansy. Things they don't mean."

"But sometimes you just know, don't you? *You* have so many siblings. *You* must know. They loved me but they loved my brother more. He was their pride and hope and the heir and so forth. And I was just a girl. I loved him, too, you know. I suppose I've always wanted to matter more than I did."

Love.

He didn't say, *There's that word again.*

He supposed it explained a good deal about Miss Titania Danforth and her quest for attention.

He'd always suspected Colin was his mother's favorite. And that Genevieve and Olivia were his father's. He didn't suppose he'd cared. There was always enough affection—and affectionate contempt—to go around in their household that it didn't matter to him. For selfish reasons, he would have happily gone to the gallows in Colin's place. To spare himself from having to watch Colin die, and to spare his mother from having to witness Colin's death.

Every day Colin had spent in Newgate had been a torment, though Ian had made sure Colin never knew this. He'd kept up the gallant nonchalance.

The fact that Colin had *escaped* the gallows was very like Colin.

"Your parents loved you, Tansy." Surely this much was true. He felt as though he could make it true with the force of his words. "Perhaps they simply worried more about you than your brother."

"Of course they loved me," she said absently. "I know they did, don't worry. Enough to threaten me—in their will, no less—with the loss of everything I've ever known or loved, unless I marry an amazing title and I'm taken care of for the rest of my life. And they didn't quite trust me to get it right on my own. Thought I might do something rash."

"I suppose they must have known you pretty well, then."

A smile started up at one end of her mouth and spread to the other, crooked, wicked. Then she laughed. Pleased with herself. Her laugh was wonderful. It was mischief made musical.

And then she sighed contentedly. "It's nice to be known," she said wistfully.

"You lost them in a carriage accident?"

She nodded.

"What were they like?"

He wouldn't know where to begin answering a question like that if anyone had asked it of him. And what she said would reveal as much about her as it did about her parents, he was sure.

She was quiet a moment, apparently giving it some thought. "Mother was always laughing. She loved to sing. She loved wildflowers. Columbine—I don't know if they grow here. They look like little paper lanterns? And aster, the purple ones. Like purple stars. Chicory, buttercups, Queen Anne's lace. The blue ones reminded her of my father's eyes. When I have a home, a permanent home of my own, I want to plant all of them in my garden to make it feel like home again. I promised Mama I'd bring a little of them home to England should I ever visit. She used to talk to them to make them grow." She was smiling now. "She thought of them as her children, in a way."

Suspicion dawned.

"Did your father smoke, by any chance?" He asked it almost disinterestedly. "Cigars, cigarettes?"

"He did! And my father . . . his laugh was the best sound you ever heard. My mother could make him laugh, but I was the best at it. His coat smelled of his tobacco . . . he rolled his own cigarettes with a particularly pungent brand he'd somehow gotten a taste for. My mother hated it." Tansy smiled faintly. "And at night he'd sneak just a bit of whisky. She hated that, too. Or pretended to. He rather liked being scolded, I think. It makes you feel cared for, doesn't it, sometimes?"

"I suppose it does," he said softly. As in his head the tumblers of a sort of lock clicked into place.

What it must have been like for her.

She *was* lonely. And, given the circumstances, resilient as hell.

He reflexively squeezed her hand a little tighter, unconsciously sending some of his strength into her.

She squeezed it back.

"I dealt with the solicitor to take care of a few stray ends of business," she said, "and I helped close up the house and pension off the servants, all but a few. A few to care for the house, a staff to care for the stables. I'd trust all of them with my life. But after that . . . do you know what it's been like, Ian? It's a bit like going to the theater. And the play we've come to see is my life. A wonderful play. But then it ends before you expect it to, and you're forbidden to leave, you're locked in the theater, and you're left to stare at an empty stage. And for all you know, you'll just sit there forever. Terrible word, forever."

"They ought to ban it from dictionaries," he concurred.

She smiled at that.

"And for quite some time it has felt like . . ." She turned to him earnestly, and he was treated to how her silvery eyes looked by lamplight, warm and hazy. ". . . It's hard to describe . . . I've been to school and learned everything there is to learn, and nothing has the power to surprise me anymore. Or to scare me."

He was stunned to realize that she was essentially describing what it was like to come home from the war.

He remembered returning . . . it was as if he'd used up every emotion he ever had, because he'd felt nearly everything there was to feel at such a pitch for so long that ordinary life felt rather flat and muted and painfully slow. He'd been willing to do nearly anything to *feel* something. And to forget.

Fortunately, Ian thought, God created French actresses and young women with flexible morals.

That rather took care of the forgetting. Climbing up trees and through windows and being ushered out of those windows at pistol point took care of the excitement part of it.

"It's a bit like that when you come home from war, too," he said slowly. He'd never said such a thing aloud to anyone. "Your senses are so accustomed to being constantly engaged and abused . . . that real life seems, for a time, inadequate and unreal and very dull. Almost stifling."

She was watching him in a way that made his heart turn over strangely. Soft and sympathetic and ever-so-slightly shrewdly.

"Is that why you have a host of mistresses?"

She was teasing.

He laughed drowsily. "*Never* a host. They're *far* too much trouble to deal with them in quantity."

She laughed softly, and suddenly he was suffused with an admiration that was almost painful. That she should *see* so clearly. That she could laugh and not judge. That her heart was accepting. That she'd confronted the utter destruction of her life with relative grace and looked forward with hope, not bitterness, not regret.

And there was a moment when he couldn't breathe, because he suddenly wanted to be worthy of her, and he quite simply didn't know how that was possible.

He'd been . . . such an ass.

"There will be a new play, Tansy." How ridiculously inadequate it sounded.

"When I marry and have my own home and family." It almost sounded like a question.

"Yes. Then." He made it sound like a promise. As if it were up to him, he'd make it happen.

And if it were up to him it would.

He was suddenly violently, irrationally yanked between two poles: The wish that she should have everything she ever wanted. To be safe and loved best of all by someone.

And the wish that she wouldn't, so this particular moment could be suspended in time. So this particular play, whatever this was, would never end.

They were silent for a time. And then she glanced down at his bare torso—his "beautiful" torso—and with a single finger, tentatively traced that scar. Delicately. Following it down, down, down, to nearly where it disappeared beneath the sheets.

He ought to stop her.

His muscles tightened with the pleasure of her touch, and with imagining what he could do to her, where he would touch her, how he would take her, how he would begin. His cock stirred. She *must* know what she was doing to him. She was still a devil, still a taker of risks, for all of that.

"I'm sorry this happened to you," she said softly. Her finger was so very near the border of the sheet, and in a moment his arousal would elevate that sheet. How he wanted to turn to her. Peel off her night rail. He could see the shadows of her nipples pushed against it, and he imagined drawing one into his mouth, imagined the little helpless sound of pleasure she would make when he sucked.

His cock stirred a little more.

"Tansy," he whispered. He slipped his fingers through her hair and drew it out, luxuriating in the silk of it, in the colors, every shade of gold there was, as her gentle fingers traced his scar. "Tansy."

"Yes?"

"You need to leave."

"Leave?"

"Out the door, and not out the window."

"Are you certain?"

"I'm certain."

"They're both dangerous routes."

She didn't need to tell *him* that. "Staying is far more dangerous than either of those. I meant what I said the other night. If you don't leave, Tansy, I *will* make love to you. It will be all, or it will be nothing. And I cannot warn you again."

The hush that fell was velvety and taut. Her wandering finger froze.

She studied him, gauging his mood, and whether to test him, and whether it was what she wanted. She had only an inkling of the pleasure that could be had. If only she knew what a razor thin line of control he walked. Knowing her, she would have risked pushing him over the edge. Because she'd just endured her own personal war, and risk and sensation were helping her to forget.

He would give nearly anything to kiss her right now.

And if he kissed her, he wouldn't stop until he'd taken everything he could.

*Stay.* It took every fiber of his control not to say it. It took every fiber of his control not to tear that night rail right from her body and lose himself in her.

"Because men are brutes?" She said this almost lightly. On a whisper.

He looked down at her. At the soft point of her chin, at her clear eyes, the generous mouth.

No, he realized. Because I want to make love to you. To *you*. Not just for surcease. Or to chase pleasure to its ultimate peak. Because I want to give *you* pleasure, to hear *you* cry out, to be inside *you*, to talk to *you* when we're quiet and spent.

On the heels of that came an even more alarming realization.

He suspected he wouldn't mind settling for simply holding her hand all night.

That was an . . . interesting . . . notion.

A very, very *unwelcome* notion.

"Yes," he agreed softly. "Because men are brutes."

She sighed and stretched. "Very well."

She slipped her hand out from his.

She shoved her hair out of her face, slid off the bed and treaded delicately as a fawn across his soft carpet, apparently enjoying the feel on her bare feet, which made him smile.

"But you can leave the night rail," he called softly after her.

She laughed softly.

She winked and blew him a kiss.

He watched her open the door, peek out, and disappear.

He'd never hated the sound of a door closing more.

He groaned and dragged the pillow over his face. It was cool. Perhaps it would lower the temperature of his feverish thoughts.

Unconsciously, he closed his fingers, as if he could capture and hold the sensation of her touch in his palm.

And that's how he fell asleep.

# Chapter 20

∽

"You're all looking unusually dazzling this morning, ladies."

His sister and Tansy and Olivia were dressed in what he recognized as their finest. Colors that set off their eyes and hair and presented bosoms and arms and the like in their best possible light. He was the brother of two sisters, and he'd known myriad women; he knew *far* more than he wanted to about such things and had been tortured by questions about fashion more than once.

"Why, thank you. You're looking remarkably alert this morning, Ian."

"You flatter me, surely," he said dryly.

"Why are you still in Sussex?" Genevieve was shrewdly suspicious.

"I've business," he said smoothly. "And I promised Adam I'd help keep the motley crew of workers organized while we finished the repairs to the vicarage. Where are you off to? Because I gather from your finery that you are off to someplace other than town."

"We've been invited to tea. Lord Stanhope is a guest of Lord Henry's family."

Stanhope.

The Duke de Neauville's heir.

The one said to be looking for a wife.

Clearly, Ian's message had been successfully conveyed and enthusiastically received.

Which ought to have made him rejoice.

And yet somehow his mind blanked, as if he'd heard news of a murder.

He realized he'd gone still, fork hovering in the air in the vicinity of his mouth. He'd forgotten whether he intended to put it in his mouth or set it down. He decided to set it down.

"Ah, the Duke de Neauville's heir. I'd forgotten there were other dukes besides yours."

"Ha," Genevieve said.

Tansy hadn't yet looked at him. She was stirring the marmalade pot as if it were one of the witches in Macbeth. Slowly, and with great focus.

"What are you hoping to find in there, Miss Danforth? I haven't heard whether you can read marmalade the way you can read tea leaves."

She stopped, looked up. There was a peculiar clutch in the vicinity of his heart when her eyes met his.

She blushed.

Slowly, beautifully.

It didn't irritate him in the least.

Which worried him a good deal.

THEY DEPARTED, AND Ian paced to and fro, feverishly, for a time.

And then he found himself heading toward the stable. He saddled up and rode out through the woods along the little tributary of the Ouse, back the way they'd come the other day. He followed the stream she'd knelt next to, slowing his horse to a walk.

He scanned for hoofprints and footprints and brush and shrubbery that might have been pushed aside or crushed. He didn't know quite what he was looking for. Anything unusual. His father had taken all of his sons out hunting at an early age, and tracking was second nature to him.

A glint caught his eye. He pulled his horse to a halt.

Something lavender and shiny.

He swung down from his horse, looped the reins into a hawthorn, trod toward the glint and stopped.

Thoughtfully, he plucked up a bonnet; trailing from it were lavender satin ribbons. He held it gingerly. He shouldn't doubt her.

Why did it matter so very much?

He strode forward, ten, twenty feet, and came to a little clearing he hadn't ridden through since he was a boy. A nondescript place, but it had inevitably changed over the years; one of the old oaks had been split by lightning and now lay on its side, and the others had grown into behemoths around their fallen comrade.

He rotated slowly, scanning the place, for . . . what, he wasn't certain. Flattened grass, from lovers rolling about? A man's footprint, a woman's footprint?

But the clearing was mostly dirt; no moss grew. It wasn't the sort of place one could comfortably tryst. Then again, he'd managed to tryst up against trees. Where there was a will to tryst, there was always a way.

Perhaps she came here the way Polly did. To contemplate nature's wonders in solitude. It didn't really sound like something she would do; then again, he'd had the blinkers ripped from his eyes recently.

Suddenly he stopped. And peered.

What appeared to be two little stakes were poking up out of the ground.

Next to two little mounds.

As though something *had* been buried.

Good God.

Even though he'd jested about it, now he was ever-so-slightly worried. He was beside the mounds in two steps.

He crouched and peered.

The earth was dark and disturbed, but in an orderly way. Not as though an animal had dug for something or churned it with hooves.

As though something had been planted.

A scrap of what appeared to be foolscap was affixed to the first stake.

In exquisite, copperplate handwriting was written the word: *columbine.*

And on the other: *asters.*

He sat back on his heels.

She'd likely planted them as a tribute to her mother.

"Damn."

The word was really more of an exhale.

He closed his eyes as a wave of something roared through him, like a dam broken.

It felt like a torrent of sunlight, and it hurt, and it felt glorious.

He knew then that the punching sensation he'd felt in the vicinity of his heart last night was really the locked gates of it being kicked open.

THE FIRST SURPRISE about the heir to the Duke of Neauville was that he wasn't *very* handsome.

Oh, he was handsome enough. He was appealing in an even-featured-possessed-all-his-limbs-and-teeth way. He was tall and long-limbed. His hair was a sandy color and his gray eyes twinkled and his complexion was free of spots. His manners were as exquisite and polished as the silver—ancient silver, passed down through generations and worth an untold fortune, no doubt—upon which they were served luncheon. Everything in the room gleamed: crystal, porcelain, utensils, upholstery, his admirably complete set of teeth.

He possessed the sort of subtle remote self-consciousness of those who knew they were very important and who were accustomed to stares.

Until he really took a good look at Tansy.

Gratifyingly, he gawked like any green lad.

Which made her cast her lashes down. Then up again.

It was a reflex, really.

"A p-pleasure indeed to meet you, Miss Danforth."

Ah, a bit of a stammer. She loved it when she made men stammer.

He was charming, really. Or really, it was what she should have been thinking.

Somewhere along the line she'd begun to interpret charm a little differently.

As challenge. Impenetrable confidence.

Occasional charmlessness, even.

He bowed low, very low, over her hand, and held it like a Frenchman, and slowly righted himself again.

"Everything I've heard about you is true."

Ah! So she was a legend already.

One day she might even be as talked about as Ian Eversea.

"WHAT THE DEVIL are *you* doing here?"

Ian whirled. Colin was standing in the doorway of the family's library with his mouth agape.

Ian surreptitiously tucked the book he'd pulled from the shelf and tucked it under his arm.

"Is it really such a shock?"

"The last time I can remember you coming in here voluntarily was when Father acquired a book featuring medical illustrations, and you thought there might be a naked woman or two inside."

"There *was*," Ian pointed out. "I was right. My suspicions were rewarded. Even though her internal organs were sketched inside her. And I never forgot how inspiring the experience was."

*Now go away*, he silently bid Colin.

No such luck.

"What are you holding, Ian?"

"Nothing."

"It appears to be a book."

"If you knew what it was, why did you ask?"

"Is it an anatomy book?"

Ian snorted.

Colin flung himself down in a chair and peered out the window. "I'm glad Genevieve will be living close. They've about settled on purchasing the estate. I'm certain you're glad your nemesis will be close, too."

"He's not my nemesis," Ian said. Rather to his own surprise.

"Inconvenient reminder that you possess a conscience, then."

"Perhaps," he said curtly.

He didn't want to continue looking through his book until Colin left. And he very much wanted to continue looking at the book. He'd visited a section of the library shelves he'd never before seen, and it had taken him quite some time to find it.

Oh, but he had, and treasures lay within. At least they were treasures to him.

Colin showed no signs of leaving. He swung a

booted leg, gave the empty brandy decanter a disconsolate shake.

"Well, then."

"Colin, may I ask you a question?"

"Why on earth are you asking permission to ask a question?"

Ian steeled himself.

"Why do you love Madeleine?" He asked it casually.

But Colin's mouth dropped open.

Even when Colin was in Newgate, pale and shackled, they'd never discussed life or death or love or loss. Ian had brought the best of the broadsheets to him. In one issue, Colin had been depicted wearing a pair of horns. He'd had it framed for Colin. Because that's what brothers were for. Every other memory was too precious to be aired in that prison cell.

So obviously Colin was surprised. "I see. I assume there's a context for this question?"

"Consider it . . . research."

Ian could see that Colin was skeptical. He could feel his brother's eyes on his back speculatively. A strange little silence passed, and Ian went still, his heart beating with a deeper thud.

"Well . . . she's the strongest person I've ever known." Colin sounded as though he was thinking about it for the first time. "She's fascinating and fearless, but she's fragile, for all of that. She sees right through me and loves me anyway and has from the first, though I'm not certain she'll ever admit to that. Because she's not as strong as she thinks she is, but she'd needed to be strong for so long that it made me want to be strong for her, a better person for her. She's so beautiful to me it hurts, sometimes, to look at her. And no one has ever before needed me, and she does. She really does."

*And no one has ever before needed me, and she does. She really does.*

It was quite a speech.

Ian stood motionless, moved and, truth be told, astonished, beyond words.

In the ensuing awkward silence, he realized there was a world of knowledge and experience his younger brother possessed that he did not. Just as Colin would never know what it was like to nearly die on a battlefield, as he had. Colin had survived unscathed. Then again, nearly going to the gallows had likely shaved years off his life.

"*And* she's as interested in the raising of cows and sheep as I am lately," Colin added.

"I guess someone needed to be. Are you sure she isn't pretending just to make you happy?"

Colin snorted. "Miss *Danforth* is interested in cows."

"If she said that, Miss Danforth was lying."

"I know, but at least she made an effort to do it, which is flattering."

There was another little silence.

"Did you come to the library today for a reason, Colin?"

*Go away now, Colin.*

"I was looking for you. I'd like to buy a mare for Madeleine as a surprise for her birthday and I'd hoped to persuade you to come with me."

"Here's my advice: if you're not buying the horse from the Gypsies, then your judgment is probably sound."

Colin gave a short laugh.

And still he didn't leave.

"Why don't you tell me why you're wondering these things, Ian?"

Bloody hell. His younger brother rivaled their cousin Adam for the ability to peer into his soul.

Ian was torn between wanting to talk and not knowing precisely how to articulate what there seemed to be no words for, primarily because it was new. A big amorphous knot of emotions and impressions, one of which was panic, another of which was glory, and there were dozens of subtler ones in between. He wouldn't even know where to begin unraveling it.

He tried.

"Colin . . . do you believe in destiny?"

"Certainly." Though Ian suspected this was a lazy answer to avoid a philosophical discussion.

"I think my destiny might be to be murdered by the Duke of Falconbridge."

Colin lifted a dismissive hand. "He can't murder you. He's family. Family doesn't do that sort of thing. At least knowingly," he added after a moment, somewhat cryptically.

"Tell that to Othello."

"A Shakespearean reference, Ian? Did you . . . actually *listen* at school?" He sounded aghast.

"Perhaps I had a knack for remembering only the things that prove enlightening later."

"Why do you think the duke will . . ."

He stopped, frowned faintly, as a suspicion began to form.

"Noooooo . . ."

"No?"

"No. No no no no no. Tell me you didn't . . . not Miss Danforth! Tell me you weren't that mad!" Colin leaped up and reached for Ian's lapels and gripped them. "Tell me you're not that suicidal! What is the *matter* with you, when there are so . . . many . . . women in the world?"

"Get off." He pushed his brother away. "Calm yourself. Of course not. It's not like that at all."

To his knowledge, it was the first time he'd ever lied to Colin in his life.

Colin was still staring at him. "Because you know Genevieve will never forgive you. And the duke may *not* kill you, but you'll always wonder, won't you? What a fun way to go through life."

He was about to say, *The duke's not a murderer*. But then cuckolding a man really was a matter of honor, and Ian wasn't certain he'd blame the duke for wanting to exact revenge . . . and if he should ever suspect that Miss Danforth had crawled into his bed last night . . .

"All right, then," his brother said. "If you *are*

worried about the duke with regards to that girl, I wouldn't lose sleep over it. After all, it's what *everyone* sees when they look at her. I imagine you're only now coming around to seeing it. And in time it'll go the way of your other, shall we say, passing fancies, no doubt."

"I see." It almost sounded like sacrilege to hear it described that way. "Well, then."

"And by passing fancies, I mean women."

"Thank you. I knew what you meant."

He was quiet.

*Go away, Colin.*

Colin regarded him with some sympathy.

"You know, marrying someone—anyone, practically—would solve the problem."

"Of Miss Danforth?" For she needed solving, as far as Ian was concerned.

"Of you."

He snorted.

"Don't marry someone dull, though," Colin hastened to add.

"Can't marry someone dull if I never get married at all."

"Forget what I said about family. Mother *will* murder you then," he said easily. "Now, come with me."

Ian sighed, and hurriedly slid *Native Flora of North America* back into place on the shelf. He would be back to study it later.

But he didn't push it *all* the way in. And when the Duke of Falconbridge entered the library a little later, specifically because he'd seen Colin and Ian departing it, he scanned the room thoughtfully. When he noticed the spine of one book poking out from the otherwise neatly aligned books, he immediately aimed for it and pulled it from the shelf.

He read the title.

And he straightened slowly and stared after where Colin and Ian had disappeared.

# Chapter 21

❧

When she bounded downstairs for breakfast the following morning, Tansy was greeted by a footman who was just taking receipt of more bouquets! How she loved flowers.

"These arrived for you, Miss Danforth," he said, smiling as she began to lunge forward enthusiastically.

But she stopped short.

And backed away two feet. As if instead of flowers, she'd been given one of the plants that eat animals, the sort that Miles Redmond had documented in his book.

At last she stretched out her hand for them, slowly, disbelieving, and the footman relinquished a colorful, casual bundle, tied with a blue ribbon.

And then her hand began to tremble as she took an inventory of the flowers:

Columbines. Asters. Marigolds. Wild roses. Bergamot. Lupine.

And the thing that stopped her breath: a trumpet-shaped flower called "shooting star."

It was like looking across a spring meadow in bloom back home.

*Shooting star!*

They could only be the gift of one person. The person who claimed he never gave gifts. At least not to women.

How had he . . . how on earth . . .

"A message accompanied them, Miss Danforth."

The message was sealed with a blob of wax but no press of a signet. She slid a finger beneath to crack the seal, and read: *I apologize if I've ever behaved like an ass.* It was the most romantic message she'd ever received.

All other messages would strive to live up to it for the rest of her days. She was convinced of that in the moment.

"And these have just arrived for you, too, miss, with the vase as well. Where would you like me to put them?"

He gestured to an exquisite alabaster vase stuffed with tasteful, towering, flawless, hothouse blooms. Roses, crimson and erect, looking like scepters, white lilies like trumpets. A triumphant arrangement only one man could have sent.

An arrangement, in fact, fit for a duchess.

Both arrangements stole her breath, for different reasons.

She opened the note that accompanied it.

*These reminded me of you. I hope you don't think me forward, but I would be honored if you*

*and Falconbridge would join me for an afternoon
picnic today.*

"I think someone is smitten." Genevieve was
smiling.

Which someone?

And which one was scarier?

SHE FOUND HIM sitting in one of the parlors, perusing a book he tucked behind him the moment she
entered the room.

"Good afternoon, Captain Eversea."

"Good afternoon, Miss Danforth."

He remained seated. His long legs were
stretched out before him, his arms folded behind
his head, and the sun was behind him, giving him
a little corona of glowing auburn. Like the embers
of a fire.

As befit a devil.

"Thank you for your very kind gift," she said.

"You're welcome."

"And for the apology."

"You're welcome."

"That must have been torture for you to write.
The apology."

He was silent.

"I can just imagine you sitting there, beads of
perspiration popping out all over your brow, your
pride writhing in torment as you selected just the
right words . . ."

He gave a short laugh. "Enough."

She smiled at him.

"Aren't you going to stand for me? Gentlemen generally do, when a lady enters the room."

And at that he drew himself slowly to his feet, and somehow the unfurling of his great length and height effectively blotted out the sunlight pouring in the window. He took two steps toward her.

As usual she felt at a loss.

"Is that better?" he said softly.

It was and it wasn't.

He was so very, very tall.

She was always so very tempted to allow him to engulf her.

"I remained sitting," he said thoughtfully, "because I liked how the sunlight poured over you as you entered the room and lit you up, and I quite simply couldn't move for enjoying it."

*Oh.*

Now he'd done it. He'd stolen her breath completely.

*She* was the arch flatterer, and she hadn't the faintest idea what to say. Like his message accompanying the flowers, this particular observation meant more than every single compliment she'd ever received in her life. She knew it was sincere.

And she once again had a sense for how he could so easily captivate women.

She didn't like the idea of him captivating women. Women.

And then she remembered: he never gave gifts.

"Thank you," she said, almost timidly.

He smiled, a slow crooked smile that ended in a short laugh, because he knew, he knew, just what he did to her.

*Beast.*

"Aren't you going to flatter me, Miss Danforth? Don't I look manly, and so forth? Don't I give the best compliments you've ever heard?"

"I'm certain you have that conversation with your mirror every morning."

He laughed again, that surprised, delighted sound. "So what are you going to do today?" He flicked a glance over her striped muslin morning dress, and she felt the heat start up at the back of her neck and her arms, her nipples perk to attention, and she knew from now on every time she stood in a room with Ian Eversea she might as well be wearing nothing, because she'd feel naked regardless.

"I've been invited to a picnic with Lord Stanhope. And Genevieve and the duke."

"Have you, now? Back to visit him so soon? And how did you find his lord, yesterday?"

"Amiable."

"Amiable," he said slowly, as if rolling an unfamiliar wine about in his mouth. "Now, given that I know you're prone to hyperbole, 'amiable' sounds like a veritable indictment."

"It's not. Did you hope it was?"

"Of course not. Amiable is all anyone can hope to be. The absolute pinnacle of personal achievement."

"And if *you* keep striving, I know one day you'll reach that pinnacle, too, Ian," she soothed.

He grinned at her.

A funny, soft little silence ensued.

"Ian . . . I've been wondering . . ."

"Yes?"

"Will you tell me more about lovemaking?"

He blinked. "Tansy. Mother of God. You have to stop *doing* that."

"Doing what?"

"Ambushing me with questions of that nature, and the like."

"It is the one way I get the better of you, and it's very, very funny to alarm you, so no, I won't."

This amused him slightly. "I did have to at least ask."

"But regarding my question . . . Don't you think I ought to be educated before I take any risks?"

Truthfully, it was a deliberate provocation. A red cape shaken out in front of a bull. She wanted to hear him talk about it.

She knew he wanted her, and knew *all* the power lay in her hands.

Too late she realized he would of course know exactly what she was doing.

He didn't like it.

His eyes went flinty. "I'm certain your husband will do it for you, when the time comes. It's his duty . . ."

*Husband.* She blinked. The word landed with a sort of thud between them. A funny little silence followed. She observed him through narrowed eyes.

She didn't like the sound of the word "duty," either, and suspected he knew it.

"*. . . and* it will be your duty to please him."

She suppressed a wince. "Perhaps it will always feel like a pleasure, not a chore," she said bravely.

"Perhaps," he said idly. "You could very well be right. But it isn't always a pleasure, you know. Not every man is a skilled lover. Not every man will make you feel as if your blood is on fire and your knees are water, and like you can't breathe for wanting him."

She froze.

*Speaking* of ambush.

Interestingly, as if he were a conjurer, her blood was now on fire and her knees like water, and she'd stopped breathing.

How did he do that? How did he know? It was desperately unfair that he knew so much more than she did. And he'd said it so easily. He stepped a little closer. Just an inch or so. She could breathe now. She was doing it admittedly faster, however.

He wasn't finished.

"Not every man will make you want to do anything he wishes because the moment he touches you your body is his to command. Not every man is capable of making you scream with bliss in every imaginable position, or knows where to touch you, or listens to your breath and your sighs to know precisely *how* to touch you, so that the pleasure you experience is the most intense. Not every man will make you see stars every . . . single . . . time."

With every word her temperature seemed to rise another degree. Her senses seemed to understand that he was calling to them, like a charmer coaxing a snake from a basket, and it was true . . . she couldn't breathe for wanting him.

How in God's name did he know exactly what he did to her?

More importantly, what on earth did he mean by "every imaginable position"?

"There are many positions?" was what she finally said, her voice a whisper.

"Yes." A curt answer.

She was speechless.

"Is that what you wanted me to say, Tansy? Is that the sort of thing you want to know about lovemaking?"

Really, he was a relentlessly cruel bastard, and yet she'd asked for it and he'd quite turned the tables on her. It really was impossible to toy with the man. She could not maneuver him in any of the usual ways.

And then she had a suspicion, which blossomed into a realization, when she looked at his hands. They had curled, involuntarily, and his knuckles were white. As though he was digging his nails into his palms to maintain control.

He was able to describe it in such detail, but he was describing how it felt for him, too.

Not in general.

With her.

With *her*.

And this seemed immense.

Mainly because she thought it might even

frighten him. The man with a bayonet scar across his abdomen who suffered over a life he couldn't save while unthinkingly nearly sacrificing his own.

"Thank you for that. It was quite edifying." Her voice was frayed, as though she'd been locked in a heated room. Which, metaphorically speaking, she was. "And *I* . . . well, I suspect that not every woman will turn your blood into lava, or haunt your every waking thought, or make you tremble when you kiss her, or lose your mind and do things you never dreamed you'd do. Like track down just the right hothouse so you could send her a bundle of wildflowers native to a very specific region. When you make rather a point of never giving gifts to women."

He went utterly motionless. Like an animal caught by a predator in a clearing.

Something like reluctant admiration flickered across his face. It was chased by something else, too: fear, or hurt, there and gone. She almost reflexively reached out to touch him, to apologize . . . for what? For seeing through him? For angering him? For subjecting him to something new?

She didn't want him to ever feel more hurt. She never wanted this brave man to be afraid of anything.

It wasn't her *fault*. It wasn't something she'd done to him deliberately, after all.

Well, not entirely.

His voice was steady. "I can assure you, some

women never know that kind of pleasure. Take a survey of your friends. You'll doubtless discover most of the married ones are mulling their household budgets whilst their husbands busy themselves on top with the act of getting an heir. And young spoiled heirs never need to learn how to pleasure a woman."

This did make her instantly flush scarlet. "You're awful."

"You don't know the half of it, I'm afraid. I'm no hero, Tansy."

She suspected she knew at least part of it. She suspected he was at least partially wrong. He was allegedly an inveterate rogue, and she'd witnessed nothing to dispel the notion. She thought of a certain sloe-eyed brunette widow and exchanged glances, and about what Mrs. deWitt had said.

It ought to matter to her more than it did.

And that was the danger of kisses, and seeing stars on a balcony at night. Her senses suddenly seemed to have dominion over her brain.

"We can limit our conversation to the weather, if you prefer," he said, when it seemed she would say nothing. "Wouldn't that be more sensible?"

"It's hot today," she said instantly.

He smiled, a slow, delighted smile. Then shook his head.

Damnation, but she liked him.

The tension loosened.

"I meant every word I said the other night. Do not play roulette with me, Tansy." He said this gently, almost apologetically. "It will be all. Or it will be nothing."

She backed away two steps. Back into the sunlight, inadvertently.

And he stood and watched her. "Like watching an angel return to Heaven."

She snorted at that. "Now *that* was blarney."

He grinned.

"Comfort yourself with the knowledge that it's all in your hands. But then, I know that's precisely where you like men to be."

He reached for his hat, lying next to him on the settee, and settled it on his head.

"And enjoy your picnic."

# Chapter 22

∽

"Has anyone ever told you that your eyes are the most singular color?"

They were walking along, side by side, across parklands that seemed never to end. Green as far as the eye could see. Once, when she was a little girl, she'd thought Heaven might look like this, but now she hoped it didn't. It was rather dull, all told. A bit safe.

And the fact that it seemed endless suddenly made her nervous. A bit like a marriage. The endless part. The "until death parts us" part.

She was somehow suddenly less certain about the safe part with regards to marriage.

"Not in so many words, no."

"They are. And when you smile . . . they're like stars."

Stars.

Seeing stars.

He *would* have to say stars.

Would Lord Stanhope make her see stars? Could he? She glanced down at his hands surreptitiously. Beautifully groomed hands. Had he ever hammered a nail with them? Defended anyone with a weapon? Had they ever trembled when he touched a woman? Did he listen to a woman's breathing in order to ascertain the kind of pleasure he could give her, and . . .

He interpreted her silence and her sudden pink color as bashfulness. "I do apologize, Miss Danforth. I hope you don't think I'm being too forward."

"Not at all. How could I object to such a thoughtful observation?"

She slid a sidelong look at the well-made young man. No lines at the corners of his eyes from squinting down a rifle or riding into the sun. His laugh was surprisingly hearty, and just a trifle irritating. Perhaps because it seemed too easily won, which seemed a very unfair thing to think. He laughed a good deal, too. Life was good to him; why shouldn't he laugh?

He'd shown himself to have a rather literal sense of humor. Better than none, she supposed. But it had thus far been difficult for her to strike a spark from it when he was so very amiable. It was only in walking and talking with him that she realized how the past few years had shaped her, carving out unexpected nooks and crevices in her character. Surprisingly, she wasn't as easy to navigate now. She wasn't as easy to persuade.

One really only discovers one's true self in contrast to other people, she realized.

Which is the only way one discovers one's true needs.

She was tempted to ask Lord Stanhope if he had any scars that told the story of his life.

Scars. Which, coincidentally, rhymed with "stars."

She drew in a sharp breath, remembering how she'd drawn a finger along the hard torso of a man, tracing a bit of his history, an event carved into his soul, while his fingers combed through her hair almost reverently, as though it was made of rare silk.

*Have you ever put yourself in harm's way for another person without thought for your own safety, Lord Stanhope?* She was tempted to ask him.

"Where did you go, just then, Miss Danforth?"

Blast. Lord Stanhope might be a bit tedious, but he was observant.

Which she supposed spoke well of him.

*And* he was going to be a duke.

The word definitely still held its glamour. Fanning out from it was a world of possibility beyond this stretch of banal, tamed greenery.

"I was imagining my eyes as stars. Such a lovely thing to say."

"You must hear that sort of thing all the time."

She smiled enigmatically. "Not as prettily, I assure you."

"Speaking of pretty, I have had the good fortune of purchasing a very fine gray mare. I think you and she would be beautifully matched."

He was matching her to a horse?

Was he about to *give* her a horse?

God help her, she wouldn't mind having her own horse here in Sussex.

Was he looking for a *wife* who would match this horse? This was a bit more troubling.

"Would you care to go riding some morning very soon?" he asked.

"I would love to, thank you. I enjoy it very much."

She peered over her shoulder. In the distance, Genevieve had kicked off her slippers and appeared to be reading to her husband, who had removed his hat and was playing, idly, with the ends of a long ribbon that circled her dress just below her breasts. Catching it, releasing it, as the breeze fluttered it.

She smiled, but felt a sharp stab of envy. Genevieve was married and she was in love with a man many people probably considered unknowable.

Then again, one might describe Ian Eversea in just that way, too.

But he possessed the key to her senses. He was waging a campaign to have her that included no promises and no future. He was likely, as the duke had implied, broken in a way.

And as she smiled up at the future Duke of de Neauville, she wondered why it didn't matter as much as it should.

ONCE AT HOME again, she sorted through the bouquets sent to her—five, this time!

She opened her mouth to ask the footmen to take a few of them down to the churchyard so the Ladies of the Society to Protect the Sussex Poor could distribute the bouquets again over naked graves.

But then she paused. And she thought about Olivia and Lyon Redmond and the loss of him, and she knew, suddenly, that the Olivia she now saw wasn't the Olivia she'd been before he'd disappeared.

And that was what Ian had been trying to tell her. Ian loved his sister, and Ian knew what "gone" felt like and he'd trusted her with that information because he'd known she would understand. And oh, how she did.

She carefully removed all of the cards from the bouquets.

"Would you please tell Olivia Eversea that all of these have come for her?"

The footman nodded as if this were an ordinary request.

She made her way up the marble staircase, thoughtfully.

And then she settled in at the little writing desk and retrieved her list of requirements, which was beginning to look a trifle worn and dirty at the edges from all the handling it had endured. Then again, she'd learned a good deal in a short amount of time.

On the surface of things, Lord Stanhope seemed to meet many of the requirements.

Funny how each day revealed a few more that seemed absolutely critical.

But the quill called to her, so she picked it up, and twiddled it between her fingers, before carefully adding two new, quite essential points.

*Must have a few interesting scars.*

*Makes me feel more alive than anyone ever before has.*

And it was this last, above all, that was significant. She'd valued very little in the past year, but Ian Eversea had both brought her down to earth abruptly as well as shown her the stars.

On the surface of things what she was about to do couldn't be more reckless. It was hardly the act of someone who had both feet planted firmly on the ground.

But it was one of the more reasoned decisions she'd made in a very long time.

# Chapter 23

※

IAN DIPPED IN AND out of sleep like a bit of flotsam tossed on a shallow stream.

She should not come to him.

He *prayed* she wouldn't come.

He woke again. Lay there in the silent dark. And felt like a bastard. An utterly worthless, lustful bastard. Who wanted what he wanted and had applied every trick of persuasion to get it.

The night stretched on.

And now he feared she wouldn't come.

He hadn't any right to do that to her. To use her own sensuality as a weapon to seduce, to persuade. To instill doubt in her future when he did, truly did, want her to be happy and to have what she wanted.

Surely he wished her a lifetime of happiness more than he wanted to make love to her.

He wasn't certain.

But if he could have one night with her. Just one night. He would have a lifetime to repent his methods. From across the sea, of course.

And the irony was that this could very possibly be the duke's revenge. To want beyond reason the one woman he shouldn't, and couldn't, and might never, have.

And as one of the longest nights he'd experienced since the war inched glacially by and she didn't come, the heaviness of disappointment finally carried him off to sleep like a stone hurled into the deep.

Sometime later—it was still dark—he awoke again and stirred. He tilted his head to the side; the wick of his lantern had burned low.

He turned his head again toward the window and froze.

She was sitting on the foot of his bed.

They stared at each other a good long time in silence.

"Am I dreaming?" he asked.

An eternity, which was likely only a few seconds, passed before she spoke.

"No." In a whisper. Hesitant. A trifle fearful. A trifle amazed.

She was there.

Wordlessly, very slowly, he pushed the blankets away from his body. He moved to her, silently. And without preamble reached for her night rail and slowly lifted it off over her head.

Her arms went up, assisting him, fell again.

She sat nude before him, her heart beating so loud the blood whooshed in her ears.

And he eased her backward, slowly, to the bed.

Her arms went around his neck. And oh, the glory of his skin touching hers. Of the heat and strength and weight of his body. She clung to him, savored the chafe of her nipples against the coarse hair scattered over his chest. He buried his face in her throat and sighed, placed a soft, hot kiss beneath her ear, and she felt herself begin to melt, to surrender utterly. And then he moved his lips to the delicate bones at the base of it, and she arched back and threaded her fingers through his incongruously soft, fine hair. She found his ears and traced them, trailed her fingers over the immense hard curve of his shoulder. Rejoicing in the fact that there was so much of him to discover.

And a sort of wildness overcame the two of them, as if nudity had turned them into the first man and woman and sex was their very first discovery.

There was to be no narration, no finesse, no coddling. He covered her as if she were a long-time lover, and she surrendered, as if in a dream, not knowing where it would lead, only that she would go wherever he wanted to take her. And in the dark silence it only seemed right, to make sense.

He found her lips, and the kiss was savage and hungry and deep, almost punishing, as if he'd waited a lifetime for this very kiss, as if she'd deprived him of the very thing he needed to survive. She cupped the back of his head with her hands and yielded to the heady dark sweetness of his mouth, stroked his hair, to soothe, to gentle him, and the kiss eased into something more languorous, more penetrating, more profound. Somehow she felt it everywhere in her body, stealing into her veins like opium. Slow, slow. As if in slowing it they could make time itself their slave, and it would stop for as long as they wanted this moment to last.

He gently pulled his mouth away and rested his forehead against hers. His breath rushed out hot and hoarse. She felt the rise and fall of shoulders.

"How I've wanted you." Half whisper, half groan, against her mouth.

He slid his lips down along the arch of her throat, lower, lower, until his mouth found her nipple and circled it hard, with a sinewy tongue.

She gasped and arched, and he did it again, then closed his mouth over it and sucked.

*"Oh, God, Ian."* A ragged whisper.

He did it again, moving to her other breast, and then his mouth went traveling, down, down, down the seam that divided her ribs, his lips and tongue and breath stopping just long enough to set every cell in its path on fire.

He was shockingly skilled. Every bit of the swift, sensual assault was deliberate, new, devastating. With his tongue, his fingertips, the slide of his palm, sensation built upon sensation, buffeting her, ensnaring her, turning her into a creature whose only purpose was to accept pleasure. She writhed beneath him, moaning softly.

He dipped his tongue into her navel, slid his hands over the soft curve of her belly, lifted her up and then parted her thighs with his hands and touched his tongue to the silky hot wetness between her legs.

She jerked at the sensation; a glorious shock.

But he didn't stop. His fingers played lightly, lightly, on the delicate skin inside her thighs as his tongue delved and stroked and circled, quickly and lightly, then slowly and hard.

She whimpered. Dear God, it was like no pleasure she'd ever before imagined. She rocked her hips in time to the thrusts of his tongue. And she could feel herself hurtling headlong into the unknown. Her words came in raw desperate sobbing shreds.

"I can't bear it . . . oh please . . . I need . . ."

She shattered in a hoarse cry, bowing upward from the force of it, and she nearly blacked out as her body bucked in the throes of it.

He raised himself over her with his arms, and with one hand guided his cock into her.

The shock of him filling her threw her head back on a gasp. He pulled her thigh up around his waist and thrust again, slowly. He dipped to kiss her, gently; he licked her nipple as he thrust and dove, almost languidly.

He withdrew. And then filled her again. The rhythm built, and with it that indefinable insistent, delicious pressure, beginning on the periphery of her senses. And with each thrust it gathered, banking, into something so almost unendurably blissful she knew it could only be released in a scream.

And then their bodies collided hard as his hips drove his cock swiftly, deeply, into her, the rhythm of his thrusts swift and pounding, his hoarse breathing and muttered oaths and her own soft cries mingling as she dug into his shoulders with her nails and their bodies raced toward release.

She threw her head back. "Please, Ian . . . please . . . I'm . . ."

He went rigid over her, and she heard his ragged cry of something almost like triumph as his release rocked his body.

HE LOWERED HIMSELF carefully. Rolled to the side of her, then collected her in the crook of his arm. Her skin, its silkiness, undid him.

"You are beautiful," he murmured.

"A compliment," she murmured. "Wonders never do cease."

He breathed into the sweetness of her hair. He pushed the silky mass of it aside and kissed her neck, and she sighed. He wrapped his arms around her body, and for a time they lay quietly. He savored the rise and fall, rise and fall, of her rib cage beneath his hands. They said not a word.

Inevitably, his hands began to wander. A leisurely journey, sliding over the soft mound of her belly, then delicately up her rib cage to her breasts. He cupped them in his hands and feathered strokes over them. Again, and again. Like a man fanning flames. Reveling in the satiny texture of her skin. Reveling in the tension he felt in her spine as desire tightened her muscles, shortened her breath, then made tatters of it. Reveling in the way she arched like a cat into his hands. She was devastatingly sensual and abandoned; she took to receiving pleasure with the instinct of a beautiful animal, and it only made him want to give her more and more and still more, and to take her every way he could.

And soon she was rippling beneath his touch, her buttocks circling hard against his hard cock. He slid his hand down over her spine and slipped it between her thighs, and his fingers slid into her silky wetness. She groaned with the pleasure of it and parted her thighs a little more, begging for more.

His hunger for her seemed fathomless. The more he took, the more he wanted.

He nipped the back of her neck and moved gently away from her, tipping her onto her stomach.

He dragged his palms down her back, then raised her hips, and unquestioningly she moved with him, trusting. He pressed a kiss at the sweet dip of skin at the base of her spine and slid his hands over her arse. He nipped one cheek gently, as if it were a peach.

And then he rose up and slid his cock between her legs, teasing her, teasing himself.

"You feel . . . so good, Tansy."

She moaned softly, and he could feel her flesh throb against him.

He did it again, sliding slowly, gently. Another tease.

She jerked from the pleasure, her fingers curling into the counterpane.

"Ian, I will *die* if you don't . . . please . . . more . . . *faster . . .*"

And then he slid into her, quickly and deeply, and he could feel her gasp, and tense. And then he withdrew, slowly, so slowly, allowing her to feel every inch of him.

She moaned, and hissed in a breath, and swore something softly.

"Beg me, Tansy," he whispered.

"*Please*, Ian. Please. *Faster*, please."

He drove himself into her, pulling her hips up hard against him, burying himself to the hilt, then sliding slowly from her.

"Please . . ." She rocked her hips against him. Nearly sobbing from the pleasure, from the sensual torture. "I'm so *close* . . ."

He did it again. Slowly. A sensual sadist.

And again.

And then he could no longer tease her, because desire had him in its teeth now. He was rigid and shaking and perspiring from the effort of control.

And so he freed them both.

He drove into her, swiftly, his hips rocking hard as he pulled her hips up against him, burying himself deeply in her faster and faster still, a relentless pounding, a mad, greedy hunger.

"Oh God . . . Oh God . . ."

She screamed her release into the counterpane, thumping it with her fists as he drove himself toward his. His release ripped him from his body, nearly blacked his consciousness. He heard his own guttural cry as if from another planet. He thought he may have said her name.

"If I had known . . ." she whispered, tangling her fingers in the fine hair scattered over his chest. Then trailing her fingers toward the hollow of his armpit. He had one arm thrown over his head.

"If you had known . . . ?" he prompted softly.

Her cheek was against his chest, and she could feel the steady thump, thump, thump of his heart beneath her cheek. An oddly precious, intimate sound. And there was the scar, the reminder that he was human and vulnerable and someone had nearly killed him.

She tensed at this, and tightened her grip a little, pulling a few of his hairs.

"Ow," he said softly.

"Sorry."

"Finish your sentence."

"How good this was . . ."

"You might have skipped being a well-bred heiress and gone straight onto being a scarlet woman?"

"Then again, perhaps not. I have it on good authority that not every man is as good at this sort of thing."

"A lot of men just climb on top and go at it."

"What a waste of so many marvelous body parts."

He laughed softly.

She kissed him on his chest. On his *beautiful torso*.

"That feels good," he murmured. Encouraging.

She drew her tongue down the seam that divided his ribs, and let her hands trail after, remembering how he'd done it to her, and how it had lit her every cell on fire.

He stirred and sighed, his fingers stroking through her hair.

"That's good," he confirmed on a murmur. "Don't stop."

She continued her progress to his flat stomach, stroking over it with delicate fingers. Lingering. Teasing. Watching, as he did, for the tension of his muscles, for the change in his breathing, in order to know exactly how to pleasure him.

She dipped her tongue into his navel, tasted salt.

His breathing was beginning to come short. His cock stirred and leaped a little as it grew harder.

And so she moved her mouth there, and drew her tongue hard and slowly down along it.

"*Christ . . .*" and then he swore something considerably more filthy than that.

She circled the head of it with her tongue and drew his cock into her mouth. And sucked.

He moaned softly, and his hands went down to tangle in her hair.

And the power to give him pleasure stirred again the desire in her. It seemed fathomless. Insatiable.

"Again?" she teased.

"And again and again," he ordered.

And so she did.

And as his cock thickened, dragging her lips and mouth and tongue over it, now swiftly, now slowly, she reveled in watching him shift restlessly, his thighs falling open, his body bowing upward, his hands curling into the counterpane, his breath short and harsh. His head thrashed back and he swallowed; the pleasure seemed well nigh unendurable, and it banked her own pleasure.

"Tansy . . . I want you to ride me."

She straddled his body, flinging her heavy mass of hair over her shoulder wantonly, and gazed down at him. The cords of his neck taut, his chest was burnished by firelight, his eyes burning.

Together they guided him into her.

He bracketed her hips with his hands and urged her to move her body up and then down again, until she understood the rhythm. And at first she moved to watch his eyes darken, to hear him beg her hoarsely with her name. And then she moved to please herself, as she had no choice: instinct drove her blindly toward it.

They rocked together until the two of them, one right after the other, saw shooting stars.

JUST AS THE light was going pearly and gray in the sky, and she knew she should return to her room, Tansy sighed and moved out of his arms. She reached for her night rail and drew it on over her head.

She sat for a moment, watching him, Ian's arms crossed behind his head, his hair tousled, his eyes drowsy and warm, a faint smile playing on his lips as he gazed back at her.

Her heart lurched.

What if . . . what if she woke up every day of her life to this view? Was it really so unthinkable? Surely no man could remain an alleged rogue for the entirety of his life? Surely Ian wouldn't mind waking up just like this, either?

But there was something on the periphery of her awareness, some little warning voice. It sounded, unsurprisingly, like the Duke of Falconbridge's. She said nothing.

She just smiled at him.

His smile grew wider, and a little more wicked, and her heart squeezed. She could feel herself blushing. Despite being clothed, and despite every delightfully wicked thing she'd done last night.

And at last Ian rolled over and sat up on the edge of the bed with a little grunt. He straightened to standing somewhat gingerly.

"It goes a bit tight if I don't stretch every morning," he said apologetically, gesturing to that scar.

She watched him arch his back and thrust up his

arms and bend backward, as he fought a grimace, and she felt her muscles tense along with him.

Not a God, then.

Or a pagan roaring to greet the day.

Just a beautiful, wounded man.

# Chapter 24

❧

Tansy clapped a hand down on her bonnet as Stanhope's high flyer careened around a bend in the road at reckless speeds. He was a brilliant driver and the horses were beautiful, copper colored and shining like new pennies, and the sun struck sparks off their haunches and manes.

"You're a brilliant driver!"

"Beg pardon?"

It was impossible to speak over the thunder of their hooves.

"YOU'RE A BRILLIANT DRIVER!"

"YOU LIKE MY HIGH FLYER?" he guessed.

She gave up. "Yes!"

He beamed at her, certain of their accord.

But when they stopped, and the horses tossed their heads and shifted restlessly in their harnesses, and the moment was no longer distractingly terrifying, and they were alone, certain dullness settled into her chest.

He was a relentlessly cheerful presence, talked only of himself but so good-naturedly that she indulged him. He certainly laughed a good deal. Something about his laugh made her feel more alone than if she were standing on a high cliff at the end of the world, shouting her name into the void to hear it echo back at her.

In all likelihood he knew he'd been born fascinating, by default, because he was going to be a duke when his father died, and he considered the ceaseless talk of himself a bit of beneficence on his part.

But better a cheerful sort than a surly sort, she supposed.

He helped her down and beamed with the pleasure of being able to do that for her, and then offered his arm to escort her back to the house.

As she moved, she could feel the night before in the stiffness of her legs. And as Stanhope led her back toward the house, she surreptitiously brushed the back of her hand against her chafed and still kiss-swollen lips, and heat rushed over her skin, just like that. In the mirror this morning she had looked alarmingly, intriguingly, thoroughly wanton, her hair in wild disarray, her eyes brilliant, her cheeks flushed; on her breast was the mark of a vigorous, lingering kiss, and remembering it now made her knees sag a little.

She'd resented the need to dress and bathe so soon, in time for Stanhope to take her out in his high flyer; she wanted to lie still, while the feel of Ian's hands and the warmth and scent of his body still lingered on her skin. Lie still and savor it until it faded like the very last note in a symphony. Lie still and try to decide what it meant to her.

And now last night had seemed real, and this jarringly cheerful, reckless outing with an heir seemed like a dream.

"I must say, Miss Danforth, I may always cherish the letter I received from Captain Eversea. I may even have it framed."

They would have that in common, she thought. They both wanted to frame missives from Captain Eversea.

"You received mail from Captain Eversea? Which Captain Eversea?"

"The one who will be embarking upon an ocean voyage soon? Within the month, I believe. Captain *Ian* Eversea."

Shock momentarily destroyed her ability to speak.

"An . . . ocean voyage?" She choked on the words. Suddenly, the ribbons of her bonnet seemed too tight.

"Oh, yes, 'round the world he's going! The sort of voyage to rival Miles Redmond's travels, from the sounds of things. He could very well be gone for *years*. With luck, a cannibal won't eat him. He looks a bit stringy to me, ha ha! Not an ounce of fat on the man."

Tansy couldn't feel her hands or feet. "Years?" she said faintly.

"One can't experience Africa and China and

India and the like in less time than that," he said knowledgeably. "So certainly, years."

"Wh-What did he say in the letter?"

Her teeth were chattering as though someone had dropped an icicle down the back of her dress.

"He suggested I might want to hurry to Sussex to meet the 'American Paragon,' as queues to meet you were long and rivals were shooting each other with arrows and the like over you. He's not given to gushing. So I knew you must be special, indeed. The man is an excellent judge of things, from horseflesh to shooting to women."

The world seemed to tilt on its axis. She stumbled.

Lord Stanhope flexed his arm and quite capably kept her from falling.

"Slippers are hardly practical for walking," he said fondly.

A faint ringing started up in her ears. Her voice sounded to her as if it was coming from a far, far off land. Africa or China, even.

"He . . . *summoned* you to Sussex? For me?"

Stanhope looked a bit worried now. "Perhaps I shouldn't have said anything at all to you. It's just that it seemed like a wonderful stroke of good fortune, and I felt as though gratitude were in order, since he did encourage me to come."

"He . . . summoned you to Sussex to meet *me*?"

She sounded like a demented parrot. She didn't care. The shock was gruesome.

"I do want to thank him, though, for aren't we having a wonderful time? I don't think he'd object overmuch."

"A wonderful time," she repeated, faintly, after a moment, like a broken cuckoo clock.

HE'D HAMMERED HIS final nail into the vicarage roof today, and after they all stood back, hands on hips, and admired their handiwork, he'd taken the crew of workmen along with Adam down to the pub to congratulate and celebrate with them.

He was surprised to see a young man named James who worked in the Eversea stables competently waiting tables.

"Captain Eversea, what can I bring you?"

"James! What a pleasant surprise to see you here. Helping out while Polly's ankle heals?"

"Aye, and it was your Miss Danforth we have to thank for it, too."

His heart stopped. He fought to keep his eyes from shifting guiltily.

"Er . . . *my* Miss Danforth?"

"The Miss Danforth who lives with the Everseas," he said, smiling. "The one who won the Sussex marksmanship cup."

"Oh, that Miss Danforth. Yes. How kind of her."

For now, Polly remained behind the bar, the better to flirt with all the customers at once. Ned, Ian decided, was going to have his hands full with her suitors in no time.

As one by one all the vicarage workmen, Seamus and Henry and Adam included, departed the Pig & Thistle for other obligations and destinations, Ian lingered. He called for another ale and nursed it more slowly than he normally would.

As he'd watched her slip out the door of his room this morning, he'd had to stifle a protest. He'd wanted nothing more than to pull her back, curl his arm around her, fold her into his body and lay there quietly on the bed, tracking the hour of the day only by the length of the sunbeam through the slit in the curtains and the color of the shadows in the room. And they would watch the sun go higher and then slowly sink again, while they made love, and slept, and made love, and slept, and talked and laughed and made love and slept.

Possibly with her hand clasped in his.

The world seemed . . . roomier . . . and kinder and more colorful and funnier today. He wasn't unfamiliar with the effects of excellent sex on a man's temper. This was like that, and yet different somehow. He felt fundamentally altered. As if he'd been sitting in a dark room for ages, and someone had casually strolled in and lit a lamp.

The only thing that would make the day even better, he thought, was if she were sitting across from him right now.

An alarming thought.

*Your Miss Danforth.*

My. Mine. He was beginning to understand the

appeal of that preposition with regards to women, and why Colin and Chase brandished it as if it were a medal they'd each earned.

And as the sun sank lower, he was aware that he was postponing returning home because he felt almost . . . shy. He recoiled from the word. *Surely* not. Very well, then: he did feel uncertain. And he'd been so very certain about everything not very long ago. There was no longer any reason for him to remain in Sussex, and it was time to return to London to complete preparations for his voyage.

And he just didn't know what would happen next. For there *would* be a "next," the awkward, fraught time between now and the moment his ship left shore.

All he knew for certain was that he wanted to see her.

And he wondered what he would read in her face when he did. Welcome? Desire? A firm and yet closed resolve to never be alone with him again, as a result of a sudden onset of regrettable sense? Regret? Would they make love again?

The bands of muscle across his stomach tightened at the thought. Of *course* it wasn't wise. But the laws of physics had been upended for him; the harder he pulled away from the notion of making love to her, the deeper and more desperate the need for her seemed.

He got up abruptly and went home.

Fittingly enough, he arrived in that neither-day-nor-night in-between hour.

His heart picked up speed the closer he came to his chamber. Once inside, he stared at the now neatly made bed.

And then he inhaled deeply, exhaled at length, and almost tenderly lifted the curtain away from the window. As if he were pushing her hair away from her face in order to kiss her.

Twilight was purpling the horizon.

She was standing on her balcony, holding a perfectly rolled cigarette and trying, in vain, to light it.

He frowned.

He would warrant she'd never actually lit a cigarette in her entire life. Rolled, certainly.

"You don't smoke," he called softly.

She froze. But she didn't turn toward him. It was a moment before she spoke.

"How would you know?"

She said it so bitterly, it shocked him.

She refused to meet his eyes. But her hands were trembling now, he saw, and she nearly dropped the cigarette.

Bloody hell. Something was terribly wrong.

He ducked back into his window, and then went through the door of her room out onto her balcony.

"May I?" he said gently.

She shrugged almost violently with one shoulder.

He took the cigarette from between her fingers.

He lit it with a flint.

A strikingly pungent smoke curled out of it, and he coughed. Her father's blend.

And she coughed.

She didn't attempt to smoke it. He handed it back to her, and she just gripped it between her fingers as if it were a spear she'd like to jab into him.

And not once did she look at him directly or say a word to him. She seemed as remote and cold as a locked room.

And then she looked up reflexively at the stars, as if seeking comfort and home, and his heart broke just a very little. Or kicked. It was hard to know for certain, because the pain was sweet.

Little things she did would always break his heart open, he felt. Always. His heart would forever be like a pond frozen over in winter cracking with the thaw.

"When were you going to tell me?" she said finally. Sounding weary.

"Tell you . . . how to light a cigarette?"

"That you're leaving. For good, essentially. More or less. In a fortnight, isn't it? Or were you just going to disappear, and hope that I considered you a figment of my imagination? A sort of fever dream?"

Oh. Hell.

"Ah. I thought you knew I was leaving."

"No." She said it flatly.

"Yes. I'm sailing soon, Tansy." He said it gently. "I did say I would be off around the world."

"You did say." She said it with faint mockery. "You just didn't say *when*."

Silence.

The ash was lengthening at the tip of the cigarette, heading for her fingertips.

"Are you going to smoke that, or . . ."

She suddenly tamped the cigarette out with great violence and whirled on him.

"And you wrote to Stanhope to tell him to hie his way here to Sussex to see me. Solving the problem of me, weren't you? Neatly disposing of me. Wave the shiny heir in front of Miss Danforth's eyes to distract her from her ridiculous *tendre* for *you*. Keep her out of the way of Landsdowne. Because she's just that shallow and just that fickle and anyone and *anything* can distract her, and here, have yourself an heiress, Stanhope, so she doesn't get in the way of anyone I actually *care* about."

In the force of her fury and hurt, he found himself becoming very, very calm, and very, very clear. It was what made him a good soldier, and why he never seemed able to stop being one.

"I of course didn't say that in so many words. And you know it isn't how I feel."

His calm seemed to make her angrier.

"Do I? How *do* you feel, then, Ian?"

He was silent. He couldn't choose from any of the words he knew, because none of them were sufficient. Of course, a single word would do the trick. But he wasn't going to say that to her now. Because he was about to lose her, and he didn't think she would believe him, and he would be gone anyway, and what good would it serve either of them?

She snorted softly when he stood there and said nothing.

"What did you do to the Duke of Falconbridge?" Her voice was bitter. "Because I know it was something. He doesn't like you."

Ah. So her goal this evening was to find as many ways to hurt him as possible.

"Did he say as much?" Not surprising, really. But it seemed unlike the circumspect duke to state it baldly.

"He implied, and I'm not as stupid as all that, Ian. Something about 'climbing' seems to come up rather a lot with regards to you. And I doubt it means anything good."

Her bitterness was knife-edged.

He didn't have the right to be angry. And so he found himself going calmer and calmer. The eye of the hurricane around them.

"What did I do to the duke?" he said musingly. "Very well. Since I have never lied to you, Tansy, and since you asked, here is what I did to the duke: I attempted to seduce his fiancée. The woman he was to marry before he met my sister. She was, in fact, quite willing. We had, in fact, been planning to tryst for some time; I climbed a tree to her chamber window, where he was lying in wait in the dark in her bedroom, unbeknownst to her. I had just climbed into bed with her, and I hadn't yet touched her when he . . . when he . . . suffice it to say he ushered me out of the window at gunpoint. Naked."

He'd delivered the words baldly, unleavened with compassion, tenderness, or apology. She *had* asked. It had happened precisely that way.

Let her do with the truth what she would.

She now knew more about him than most of the people he'd known his entire life.

Tansy had gone utterly silent, listening.

Utterly still.

He couldn't even sense her breathing.

He saw the curtains rise a little at her window, which were open just an inch.

Windows seemed to play an inordinate role in his fate.

"You . . . *knew* she was his fiancée?"

Her voice sounded scraped raw. As if she could scarcely speak in the wake of that confession. She was aghast.

"Yes."

More glacial, ominous silence.

"Why? Why did you do it?"

And suddenly the fury broke through.

"Because she was beautiful. Because she wanted me. Because I wanted her. Is that what you want me to say, Tansy? Because the duke was rumored to be a dangerous man, and I liked the idea of risk. Shall I quote *you* on the subject of risk, Miss Danforth? Shall I remind you that you climbed in my window, and that you allowed me to lay you back on my bed, and allowed me to lift your night rail from your body, that you slid your hands into my shirt, that you—"

She'd jerked away from him as if he'd thrust a torch into her face.

"*Stop* it. Don't you know, Ian . . . the duke is a *person*. He'd lost his child. He'd lost his wife—"

"Don't you know he was rumored to have *killed* his wife? The rumor didn't arise from nowhere. No one is suspected of that unless people have reason to wonder. He's no saint, Tansy."

"What utter shite, and you know it! Of course he's no saint! Who *is*? Certainly not you. And it's hardly an excuse, and you know that, too. But he'd hoped to marry again and rebuild his life. And you *took* that from him. No wonder he thinks you're *broken*. You took it because you *could*. You took it simply because you wanted it."

Broken? He supposed he was.

He gave a short, dark laugh.

"It wasn't quite as simple as all that, Tansy. Nothing ever is. And if you take a deep breath and think it over, you'll know I'm right. You knew who I was before you came to me. I have *never* lied to you. Never. And I have never promised a thing."

But she wasn't in the mood to listen. She was in a mood to hate him, and she needed the hate to distance herself from him. Like a boat she could leap into and push away from a dock. As if that would make any of this less painful.

"You always do get what you want, don't you, Ian? You wanted me, and you in all likelihood did exactly what needed to be done to *have* me. Was it the risk that made me so appealing? Or did you want to shame the duke again?"

He was silent. Long enough for her words to reverberate, long enough to allow her to hear what she'd just said, and to shame her just a little. She knew they weren't true. She was just flinging shards of words. She hoped a few of them struck him. She wanted to hurt him.

She succeeded.

But he knew better than she did how to withstand pain.

"I never *wanted* to shame anyone," he said quietly.

She was breathing quickly now. She gave her head a rough shake.

"Look me in the eye and tell me you're proud of everything you've done, Tansy. Look me in the eye and tell me you thought about the hearts you might be stealing or breaking with flattery and flirtation. Look me in the eye and tell me that you carefully thought through the consequences of every one of your actions. Particularly the actions of last night."

She didn't turn to him. "Yes, damn you," she said brokenly. Sounding furious. "I thought last night through. Did you?"

"Yes," he said tersely.

The break in her voice nearly undid him.

They regarded each other unblinkingly, from a distance of just a few feet. There might as well have been an ocean between them.

"Tansy." He tentatively stretched out a hand. He wanted desperately to gather her to him.

"Please don't touch me."

His hand dropped.

"You always do get what you want, don't you, Ian? You wanted me, and you in all likelihood did exactly what needed to be done to *have* me. It's all about the *getting* of someone, isn't it? God forbid you should *give*." He couldn't believe she thought any of these things were true. She just wanted to lash out.

He waited again, and though he was certain nothing he said would matter at this point, he chose his words carefully, succinctly. So perhaps she would remember them later, when her anger had ebbed.

"I will tell you a few things that I know to be true. I wanted you, Tansy. I want you now. I will want you until the day I die. I never promised or implied a thing other than that. You wanted me, too. The duke will never allow me to marry you. And I am leaving."

He could feel her take each word as a blow. And he'd delivered them that way. Irrefutable facts, all incompatible with each other.

She stood, utterly motionless, her face peculiarly set, and yet peculiarly crumpled, as if she was made of melting wax.

"And *you* . . . are probably going to marry a future duke. Take comfort in that, Miss Danforth. And you're welcome for that, by the way."

He could do bitterness well, too.

She jerked her head away from him. Stared off toward America, or Lilymont, or someplace that felt like home. Someplace that wasn't him.

And if he wasn't broken before he set foot on the balcony, he felt broken now as he left.

# Chapter 25

✲

As usual, it didn't take long for word in Sussex to spread: Miss Titania Danforth was being courted quite determinedly by Lord Stanhope, and wagers were being made over how long it would take him to make her his bride. If the way he drove his high flyer was any indication of his courtship style, those that had "before the month was out" stood to win.

It was generally understood that the competition, which was considered legion, didn't stand a chance, and that sending flowers to her and the like was a quixotic exercise, and yet they continued to straggle in, for one just never knew. It was the same philosophy the ton at large took to Olivia Eversea. It was like an investment. Best to keep a hand in. The winds of fate were fickle.

So flowers still abounded in the Eversea house.

Which meant the Everseas saved a good deal of money on decorations for the Grand Ball.

TANSY STOOD WITH Annie in front of her wardrobe and scrutinized her row of dresses as though

Tansy was queen and she was choosing her ladies-in-waiting.

The abigail's face was radiant and abstracted. And at last she turned to Tansy and blurted, "Oh, there's something I just must tell you, Miss Danforth. We're to be wed in a week! My James and I!"

"Oh, Annie! That's wonderful, wonderful news!"

She turned and gave the abigail a swift little hug, which made both of them blush.

"It has made all the difference, the money from waiting tables at the Pig & Thistle. Ned Hawthorne thinks James is ever so good with the customers. We cannot thank you enough for recommending him."

"So lovely to hear. I hear 'Titania' makes a fine second name for girl babies," she teased.

Annie blushed scarlet at this, and she seemed momentarily speechless with pleasure.

"Well, we should dress you tonight as if you're already a duchess, Miss Danforth," she finally said.

Tansy went still.

But then, naturally, gossip had entered the bloodstream of the Eversea household, and of course the servants would know about Stanhope's attentions.

She immediately squared her shoulders, as if the courtship was a lead-lined cloak.

She'd scarcely made an effort to charm anyone in the last fortnight or so, but it wasn't as though Stanhope or anyone else had noticed. He chattered happily when they went out walking, or drove recklessly in his high flyer, or he rode alongside her.

Meanwhile, she hadn't seen Ian at all.

She supposed he was busy with preparation for his round-the-world journey. She tried very hard to be very philosophical and mature and sophisticated, to think of her time with him in terms of fleeting, startling beauty—a sunrise, a sunset, that sort of thing. When that failed to console her, she tried to poke the embers of that righteous, incinerating anger with which she'd driven him off the balcony the other night. But that failed, too, because that particular fire was dead. Because he'd been absolutely right, of course, and it was ridiculous to be angry with *him* for something (granted, remarkably stupid and selfish) he'd done before he met her. To be angry at him for being who he was. She understood what drove him, perhaps better than anyone ever had. She'd already forgiven him.

And she didn't think he was that person anymore, either.

It seemed, then, that all that was left to her was to suffer, silently, for as long as . . . well, until she no longer did. Presumably at some point in the history of her life she no longer would suffer, or at least she'd arrive at some effective way to manage what right now seemed gruesomely unfair and nearly intolerable.

The two of them would just have to join the

annals of star-crossed lovers, she supposed.
Tristan and Isolde. Romeo and Juliet.

Olivia Eversea and Lyon Redmond.

It was far more romantic-sounding in books.

In reality, it was ghastly.

And besides, he certainly hadn't said that he
*loved* her. *I will want you until the day I die*. He'd
said *that*, but not a word about love.

Would it be better if he'd said it?

Yes, she'd decided. It would have been. She
wasn't certain whether he *did* love her, or whether
he would even recognize it if he did, and it was
this that gave her a spine, and this that got her
through the ensuing fortnight of Stanhope's
courtship, and this that propelled her from bed
each morning since that night on the balcony, and
this that made the notion of life without him just
an infinitesimal fraction more bearable.

It was, however, a mercy that Ian was leaving the country. Because to marry someone else
while they shared the same continent, breathed
the same air, looked up and saw the same stars,
seemed . . . ridiculous. Counter to natural law.

And yet to *not* marry, and marry brilliantly,
seemed not only a betrayal of her parents' wishes,
but of the duke . . . and herself. Her parents had
wanted nothing more than for her to be safe and
cherished and settled. To have a home and family
and permanence once more.

And God help her, it was what she wanted, too.

But tonight . . . in all likelihood, she would

have to see him tonight. At least out of the corner of her eye.

She shook herself from a reverie and turned to Annie, who was watching her with a disconcerting look of sympathy, which fled instantly.

"What would you wear, Annie, if you were going to see a man for the very last time, and you wanted him to never forget you, and for every woman he ever saw after that to pale in comparison to the memory of you?"

Annie's expression then made Tansy realize that yes, servants observed everything. They knew who slept where, and how crumpled the beds were in the morning, and she realized that footmen who moved silently through the house must notice glances exchanged. They must know.

The abigail suddenly reached out impulsively to squeeze her hand.

And then she whispered: "It won't matter what you wear, miss. He will never, ever forget you."

IAN DIDN'T WANT to go to the ball.

He didn't want to watch Tansy dance with other men and he didn't want to dance with any other woman. But he was no coward, he generally had very fine manners and a sense of duty, and so he shaved and dressed scrupulously and went and stood in the ballroom. His mother had insisted; if he was going to go off again on an around-the-world trip, she wanted to see as much of him as she could before he did. He never could deny his mother what she wanted.

So he managed to smile and bow and say appropriately banal things to the people who passed by. He'd been through worse evenings, by far; he would survive this one. He would just keep moving through the ballroom, smiling, nodding. That way, if anyone were to say, "Have you seen Ian?" many were bound to nod yes, and assume he was dutifully participating. He was nothing if not a strategist.

And then tomorrow he could leave for London. Distance would help. Like opium, it wouldn't eliminate the pain, but it would certainly help to muffle it.

The glittering ranks of ball-goers swelled. Everyone he knew, clad in finery he'd seen event after event, poured in. After all, everyone wanted to be present when it was rumored that the duke's ward, Miss Titania Danforth, who had been such a disturbance upon the calm waters of Sussex society, would become engaged to someone who would *also* become a duke. What marvelous symmetry, some sighed. Certainly it was destiny.

Ian hadn't yet seen her.

He hadn't, in fact, seen her for almost a fortnight.

Or for twelve days, four hours, thirty-two minutes, and forty-one seconds, to be precise.

He'd looked at his map this evening, but then

shoved it aside and whiled away some time doing those particular calculations instead.

During that calculated time, he had returned to London and begun purchasing supplies and commissioning clothes appropriate to a trip to Africa and all the points in between. And during that time, he supposed she'd been whisked about in a high flyer and taken on picnics and walks and the like. He hoped, quite uncharitably, that she was bored, and that she thought about him constantly, because if she was going to forget him, there was time enough to do that *after* he sailed away.

And then he hoped—and the very nature of the selflessness amazed him—that she wasn't too bored, because the very idea of her unhappiness, of her sparkle dimmed for any reason, filled him with something close to panic. As though his own life was imperiled.

"What the devil are you glowering at?"

Colin, one of the circulating ball attendees, stopped in front of Ian and stared.

"I wasn't glowering," he said reflexively.

"I beg to differ. You've quite frightened all the young ladies standing across from you."

Ian blinked. There *were* young ladies standing across from him. And each of them had wide eyes and pale faces. Well, then.

"Ah. I think I need to visit the loo," he said bluntly to Colin, who made a sympathetic face as Ian stalked off down the hallway, toward where he'd interrupted Sergeant Sutton in the act of trying to persuade Tansy of their spiritual accord. Not toward the loo, just away.

And then someone stepped out in front of him.

He froze.

A beautiful brunette with a decidedly pouting lower lip. Alarmingly, it took him a moment before he recognized her.

He'd nearly forgotten about her altogether.

And there really was no reason to avoid her now.

"My apologies, Lady Carstairs, for not writing to you earlier. I've been unavoidably detained by business both in Sussex and London. But I am so pleased to find you here."

"I shall endeavor to forgive you. Some things are enhanced by anticipation."

Anticipation.

She *would* have to say anticipation.

It was as though someone had thrust an arrow into his gut.

He froze for a moment.

"Is something amiss, Captain Eversea?" Her hand went up to touch his arm.

"No. Not at all." He managed a smile. He stared down at her hand resting on his arm, and he was tempted to flick it away. It was a lovely hand, elegant, well-tended. It looked wrong there, somehow, like a spider. "Why don't you tell me where your rooms are."

"The second floor. The third from the stairway."

They heard footsteps then, clicking down the hallway.

A woman's footsteps.

Lady Carstairs ducked away. "Until then," she murmured, and slipped with the skill of someone who was accustomed to slipping away, her fingers trailing his arm.

Ian turned abruptly, toward the sound of the footfall.

And went still.

Tansy stood there.

She'd been watching him.

Her face was white.

They simply stared at each other for some time. The pleasure in simply looking at each other, being in each other's presence, was barbed with unspoken things.

She had no right to that expression of betrayal.

And yet . . .

At last he spoke.

"And what can I do for you, Miss Danforth?" he said quietly. Curtly.

It felt strange. As though he were speaking his native language for the first time in a long time, after speaking another to everyone else.

For twelve days, four hours, thirty-two minutes, and forty-one seconds.

And it was a relief just to be near her. Suddenly, gravity seemed much less oppressive.

She didn't say anything for a time. She was apparently mustering nerve. How unlike her to need to muster nerve.

"Are you going to make love to her?"

He nearly swore. Damn her and her penchant for ambushing him with questions.

He'd do nearly anything to take that expression from her face, and yet . . . And yet he wanted to shout at her for being naive. Things were as they were.

"Are you going to marry a future duke?"

The voices of the partygoers echoed like the remnants of a dream. One of those voices was that of the future duke. The young man with the lofty fortune, the influence, the money, the title. A young man who had likely never cuckolded the Duke of Falconbridge.

"Probably," she echoed, her voice frayed. Ever so faintly anguished. Defensive.

And angry.

His head went back hard. Then came down in a nod.

And then he shrugged.

There they had it, after all.

More relatively absurd silence ensued.

And Lady Carstairs was waiting for him in her room, and in minutes, in all likelihood, she would be tapping a satin slipper in impatience. He imagined the lush white curves of her body beneath his practiced hands. He imagined the moans and sighs he knew how to elicit. He would wrap one of her thighs around his waist and take her swiftly against a wall or in a corner. That glorious pleasure and forgetting could be had in burying himself in her body. Temporary surcease.

Tansy didn't move, didn't speak.

He moved so abruptly, toward her, she flinched.

"What do you want from me, Tansy?" His voice was low, furious, urgent.

She clasped her hands in front of her. He looked down at the little white knot of her fists and up at her white face. Two hectic spots of color appeared high in her cheeks.

He wanted to touch her to soothe that color away.

He didn't dare.

He waited.

And waited.

And when her voice came, it was whisper thin. "I don't want you to make love to her."

He sucked in a sharp breath. He took the words like an arrow. The sort that murders.

And the sort that Cupid shoots into its victims.

There were so many things he could say. He could point out hypocrisy and futility and fairness and rightness. He could point out, yet again, that while she was wise in some ways, she was naive in the ways of the world and that men had needs and all that nonsense, and she had no right, no right, to stand there with that look on her face. That everything said about him was true, and she knew it. He could say that she had driven him to it. She had no right.

*Too bad for you, Tansy.*

It was the most merciful thing to say. It would allow her to go her way and him to go his, which was as it should be. Allow her to loathe him a little, and then a little more, and then finally forget.

It was what he meant to say, anyhow.

"Then I won't."

Is what he said instead. Very gently.

It was tantamount to a confession.

He didn't know who he was anymore.

All he knew is, he wanted her to have whatever she wanted. No matter what it was. No matter what the cost.

And having just sealed his fate, he spun on his heels and left her just as her lovely face suffused with a nearly celestial light, because he didn't think he could bear to look at that, either.

DURING A LULL between dances Stanhope sidled up to him, his handsome young face open and shining. He had a petulant chin, Ian decided, with a surly lack of charity. There was just something about it, the way it sat there, unblemished and square, that bothered him immensely.

"I just wanted to thank you, Eversea, for your letter informing me about Miss Danforth."

"No need," Ian said curtly.

"Oh, please don't deny me the pleasure of my gratitude," he said quite grandly, looking pleased with the choice of phrase.

"You're going to be a duke. Far be it for me to deny you a thing."

Stanhope looked momentarily a little uncertain at this, and then he nodded, missing irony completely. Then again, irony is a defense for those who are at least occasionally disappointed, Ian thought, and surely the young lord hadn't yet experienced anything of the sort.

"I do think my courtship of Miss Danforth has gone well. Very well, indeed."

"Has it?" Ian grit his teeth.

"It was easy, old man. Really, there was nothing to it." He snapped his fingers. "A few bouquets, a few compliments about her eyes and the like, a few rides in the old high flyer, and she's mine! She's a simple thing, really."

"That easy, was it?"

"Certainly. She's young yet, and so her personality is still forming. Though she's cheerful and agreeable. I suspect she can be molded."

"Ah. So she's that malleable, is she?" He wasn't aware, but his volume was increasing exponentially with each sentence he uttered. No mean feat when speaking from between clenched teeth.

"Oh, of a certainty, sir," Stanhope said gravely, on a confiding air. "Oh, she isn't perfect. She's a bit vain and frivolous. A bit vapid, I think, and a bit shallow. But that's due to youth. A few babies will change all of that. And Lord, but she *looks* perfect."

Ian spent a moment in blank, furious speechlessness.

"Vain? Frivolous? Vapid? Shallow?" Ian hissed the words as if they were darts he were hurling into a board. Stanhope blinked at each one. "Have you . . . seen a mirror lately, Stanhope?"

"Ha ha!" Stanhope laughed. He did laugh an inordinate amount. "Oh, ha ha, Eversea! Witty. But she is beautiful," he pointed out. "She'll be a *marvelous* ride, and my heirs will be incredible looking, don't you think?"

"Did you just call Miss Danforth . . . a marvelous ride?"

"Yes."

"A . . . marvelous . . . ride," Ian repeated slowly, flatly. As if learning new vocabulary.

A red haze was moving over his eyes.

"Yes?" Stanhope was a little confused now.

"And you think she's vapid, shallow, and frivolous. *She* is." He said this as if he were trying to record the duke's words for posterity. As if he wanted to get them precisely right.

"Well, yes," Stanhope hastened to reassure him. "But then most women are. The dears. What would we do without them, right, Eversea?" He gazed out over the ballroom at all the other women he might have had so easily, given his title. "And I know you *never* do without them."

Ian stared at him the way he would stare at a cobra he intended to shoot to smithereens.

For a good long time.

Without blinking.

Stanhope looked at him, began to turn back toward the ballroom, and then recoiled when he really got a look at Ian's expression.

"You're worrying me a bit, Eversea. You haven't blinked. You're a bit young yet for apoplexy, aren't you?"

"You *should* be worried, Stanhope," Ian said pleasantly.

Stanhope looked down and noticed that Ian's hands were clenched into knots. The better to launch into the jaws of young lords.

"Did you think . . . Oh, I meant no insult. She's a grand girl. Splendid. I was certain I made that clear." He gave a short nod. He seemed to think this took care of it.

"That's all you can say? She's a *grand* girl?"

And now Ian was shouting.

And conversations in the periphery ceased as people craned to hear.

Stanhope was now clearly baffled, and his feet shifted uneasily. "What higher compliment can I pay? What else is there, really?"

"What else is there? WHAT ELSE IS THERE?" And suddenly he was breathless and hoarse. "She . . . apologizes to flowers. She talks to the stars. She rolls a perfect cigarette. She *thinks* about the servants. She smells like a bloody meadow. She shoots like a rifleman. She rides like a centaur. Just being able to make her laugh is like . . . winning a *thousand* Sussex marksmanship cups. *Better* than that, you pompous, *whinnying*, RIDICULOUS *ARSE*."

He was distantly aware that it sounded almost as though he was speaking in tongues, in a series of non sequiturs. That he was gesticulating incredulously and possibly somewhat threateningly. That Stanhope was staring wide-eyed at him, and that the brightening he detected in the room around him might just be the whites of dozens of eyes as they widened, too.

He didn't care. They were visions of her, memories, all queued up at the exit of his mind, every last one of them significant, like linked dreams, and he couldn't stop them. And yet none of them were adequate. None of them added up to the girl.

Stanhope took another step back.

"Er . . . the whites of your eyes are showing, Eversea . . ."

"She has a wit that can cut right through a man. She's . . . oh, God, she's gentle. She's more forgiving than she ought to be and kinder and braver and wiser and more loyal than you'll ever be, you worthless, mewling, OVERBRED, *FATUOUS . . .*"

He trailed off when he realized that he had quite an audience.

All silent.

All utterly rapt.

"Eversea," someone muttered in resignation.

"What a pity the syphilis has gone to his brain," someone whispered. "That must be it."

"I haven't lost my mind!" He said this a little too loudly. And then added, "And I don't have syphilis!"

He *had* lost his mind.

And to the end of his days he would regret shouting "I don't have syphilis!" in a crowded ballroom.

His brothers would never, ever let him forget it.

The silence that followed was laden with doom.

Young Stanhope stepped toward him and said quietly, "I say, Captain Eversea, perhaps you ought to retire for the evening? I'll overlook the insult if you apologize. She's enough to addle any man's brains. Just look at her in that dress. Like an angel, she is."

Ian almost sighed.

How very pleasant it would be to shoot this man, he thought idly. How easy it would be to say, "Name your seconds." He *would* kill him. There was no question about it. But Stanhope's only fault was that he'd never *needed* to develop character, and likely never would. Stanhope was the most important thing in Stanhope's world, and that was the lens through which he saw everything and everyone.

And yet Stanhope had enough breeding to forgive him, and this was nearly intolerable.

Ian looked across the crowd and his eyes met Tansy's wide blue-gray ones. And immediately he felt her everywhere in him.

The expression in them nearly buckled his knees.

And yet . . . if he did kill the young heir, he would destroy her reputation and future, not to mention his own.

He sought out other pairs of eyes. Genevieve was staring at him with two hot spots of disbelief high on her cheekbones.

She shook her head just a little, to and fro.

Falconbridge was watching him, too.

Ian met his eyes evenly. He'd thought to read murder there.

But he saw nothing of the sort. He in fact couldn't read the duke at all.

For a moment he held that fixed gaze. Unapologetically. Defiantly.

And suddenly he knew what he had to do.

It was as clear, almost painfully clear, as if a blind had been yanked up in his bedroom on the morning of the worst hangover of his life.

But then it was exhilarating. And so very, very simple.

But first things first.

"I apologize, Stanhope."

He turned on his heel and walked out of the ballroom, and that was a sound he would never forget, either: his boot heels echoing on the wooden floor as everyone watched him walk away.

"MADNESS. THAT'S ALL it was. You know how old soldiers can be. And you can inspire anyone to madness. You're very lovely, my dear."

He'd taken to calling her "my" this and "my" that, and every time he did, Tansy wanted to swat him, which surely wasn't the way she should feel about someone who was allegedly about to propose to her.

"He's not old," she said sharply.

"Old*er*," Stanhope indulged placidly. Amused with her, apparently.

There was a certain peace in knowing she was about to be proposed to. It would mean that years of upheaval would end. Life would take on a certainty it had lacked for too long. She would acquire a husband who could be managed. She would obtain what remained of her parents' fortune. She would never want for anything. He hadn't yet tried to kiss her, but she knew, thanks to a waltz or two, that he smelled of starch and almost nothing else, and she suddenly had grave difficulty imagining him naked or breaking wind or roaring in the morning.

Or kissing her.

Or making love to her.

The night had continued after Ian's outburst, and the dammed conversation had flowed again to fill in the brief shocked silence, and then everyone had drunk and danced enough to mostly forget about it.

Ian, she was certain, had left the ball entirely. She knew he wasn't in the ballroom as surely as she was certain she would know if the sun suddenly disappeared from the sky.

She'd stayed. For a short time.

She was certain she'd held conversations and danced dances and fielded and issued compliments, but she couldn't remember any of them when she returned to her chambers. She'd begged a headache, and allowed Stanhope to believe it was nerves.

And Stanhope had parted from her, telling

her he'd arranged to call upon the duke at eight o'clock the following morning.

When she was in her room again, she leaned her cheek against the wall as if she could hear Ian's heartbeat right through it.

He was leaving tomorrow. Or so she'd heard.

She finally made herself undress and crawl into bed, but she didn't sleep at all.

Finally, when it was just past dawn, she tipped herself out of bed and followed the little road of light to the window.

But he wasn't outside on his balcony.

And so she sat down and took out her list of requirements one final time.

She emphatically crossed out *of fine moral character* and carefully—and very painstakingly in even, small letters, smaller now, because she was running out of room—wrote something else there instead.

She blew on it impatiently, waiting for the ink to dry.

Then a tear plopped on it, and she was forced to carefully blot it, and wait even longer, which was maddening.

And then with a sort of blind purpose she snatched it up and carried it down the hall to the office where the Duke of Falconbridge liked to conduct business.

She gave a sharp rap on the duke's door. Sharper than she'd intended.

"You may enter," he called. Very alert for that hour of the morning.

He looked up and began to rise.

"Titania." He sounded surprised.

She curtsied, but otherwise wasted no time on the niceties.

"This is my revised list, Your Grace. I wanted you to have it."

He reached out and gingerly took it. She supposed it was starting to look a little disreputable.

"From the looks of things, it's grown quite a bit."

"As have I."

She had the satisfaction of seeing the duke blink.

She whirled and left without being dismissed.

Falconbridge's eyes fell to the item that was clearly the newest.

*Defends me in a crowded ballroom at the risk of his own dignity, because he knows me and loves me better than anyone ever has and ever will, even if he can't say it.*

*Yet.*

# Chapter 26

❧

By eight o'clock in the morning, Ian had already been awake for four hours, accomplishing something that would surprise a good many people.

He immediately took himself up to the room Falconbridge had been using as an office during his stay.

The duke's door remained shut. The clock had yet to strike eight.

"What ho, Stanhope."

For there Stanhope already sat, just as a footman had told Ian, jouncing one leg nervously.

When he saw Ian he shot to his feet and then staggered backward a few steps.

"Eversea."

He looked nervous. As well he might. For numerous reasons.

Ian, however, was all soothing contrition.

"I'm sorry again about last night, old man. I drank a bit too much, and you know how it is when you've worked a bit too hard . . ."

He was utterly certain Stanhope hadn't worked a day in his life.

"Certainly, certainly."

"Nervous?" Ian smiled enigmatically.

"Well, of course. Ha. I'm about to ask for Miss Danforth's hand in marriage." He *was* decidedly green about the mouth.

Ian whistled, long and low. "Marriage is forever."

*Forever.* A portentous word, forever.

"Ah, yes. I know. Long time, forever."

"It is, indeed. It is, indeed. Listen, old man, I was sent to tell you that the duke isn't actually in—he's waiting for you instead at the vicarage. He's there on a bit of parish business and the notion took him—he'd like you to meet him there."

"The vicarage?" Stanhope was confused. "The Pennyroyal Green vicarage? I was certain he would have liked to speak to me here. We made an appointment last night, you see, and when the footman admitted me I was directed to wait right here."

"Ah. I think it was an impulsive decision on Falconbridge's part, and perhaps word hasn't yet reached all the servants," Ian improvised smoothly. "I think he thought the vicarage would more accurately reflect the gravity of the event. Confer a little more of the sacred upon it."

"Ah. Certainly, certainly. I can see that, I suppose. Very well, then. Thank you for conveying the message, Eversea. No hard feelings about the night before?"

"None at *all*." Ian smiled.

Stanhope glanced at the door of the office uncertainly.

He glanced toward the stairwell.

"You'd best hurry. He dislikes tardiness. Considers it a character flaw."

"Thankfully I have my new high flyer."

"*Thank*fully." Ian sounded relieved.

"Good day, Eversea, and thank you."

He turned and hurried past him, jamming his hat down on his head.

"Thank *you*, Stanhope."

And Ian settled into the chair to wait, and put his hand over the pistol in his pocket.

THE DUKE'S MOOD was edging toward foul, because he'd just opened a message this morning from the solicitor responsible for Lilymont's sale. It had been sold just that morning.

Bloody hell. He knew Genevieve would withstand the disappointment, but there was nothing he loathed more than disappointing her.

Deciding Stanhope had in all likelihood marinated in his own nerves long enough, and that he could probably expend a little of his mood upon the boy, the duke called him in.

"Enter, please," he said irritably.

A clean-shaven, crisply dressed, white-faced, granite-jawed Ian Eversea slowly walked in, clutching his hat in one hand.

And a pistol in the other.

Ian strolled deliberately over to the desk and lay the pistol on it.

"I'd like you to be able to make an informed decision, Falconbridge," he said, "after you hear what I have to say. We will settle everything between us here and now. And then if you wish to shoot me, I'd like you to have that option."

The duke stared at him. Ian had the satisfaction of knowing he'd at least nonplussed the man a little.

Something darkly amused twitched across the duke's face. Then he gave a subtle nod. "Very well. What can I do for you, Eversea?"

The tone wasn't . . . warm. To say the least.

"I'm here to speak to you about Miss Danforth."

There was a silence.

Ian fancied it was the sort of silence once experienced before the guillotine dropped.

"What about Miss Danforth?" His tone was deceptively casual. But the vowels were elongated. Nearly drawled. It was the duke's way of warning him. His eyes flicked over to the pistol.

"I would die for her," Ian said simply.

Drama was as good a place to begin as any.

The duke blinked.

Ian didn't wait for the duke to speak. "But it will never come to that, because I, more than anyone, am uniquely qualified to keep her safe all of her born days. Because I love her. And I know her. I know her heart. No one will ever love her better. I will endeavor to deserve her every day of my life."

The duke's fingers took up an idle, slow drumming on the edge of his desk.

He said nothing. He hadn't yet blinked.

"I know you've cause to despise me, Falconbridge. I know you've cause to doubt my honor. To apologize for my past offenses against you only now would seem self-serving. But I *am* sorry. I was driven then by motivations I can scarcely explain to myself, let alone you. But one reckless night should not define a man for a lifetime. If you can look me in the eye and tell me your soul is stainless, I'll leave now. And if you can look me in the eye and tell me that you don't think I deserve happiness, I'll leave now. And if you truly believe I cannot make Tansy happy, I will leave now. I don't know if she loves me. But I love her. And I would die for her."

The duke listened to this with no apparent change in expression. The silence was a palpable thing. Brittle as glass.

"I thought you were leaving, Eversea." He sounded pensive. "A trip around the world."

"*She* is the world. She is *my* world."

Something glimmered in the duke's eyes.

"And what about your savings?"

"I think you may have already guessed what I've done with them."

Falconbridge gave a short laugh. Surprised and seemingly perversely impressed.

"Very well. What do you want from me now?" The duke's voice was a little abstracted. He sounded, in truth, fascinated.

"I've come to ask you for the honor of Titania's hand in marriage."

There ensued a silence so long and painful it was as though time itself had been stretched on the rack. Ian worried for a moment that he'd given the duke apoplexy, and would now have his death on his conscience, to boot.

And then the duke stood up slowly.

Ian didn't budge.

He moved deliberately around the desk. Not quite in a stalking fashion. More of a careful one. As if giving himself time to change his mind about what he was about to do.

Ian consoled himself that the man hadn't snatched up the pistol.

He stood directly in front of Ian, eye-to-eye.

Ian stood his ground. He didn't like knowing that he could count his brother-in-law's eyelashes if he so choose, but he didn't blink.

Which is why it took him a moment to realize the duke was holding something in his hand.

The last time the duke had slinked toward him like that he'd been holding a pistol.

This time he was holding what appeared to be a sheet of foolscap.

"Titania delivered this to me this morning. It's a list she made of requirements for a husband. She thought it might be . . . helpful . . . to me."

He handed the sheet to Ian. Urged him to take it with the launch of one eyebrow.

Ian eyed him skeptically.

He took it between his fingers.

The duke gave an impatient jerk of his chin, urging him to read.

So Ian bent his head over it.

His heart lurched when he saw that her fingerprints darkened the edges. And that it was stained faintly by what he suspected were tears. Despite this, he could read it well enough.

And by the time he'd read all the way to the bottom, the foolscap was rattling.

Ian's hands were trembling.

He took a long, slow breath and looked up at the duke. "I think it's fair to say she loves you, Eversea." Falconbridge sounded ever-so-slightly resigned. But surprisingly, his voice was gentle.

Even amused.

Ian found he could barely breathe.

"And our accounts?" he managed finally.

A hesitation. "Are even."

Ian gave a short nod.

"Very well. My life is in your hands again, Falconbridge. What will you do with it this time?"

"TANSY, WHY DON'T we go for a drive?"

Tansy jumped. She'd managed to dress herself, and had taken a single cup of tea in her room, and picked the scone Mrs. deWitt had sent up into powdery smithereens. It now lay untouched on a plate. And she had stayed put, jumpy as a prisoner about to be led to execution, which was hardly the way she ought greet the day she might very well become engaged.

"But . . ." Suddenly, she didn't have an excuse.

And going out seemed better than staying in. And movement better than not moving.

Movement. Ian was likely on his way to London, anyway. He could even now be standing on the deck of the ship.

Genevieve looped her arm through Tansy's and tugged. "Come. It's an *excellent* day for a drive. Some might even say a transformative day for a drive."

SHE STARED LISTLESSLY out the window as Penny-royal Green scenery unfurled.

Genevieve pointed out landmarks.

"Look, there are the two oak trees entwined in the town square! There's a legend about them, you know."

Tansy didn't care.

"Doesn't the vicarage look lovely with all the new repairs? And look, there's Miss Marietta Endicott's academy. They've added a wing since you were a little girl. Do you remember it?"

She shook her head noncommittally. She remembered it. Vaguely. She just didn't want to *discuss* it.

"Now we're passing the O'Flahertys' home. It certainly has improved over the past year or so. They've a new roof and paddock fence."

Who were the O'Flahertys'? Why should she care about their paddock fence?

She began to wonder where on earth they were going. It had begun to feel less like an idle drive

meant to distract her and more like a means to a
destination.

But then Tansy straightened as the scenery
began to look a trifle more familiar. Just something about the jut of the rocks to the left . . . the
slight rise and curve in the road . . .

A peculiar tingle started along the backs of her
arms.

"Where are we going, Gen—"

When the house came into view, she gasped.

"And look. Here we are at Lilymont," Genevieve said quite unnecessarily. "It occurred to me
that you hadn't seen it since you were a girl."

"No," Tansy managed.

She was helped down from the carriage by a
footman and began drifting toward the house,
reflexively. It looked the same, if a bit in need of
paint and a bit of weed-tugging. The mellow stone
walls still glowed amber in low sunlight. The
windows all glinted at her, like smiling eyes. She
could almost imagine her five-year-old self and
her brother gazing down from one of them.

Genevieve remained next to the carriage.

"And look," she said, "the garden gate is open."
She pointed at it.

Tansy turned. The wooden gate was ever-so-
slightly ajar. As if it had been anticipating her arrival.

"Do you mind?" Tansy turned to Genevieve eagerly. "May we?"

"Yes! Let's do have a— Oh, drat! I've just

dropped my glove in the carriage . . . you go on ahead, Tansy, I'll be right on your heels. I know you're eager to see it."

Tansy gave the little gate a push to open it wider, and stood motionless at the entrance.

Her childhood came back at her in a rush that gave her vertigo. Everything had gotten larger and woollier, but the path was still there, obscured as it was by tufts of grass, and all the beloved trees, and the ivy still spilled over the walls, and there was a man standing in the garden.

There was a *man* standing in the garden!

"Ian."

Her hand flew to her heart. It was more a gasp than a word. It had leaped into her throat so swiftly she thought it would choke her.

He didn't say anything for a good long time. They stared at each other like witless people who had never before encountered another human.

"Am I dreaming?" she said finally, softly.

"No."

She jumped and swiveled around at the sound of the carriage pulling away at a swift clip. She took a step toward the gate, and froze.

And turned around again.

Her heart began to hammer.

"Please don't leave without hearing me out, Tansy."

"Well, I can't leave," she pointed out, practically. "I do believe I've been abandoned here."

He began to smile.

She turned away from it, because his smile was almost too beautiful to bear.

And restlessly she began to move.

She could scarcely hear her own footfall, or the birdsong, as she wandered wonderingly into the garden over the woolly overgrown ground. She touched a flower. And another. She stretched out an arm and lovingly drew her fingers along the warm stone of the garden wall. She set one foot in front of another along the path. And yet she couldn't look at him. She didn't dare look at him. Not yet.

What if it *was* a dream? Tears began to prick at the corners of her eyes. To have everything she wanted, and only to wake up, would be cruel.

But she was no coward, and so she stopped and turned.

The expression on Ian's face turned her knees to water.

"Why are we here, Ian? Shouldn't you be preparing to board a ship?"

His voice was gentle. "First, I want you to know that Lilymont is yours. It belongs only to you. If you want it. No matter what you decide your future will be."

Her heart stopped.

"You bought this house . . . for *me*?"

"I bought the house for *us*, but if there is no us, it belongs only to you."

She stared. "I don't under—"

"I love you." He sounded almost impatient.

He delivered the words like a musket shot.

Time seemed to stop. The birds ceased singing. The words echoed in the quiet garden.

Magic words, those words: she felt them everywhere in her body, slowly, like tiny candles lit one by one in every one of her cells. And then suddenly she couldn't feel her limbs, or the ground, and she would not have been surprised to look down and see a cloud beneath her slippers.

"What did you say?" she whispered.

Only because she wanted to hear him say it again.

"I love you. I love you. So much it amazes me I've managed to live this long without you. I used to think that in order to find peace, I needed to keep moving, to keep searching, until I'd exhausted every corner of the world. But . . . Tansy . . . *you* are the world to me. *You* are my home, and, quite ironically, my peace, though I haven't truly known a moment's peace since I've met you. Which I quite like. And if you would do me the honor of being my wife, I will always love you better than *anyone* in the world, until our children come, and then I will love all of you more than life. I will devote the rest of my days to doing my best to making you happy. You must marry me, unless, of course, you'd like to see me perish. Will you?"

She couldn't yet speak. She was memorizing his beautiful face, and the way the light and shadows were just so, so she could savor the memory the rest of her days.

"That was quite a pretty speech, Ian," she said finally.

"Thank you."

He looked quite apprehensive now.

"Much more coherent than the one you gave at the ball."

"Thank you," he said again, sounding clipped and tense.

Ah, but she shouldn't tease him.

"What if I said I didn't love you?"

"I would say you were lying," he said, and produced her list with a flourish. He dangled it in front of her.

She stared at it openmouthed.

And now she was blushing.

"Falconbridge gave it to me. I have his blessing. So you might as well say it, Tansy."

She inhaled deeply, reached out and took his hand.

His was shaking a little, but then, so was hers.

Now that he had her hand, he pulled her abruptly close. Up against the sheltering warmth of his body. Wrapped his arms around her. Slid his hands down over her back, as if to claim her, as if to prove that she was real and she was his.

"Say it," he whispered.

"I love you," she whispered. "I will be honored to be your wife. And I think the only way my name will ever make sense is if the name Eversea follows it."

He kissed her to seal that promise. It was gentle, that kiss, and slow, and deep, and it bound the two of them, soul to soul.

When he lifted his mouth and rested his forehead against hers, she whispered, "I think I saw stars."

"Of course you did. And I will make sure you do. Every. Time."

IAN OBTAINED A special license so they could be married in spring in a modest clearing in the forest that had nothing much to recommend it apart from the profusion of brilliant wildflowers, all of them American expatriates. He had referred to the book in the library and planted even more of them than she had, as a surprise for Tansy.

And all those American flowers made her feel as though her parents and brother were there with her.

A crowd of townspeople gathered to witness the marriage, as did innumerable Everseas, including Sylvaines who rode into Pennyroyal Green for the occasion, and the servants. Reverend Adam Sylvaine conducted the service, and even he couldn't get through it without pausing to clear his throat suspiciously.

*Everyone* wept, for different reasons. Really, said the magnanimous, it was very big of Ian Eversea to take Miss Danforth out of circulation, as she'd caused a temporary insanity.

And every man who acted like a fool was forgiven, since Ian Eversea had clearly acted like the biggest fool of all, and in doing so had won the equivalent of—as he legendarily said—a thousand Sussex marksmanship cups.

"Beautiful scenery, don't you think? Such astonishingly colorful flowers. Such a lovely day for a wedding. So warm and bright and clear. Didn't she look beautiful? I never thought I'd see the day when Ian would agree to be legshackled. He even took the promotion for the East India Company, so he'll be in London part of the time. But she certainly is lively. He's unlikely to be bored."

Olivia was nervous. She was prattling inanely, and she *never* prattled, let alone inanely. Landsdowne was so quiet, and it was a full sort of quiet, the quiet of the preoccupied. The quiet of preparation. He was either going to tell her that they were through, that it was no use. Or . . .

"By rights it ought to rain right—"

"Olivia."

She stopped. And took a deep breath.

"I know you don't love me," he said.

She nearly choked. Shocked. "I . . ."

He saved her. "But I think that one day you will. And until then, I would be content to devote my life to making you happy. For your happiness is mine."

"Oh . . ." And now her breath was lost completely.

He paused and turned.

"Olivia . . . my dear, beautiful, Olivia . . . would you do me the honor of becoming my wife?"

She stared at him as if she'd never seen him before. Her hands went up to her face.

And fell again.

It wasn't as though she hadn't known this might happen.

She looked up at Landsdowne.

He had become dear, or he had become familiar, and sometimes those two things were one and the same.

She told herself this.

She didn't know anymore.

She wondered if she ever *would* know.

It was only one word, she thought. A word upon which her entire future would turn. The word would decide whether or not she had a future. She need only open her mouth and say it.

It was simple as the flip of a coin. She told herself that.

Her heart pounded like a fist against a wall.

"Yes," she told him softly.

She laid the word down. It felt strangely weighted to her. Like a monument.

Or a tombstone.

He closed his eyes and mouthed, *Hallelujah*.

And he took a long, shaky breath. His face was brilliant with happiness.

And there was that at least: she had the power to make someone else supremely happy, and it was as close to happiness as she'd felt in a very long time.

And maybe one day she wouldn't be able to tell the difference.

"I should like to kiss you now," he said.

"I should like that, too."

She found that this was true.

He gathered her into his arms.

And in that moment she felt like a girl. It had been a long time, a very long time, since she'd been kissed. And if a tiny corner of her heart where she kept a memory in a dungeon howled betrayal, she ignored it. Lyon wasn't here, and Landsdowne was, and she was still young.

DROWSY, THOROUGHLY SPENT, happier than any two people on the planet had ever been since time began, or so Ian emphatically claimed, he and Tansy twined their limbs and rested after the fourth bout of married lovemaking in their new home.

"I wanted to give you something when we were alone, Tansy. Close your eyes and hold out your palm."

"Very funny, Ian. It's so large I'd have to hold out two palms to hold it."

He laughed. "Just do it, please."

She closed her eyes, and he trickled something that felt like a very fine chain into her hand.

"Open your eyes."

She gazed down into a fine little pool of gold. She used her little finger to scoop it up, and lifted. It was a necklace.

Dangling from it was a tiny gold star.

He was rewarded when her eyes began to shine with tears and then she laughed.

"A gift! Of all things, yet *another* gift from Ian Eversea."

"I've discovered I've developed a taste for giving them."

Wonderingly, she ran her thumb over the tiny, simple, exquisite little star. Not expensive. But perfect.

"It's etched!"

"Turn it over, Tansy, and read it."

She turned it over and read it aloud: *"Forever."*

"My favorite word!" she said delightedly.

"Mine, too. It's *our* word now."

*At Avon Books, we know your passion for romance—once you finish one of our novels, you find yourself wanting more.*

May we tempt you with . . .

- **Excerpts** from our upcoming releases.

- Entertaining **extras**, including authors' personal photo albums and book lists.

- Behind-the-scenes **scoop** on your favorite characters and series.

- **Sweepstakes** for the chance to win free books, romantic getaways, and other fun prizes.

- Writing **tips** from our authors and editors.

- **Blog** with our authors and find out why they love to write romance.

- **Exclusive content** that's not contained within the pages of our novels.

Join us at
**www.avonbooks.com**

**AVON**

*An Imprint of* HarperCollins*Publishers*
www.avonromance.com

Available wherever books are sold or please call 1-800-331-3761 to order.

FTH 1013

## Give in to your Impulses!

**These unforgettable stories only take a second to buy and give you hours of reading pleasure!**

Go to *www.Avon*

Available wh

IMP 0811